"And what do we have here?"

Nerves gripped her as she recognized the viscount's voice. "I was just picking up a book. I couldn't sleep."

"It's late to be out. People could get the wrong impression." His breath tickled her neck, and she involuntarily moved back against him. "Or have the wrong intentions."

Her muscles tightened. She stepped away and twisted to face him. "That they could. You should heed your own advice, my lord."

She was pleased to note that her voice was cool and calm, in direct contrast to the rest of her body.

The viscount let go of her and leaned negligently against the doorframe. "And why would I do that? Of what do I need to take heed?" He leaned forward, his lips inches away from hers. "This is my domain, and I can take what I want. . . ."

Other AVON ROMANCES

Coming Soon

And Don't Miss These
ROMANTIC TREASURES
from Avon Books

Anne Mallory

The Viscount's Wicked Ways

AVON BOOKS

An Imprint of HarperCollinsPublishers

AVON BOOKS
An Imprint of HarperCollins*Publishers*
10 East 53rd Street
New York, New York 10022-5299

Copyright © 2006 by Anne Hearn
ISBN-13: 978-0-06-087292-2
ISBN-10: 0-06-087292-6
www.avonromance.com

First Avon Books paperback printing: April 2006

Avon Trademark Reg. U.S. Pat. Off. and in Other Countries, Marca Registrada, Hecho en U.S.A.
HarperCollins® is a registered trademark of HarperCollins Publishers Inc.

Printed in the U.S.A.

10 9 8 7 6 5 4 3 2

To Dad,
who never failed to tell
the monsters in the closet
to "quiet down in there,
it's time to go to sleep."
Love you.

Special thanks to
Mom, Matt,
Selina and Paige.

Chapter 1

Patience Harrington shivered with excitement and anticipation as she stared at the massive doors adorned with pointed crowns, sinister ravens, and trailing ivy. The work of the carvings was intricately and painstakingly detailed, as if hewn in offering to an ancient god of the underworld.

Lightning split the sky, illuminating the courtyard, turrets, and stone carvings of the night-shrouded castle. A thunderous boom shook the ground beneath her feet, causing her to wonder if Hades was just then reaching up to seize his gift.

The bestial sculptures lining the courtyard called out to her. Protectors fending off evil spirits. Heroes slaying dragons. Warriors surging into the fray armed and ready to best the enemy.

A low groan shifted her attention back to the castle's magnificent doors as one slowly swung open. A distinguished figure stood backlit in the doorway—an archangel welcoming them to heaven—or a demon summoning them to hell.

The figure motioned them inside.

Patience took an enthusiastic breath, pushed up her spectacles, and walked into the large, marble vestibule. A towering ceiling and stark frescoes were her first impressions of the main hall. The ceiling captured the fierce battle between the ancient Greek gods and the Titans. The battle with Cronus was at center, the hundred-handed, fifty-headed Hecatonchires, the Gigantes, and Cyclopes forming a ring of arms, heads, bodies, and eyes around the edges. The shadowed gods cast their eyes upon the travelers as if to judge their worth.

Patience reveled in the feel of the art and of the myth. Of the pure atmosphere of the lightning-kissed illusions and the rumblings as the sky stroked the earth. This was the real joy of her work. The feel of it. The imaginings. The true sensory experience. Later she would delve closer to poke and prod, to examine, dissect, and discuss, but for the moment she would simply feel and enjoy.

She was jostled from behind as one of her fellow travelers pushed forward to escape the storm and enter behind her. She realized the great doors had only been opened partway, to keep out the sheeting rain, and that she was blocking the entrance. She immediately shifted to the side, giving the jostler an apologetic smile and lift of her shoulders. It was just her luck that it was Mrs. Tecking, the person least amused by Patience's somewhat frequent flights of fancy.

Chastened by the glare she received from the impatient blonde, Patience stepped aside before continuing her perusal of Blackfield Castle's entrance hall.

A cantilevered staircase dominated the space, its mahogany railing rising majestically upward. Newel warriors guarded each landing, warning invaders of dire consequences if they continued their ascent.

Colorful rugs, fierce statues, decorative entrance tables, and priceless paintings framed in gold leaf adorned the floor and walls around, under, and over the grand staircase. Strange-looking sconces cast a golden light that alternated between somber and soothing depending on where she looked. Patience was impressed by the way the hall could feel both intimidating and inviting at the same time.

"Welcome to Blackfield Castle, I am Kenfield, Lord Blackfield's butler," the distinguished man who had opened the door announced, as Patience finally had the presence of mind to shake out her sodden skirts.

"Foul weather we are having," her cousin John remarked cheerfully, as he reached out a lanky hand to pass his walking stick, greatcoat, and hat to a footman. His sandy brown hair was damp around the edges and had already started to curl. Chocolate brown eyes absorbed the room much in the same way that Patience's had. "It's wonderful to be here."

"Indeed," Mr. Frederick Tecking said in his dry and somewhat absentminded fashion, his hazel eyes focused single-mindedly on a marble statue of Minerva in one of the hall's nooks. It was the first comment he had made in nearly an hour, and it was not surprising that it had taken a Roman antiquity to do it. "Odd chandelier though," he muttered, never taking his eyes off the statue.

Patience blinked and looked up. An enormous cut-glass chandelier hung from the ceiling. And Mr. Tecking was right. There was something unusual about it.

Before she could discover what it was, the butler gestured to a room on the left. "Please make yourself comfortable. Dry yourselves by the fire. I will inform Lady Caroline of your arrival, and your servants will be shown to their quarters."

Patience smiled as she watched her maid Tilly, who looked as excited as a woman a third her age, scoot down the hall. She, too, had looked upon this trip as an adventure.

The servants climbed the stairs as Patience, John, and the Teckings walked into the ornate room. A fire blazed in a large fireplace. A plaster frieze depicting nymphs and woodland creatures rose above the chimneypiece and surrounded the hearth. A large variety of furniture was positioned in front of the fire, and Patience's three traveling companions eased into the comfortable settees, relaxing after the last miserable hour of their journey.

Patience, on the other hand, began to examine the frieze. Tiny leaves and intricate vines were

exquisitely crafted along with the nearly animate sculptured forest creatures. She ran her fingers along the edges, marveling at the artisan's
skill.

"Please do sit down, Miss Harrington. You're
making me extremely nervous."

Patience restrained a sigh. "Do excuse my excitement, Mrs. Tecking. This is so wonderfully
done." She continued to study the lovely carvings beneath her fingertips.

"I daresay, Miss Harrington, you will have the
next three weeks to study the woodwork, the
plaster, and artifacts to your heart's content, but
only this first chance to make a good impression
on Lady Caroline and her nephew Lord Blackfield. Wouldn't you say, Freddie?"

Mr. Tecking absently patted his wife's hand.
"There, there, dear, it's been a long trip. You're a
bit overwrought."

Mrs. Tecking's pinched features pulled
tighter, her icy eyes narrowed; but she quieted as
usual under her husband's attention, as infre-
quently as it was given. Patience released a long
sigh and sat on the plum settee John was occu-
pying, his long legs stretched out in front of him.
She didn't want to cause problems, although no
matter what she did, problems seemed to follow

her with the tenaciousness of one of Lady Shickles's feral poodles.

Kenfield returned with a tea service minutes later, and Mrs. Tecking promptly volunteered to serve. Patience turned to the butler, but before she could speak, a tremendous boom reverberated through the room. Mrs. Tecking jerked, nearly spilling the contents of her cup.

A footman rushed over and whispered something in Kenfield's ear. His face remained impassive, but his shoulders tightened.

"Excuse me please, ladies, gentlemen. Lady Caroline will join you shortly." With that, Kenfield strode from the room.

Patience shut her mouth with a snap. Her need to use the retiring room had been increasing for the past hour, and now that she was safely inside the castle her body had decided that the need had suddenly become pressing. Listening to the steady downpour of rain was not helping matters.

She tried to concentrate on something else. Anything else. She noticed that the chandelier was smaller than the one in the entrance hall, but it, too, was odd-looking. She crossed her legs. Crystal jars hung from the branches. She uncrossed her legs. Whatever would the jars be used for? She shifted uncomfortably to the left. And where were the candles hidden?

She shifted right. Trying to distract herself wasn't working. She tried to join the conversation instead as they talked about their impressions of the castle so far, a grand country estate as opposed to the drafty fortified castles of old. Patience just wished there was a moat. Unfortunately, moats made her think of water, which caused her to pinch her knees together.

"Did you see the fourteenth-century stonework?" Mr. Tecking asked.

"Or the thirteenth-century tapestry?" John added.

Patience forced herself not to rock about like a child, but her efforts grew futile, and she stood. "If Lady Caroline arrives before I return, please make my excuses."

John cast her a sympathetic look, but Mrs. Tecking frowned. "Miss Harrington, surely you can wait a few more minutes until our hostess arrives."

Patience, never known for living up to her name, tried to give the woman a disarming smile. "No, Mrs. Tecking, I'm afraid not. I won't be five minutes. No need to worry."

"But—"

Patience slipped through the door and into the hall before anyone could remind her of what had happened the last time she had gone unaccompanied in a foreign house. Part of the reason her father had sent her on this trip was to remove her from London and allow the gossip to die down. Not that she wasn't a skilled antiquarian—she was perfectly suited for this expedition regardless of the gossip.

But as naive as she sometimes could be, she had seen her father's relief and excitement. He felt the trip was a twofold blessing. The first was the cataloging and acquisition of the Ashe largesse, Lady Caroline's generous donation to the museum. The second, and more important, his happiness at removing his beloved child from the distasteful rumors running rampant through the city.

Patience pushed the rumors from her mind. She had dreamed of this trip for weeks and refused to allow the unpleasant thoughts of London to ruin her grand adventure. And at this very moment her grand adventure consisted of finding a room and a pot. Not necessarily in that order if she were forced to wait twenty minutes more.

Any of the servants should be able to assist

her. Actually, the butler should have guided their party to the appropriate area on their arrival. He was obviously preoccupied.

His preoccupation seemed to have spilled over to include the footmen. She was disgruntled to find no one present in the hall, where only twenty minutes before there had been at least fifteen servants bustling about. She peered in each direction and called out a greeting, but the only response to her overture was the steadily falling rain and crackling thunder outside.

Thinking about the rain again was not helping her condition, so she decided to take matters into her own hands and investigate. She reasoned that she should encounter a person by walking down the hall with the most light.

Heading down a well-lit hall, she called out greetings. Beautiful tapestries and paintings dominated the walls, and small alcoves with statues and armor were nestled at random intervals. She vowed to return when she could better appreciate the work. John loved medieval tapestries, and she would definitely tell her cousin where to find such a large and beautiful assortment.

Where was everyone? The hall branched out. Two paths were lit equally by ornate sconces, so she proceeded left. Twice more she turned left, and Patience decided that maybe it was time to stop searching for a person and begin looking for the room herself. Lifting a hand lamp conveniently placed halfway down the hall, she opened a nearby door, poked her head inside, and barely contained a shout of glee as she found what she had been searching for.

After taking care of her immediate needs, she perused her surroundings more seriously. Strange handles, knobs, and cords rimmed the room. Patience reached out and pulled a handle on the left. Whoosh. She couldn't be sure with the torrential storm raging outside, but it sounded like a gush of water emanating from somewhere in the walls. She pulled it again. Whoosh. And again. Whoosh.

It was a funny noise, so she pulled it twice more before moving to the knob on its right. She turned the knob a few times, but nothing happened. After that was a cord that hooked into the wall. She gave it a tug and heard a click, but disappointingly, nothing appeared to happen with it either.

Next in line was an intricate conglomeration of machinery attached to an arm. She pulled the arm and was surprised when a small stream of water poured into the hand bowl. She pulled it a few more times, running her hand beneath the cold spray. The bowl was nearly full, so she abandoned it and grasped the last handle.

A thump alerted her to look at the chamber pot as the bottom opened and the contents dropped. When she let the handle loose in surprise, the bottom slammed back into place. She stared open-jawed at the empty pot. A chamber pot that emptied itself? Where did the contents go? She peered around it and even tried the handle a few more times, trying to see beneath. In her haste upon entering she hadn't noticed anything odd about the pot, but now she could see it was composed of separate pieces.

She shook her head. The light was too low. She'd have to come investigate during the day. She gave the whooshing handle one last tug, her mouth curling as the whoosh moved from one side of the room to the other. It wasn't polite conversation, but she would have to come up with a suitable way to ask someone about the devices. Perhaps Tilly could ferret the information from the castle servants.

Patience began to retrace her steps to the drawing room when another boom of thunder caused her to jump. The storm was not abating. She smiled as she listened to it raging outside.

The shadows hugged the walls, and her fertile imagination conjured up images of ghosts and beasties that could be waiting around the castle's corners prepared to leap upon a distracted traveler. Phantoms and ghouls springing in her mind, she was unsurprised to hear the creaking sound that came from within a room on her right. It was a distinctive sound, like a window opening. A window opening for a ghoul to enter.

She paused. Yes, there it was again.

The same curiosity that had caused her to open the door at the Speckling Rout when she had heard moaning and stifled screams, only to discover Lord Seagram doing interesting things to Lady Hillshine, prompted her to open the door here too.

Except for a faint light cast by a softly banked fire in the grate, the room was dark.

Patience stopped, listened, then cautiously slipped inside. A window *was* sliding upward. A flash of lightning highlighted a figure wearing a pointed collar drenched in blood as he grasped the open window ledge. A scream stuck in her throat as the vampire hauled himself up and over the sill, his long cloak slithering behind.

Recovering from her initial shock, Patience grabbed the first objects at hand, statues that had been displayed on twin pedestals near the door. Arms outstretched, she crossed the statues before her.

"Stop! Fiend!"

The vampire dropped to the floor and raised his dark head in surprise. "Who the devil are you?"

She shook the statues at him, keeping them in a crossed position. "Go on, get out of here. The lord of the castle and his servants will be here shortly. Best get out while you still are able." Her voice wavered as the figure stepped forward.

He snorted and brushed water, not blood as she had initially thought, off his sleeves, before removing his wet cloak and casting it aside. "Now that would be amusing. Go tell the lord of the castle that I'm waiting."

Well, he wasn't acting like she assumed a vampire would, but he certainly looked the fiend, shadows clinging to his form, cloak enveloping him in darkness. She wasn't going to get close enough to examine his teeth for verification though.

"Well?" he asked, a touch impatiently.

In her imaginings, vampires weren't impatient. They tended toward guile and seduction. Hence, the intruder obviously wasn't a vampire, but a . . .

"Thief!" She exclaimed. A thief obviously touched in the head. In the latest novel she had read, the heroine had successfully negotiated with the insane madman and appealed to his better nature. "Go on, leave now before they arrive, and you won't get hurt or jailed."

Firelight illuminated sardonic features. "You're going to hurt me with those?" He pointed to the statues before turning his back, completely ignoring her.

"Wh-what, yes!" She waved them, not needing to hold them crossed anymore since she had ruled him out as a vampire, but he didn't seem impressed or concerned.

What to do next? As a guest at the castle, she felt obliged to prevent a robbery, but she wasn't foolhardy enough to think she could do this man bodily harm. He outweighed her by at least four stone. A well-muscled four stone from the breadth of shoulder and fit of his trousers. She would need help in her adventure.

The thief lifted two logs from the firebox and placed them on the coals. Grabbing a poker, he shifted the wood and stirred the embers, nursing the fire to life. Patience shivered. The long trip, the chill of the night, and her nerves finally caught up with her.

He must have seen it. "Miss Whoever-You-Are, put those statues down and come sit by the fire before you collapse." He ran a hand through his drenched hair, spraying droplets of water in every direction. Clumps of raven locks fell across his face in a decidedly wicked manner. He turned and opened a lacquered cupboard.

Thieves did not light fires, then rummage through liquor cabinets. At least none in her frame of reference. Her imagination once more disappointingly turned to reality.

He seemed to find what he was looking for and poured himself a glass. "Port?"

She shook her head, and he sat down and swallowed a healthy portion. "I'm not going to harm you. The door is partially open, and you can always scream for assistance. A loyal retainer is bound to come running," he said softly, but added with a sneer, "I can assure you that my intent is not to steal any of the viscount's priceless relics."

He motioned to her. "Come and sit down. I don't bite. Much." He raised a mocking brow and revealed a mouth full of straight white teeth without a point in sight.

Intrigued, despite herself, with the miscreant, who was obviously not a thief or vampire, she sat in a chair across from him and maintained a firm grip on both statues.

He wasn't classically handsome, but there was a definite virility to his features, a rakish quality, that probably earned him a faithful following among her gender. Dark, slashing brows and brooding features. Perfect for a dark, yet heroic and redeemable vampire. Yes, the kind of man who would love deeply, and perhaps tragically. The kind of man—

"Invited by Caroline, were you?"

Caught in her musings, she looked at him in surprise. "Ah, yes, were you invited as well?"

He snorted, but continued to drink. "I'm sure to be on the morrow. Can't have female guests at the castle without my attendance."

"I'm not sure I understand, sir."

He waved a hand in dismissal without answering. He drained the glass and set it down on the table with a thud. Lounging back in the chair while tapping a finger on the arm, he openly studied every detail of her traveling attire. She stilled her hand from smoothing the skirt. She now understood how the antiquities she examined would feel if they were animate—cataloged from top to bottom. His eyes lingered on her lips, then rose back to search her eyes.

"What are you doing back here, in any case? Shouldn't you be with a chaperone?"

Patience shifted uncomfortably. "Yes, well, it was a long trip and the servants disappeared before they could direct me to the necessary area."

His eyes lit with amusement. "So you endeavored to find the ladies' area on your own?"

"Yes," she said a bit defiantly.

He leaned forward and did another slow perusal of her body. "I don't know that I believe you. Seems more likely that you were looking for someone. A rendezvous, perhaps?"

His words were no worse than any of the others in the last few months. But still, they stung. Patience stood. "I did no such thing. But I think I'd best find someone who knows you. I have only your word that you should be here."

His hand shot out and gripped her chin before she even realized he, too, was standing. "Oh, but I can't let you leave just yet. You are the first interesting woman Caroline has brought this way."

Despite her pique and general, although sometimes skewed, preservation instincts, the scent of something spicy and warm and the touch of his hand as he dragged it along her jaw caused fairies to dance in her stomach.

"I'm not sure . . ." Patience's voice faltered as he leaned toward her. The firelight slashed across his features, and the mischievous look in his eyes mesmerized her as if she were in a vampire's enthrall. The fairies began a rousing jig as she was drawn to him.

Knock, knock. "My lord?"

The man drew back and looked at the door, his hand still moving across her jaw, his thumb skimming her bottom lip. "Yes, Kenfield?"

About to move into his fingers' caress, she froze in sudden recognition. Startled eyes locked with his. "You—you're the viscount?"

One eyebrow rose. "At your service, Miss . . . ?"

"Harrington," she whispered, shock holding her immobile.

Kenfield pushed open the door, and only a slight twitch belied his own shock at seeing Patience with the viscount in a nearly closed room. "My lord, Lady Caroline is in the drawing room attending to some of the guests."

19

"Ah, yes. I saw the coaches. I suppose you came with them?" The viscount directed the question to Patience.

Now that she had time to assimilate the information, she couldn't believe she had missed the obvious. Of course, his entry through a window had thrown her for a loop. Why in Hades had he not used the door? The viscount *was* reputed to be eccentric, but Patience hadn't heard he was crazed.

The viscount was eyeing her, obviously amused, and she realized he had asked her a question. "Er, yes, we all came together."

"What was the excuse this time? Come to see the summer wildlife? The rose garden? Aunt Caroline's collection of posies?"

"Pardon me? I don't understand." Then it dawned on her what he was implying. She pulled herself upright. "We are here to catalog George Ashe's collection."

The mocking smile, and in fact all of the amusement, abruptly dropped from his face, a cold, chilly look replacing it. He looked at the butler. "So the catalogers have arrived?"

"Yes, my lord, I was going to remind you earlier, but you were out. We tried to find you when they arrived." He didn't have to repeat "but you were out," but it lingered in the air. Where had the viscount been on such a night? And why had he returned through a window?

"Thank you, Kenfield." He turned back to Patience, a cold mask in place. The mocking look had returned, but without any of the earlier warmth. "So you are here to catalog my uncle's relics. We should return you to the drawing room, Miss Harrington. Surely your fellow travelers are worried."

He moved toward the door, and she followed, confused and trying to reason why he had gone from amused seducer to forbidding lord so quickly. Was he upset over the donation of the collection? But, no, George Ashe had been dead for over a year. It was reputed that the viscount was on excellent terms with Lady Caroline, George's widow. Surely if Blackfield had wanted to keep the collection, Patience's group would not be there to catalog and transport it. Had he changed his mind? She had never heard of him being interested in antiquities.

The butler shut the door behind them and followed the viscount, who was walking quickly, almost as if he were trying to put as much distance as possible between Patience and himself. When they reached the main hall, the viscount mockingly swept his arms toward the drawing room.

"Enjoy your stay at the castle, Miss Harrington."

Feeling completely confounded by his behavior, she nodded and walked to the drawing room. She was within five paces when a whispered voice near her ear stopped her. "If I could have my Canovas back, Miss Harrington."

She turned quickly to find him right behind her, his features cold and inscrutable. Flustered, she thrust the Canova statues into his outstretched hands and walked into the room.

Thomas Ashe, tenth Viscount Blackfield, watched her disappear into the drawing room, obviously confused by his abrupt change of demeanor. He admired the regal way she moved, shoulders back and head held high, spectacled dark eyes staring straight ahead. She moved with poise, not even the black tendrils escaping from her floppy bun disturbing the picture of quiet confidence.

It was good that she was an antiquarian. He had felt something. A spark. And sparks were dangerous.

He had forgotten himself for a moment. Yes, dangerous indeed.

Thomas glowered at his sedate-looking butler and thrust the statues into Kenfield's out-stretched hands. His valet hurried down the stairs, and Thomas's scowl changed to grati-tude at how quickly Kenfield had informed his man of the need to change garments. Grumbling about the indignity of dressing his master in an entrance hall, his valet assisted him into a dry jacket, tied a loose cravat, and fiddled and fussed with his clothing. Thomas knew that if he were to return to his quarters to dress, he would never make it back to greet his guests be-fore they retired. And Miss Harrington was sus-picious already.

Thomas heard the last bit of conversation in the drawing room, shooed away his valet's min-istrations, and muttered, "Let's get this done."

He walked into the drawing room.

Chapter 2

Feeling a bit flustered from her encounter with the viscount, Patience smiled nervously at the elegant woman standing near John and the Teckings.

Lady Caroline was an attractive, diminutive woman with upswept deep brown hair generously streaked with silver. She had friendly light blue eyes and a gracious manner.

Lady Caroline glanced behind Patience, and Patience wondered if the viscount had been seen by any of the room's occupants. When the lady's eyes focused back on her, a speculative gleam appearing in their depths, Patience concluded at least one person had observed Blackfield. Patience held her breath, waiting to see if Lady Caroline's expression turned to disdain.

Instead, she was rewarded with a genuinely warm smile. "Ah, you must be Miss Harrington, Arthur's daughter. Welcome, my dear, to Blackfield Castle."

Patience returned her smile and walked across the plush red-and-brown Aubusson rug. Her hand was clasped warmly by the older woman, and Patience felt drawn to her immediately, understanding at once why her father had always spoken well of her. "Lady Caroline, it's a pleasure finally to meet you. My father has spoken so highly of you."

Color flushed Lady Caroline's cheeks as she sank into a high-backed burgundy armchair and motioned for Patience to sit next to her. "Oh, my husband George and your father maintained a lively correspondence and friendly rivalry. I have continued to communicate with your father since George's passing."

Patience arranged her celery green skirt as she sat in the chair next to Caroline's, the smooth velvet feel of the chair's upholstery was soothing even through Patience's gloved hands. "He sends his warmest regards and regrets that he was unable to accompany us. Nothing but an emergency would have prevented him from personally accepting your generous invitation and bequest."

"I hope he is well?"

"He is, thank you. He was summoned to appear before Parliament on behalf of the museum. He requested that I issue you an invitation to dinner the next time you are in London."

"Excellent. I look forward to seeing him again." Lady Caroline gestured to the tea set. "Your trip was well?"

Patience accepted a cup. "As well as can be expected on such a difficult night."

Lady Caroline extended a bejeweled hand in distress. "I apologize on behalf of the staff for not seeing to your comforts sooner. We had a slight mishap that required their immediate attention."

Mrs. Tecking smiled obsequiously. "Their service was excellent, Lady Caroline. It was naught of their doing."

Patience turned an apologetic smile on their hostess. "I'm afraid the trip was a mite long for me. I'm unaccustomed to traveling in a coach for such an extended period. I apologize if I overstepped myself."

Lady Caroline smiled in understanding and patted her perfectly coiffed hair. "Nonsense. Unless we are hosting royalty, we tend to be quite informal here at the castle. Long carriage excursions can be quite tiresome. It's one of the penalties of living so far from London."

"When one is accustomed to the ways of the ton, such excursions are commonplace," announced Mrs. Tecking, sending a pointed look in Patience's direction.

John gave Patience an amused glance and diverted the conversation.

Patience's smile grew somewhat pained. It wasn't as if she didn't *know* the decorum and ways of the ton. So she had her fair share of disasters. Didn't every debutante and newcomer to the social scene?

It wasn't her fault that she enjoyed discussing the adornments at a ball rather than the people. And really, one would think that a faux pas here and there would be forgiven and forgotten. She had not actually *known* the Countess of Lockely wasn't pregnant. Or that the Earl of Montooth wasn't *really* interested in a dissertation on the role of cats in Egyptian society during her first (and last) night at Almack's.

After all, the man *had* expressed interest in antiquities. How was she to know that people said things they didn't mean? Her father hadn't raised her to simper and bandy platitudes.

And if she had known that the old Marquess of Antleberry was nicknamed "Randy" for a reason, she would never have followed him back to look at his "antiquities." Antiquities, indeed. It had just been her bad luck that a group of people had chosen that moment to enter the solarium, just when she herself had turned around to see the marquess's antiquities in full view.

Traversing London society had been an enlightening disaster. But honestly, one would think, judging by John's expression and Mrs. Tecking's mutterings that they expected further faux pas.

Lady Caroline smiled. "Now that you are here, we can discuss your plans for the next few weeks."

Patience nodded, and Lady Caroline refilled her cup with a dark Darjeeling tea, her favorite.

"Your father speaks very highly of your abilities to organize, catalog, and lead. Quite a compliment from such an astute scholar. It is very unusual for the responsibilities to fall on the shoulders of one so young, but I'm delighted that you are here, and the work can begin."

Patience felt a warm burst of love toward her father. Since he was in London attending to business, the task of coordinating George Ashe's bequest fell to her. As Lady Caroline expressed, this was an unusual appointment for one of her age and gender. She knew that her father had wanted her on the assignment, in part to get her away from the gossip associated with the Antleberry incident. However, he had praised her skills to the museum director and board, and they had announced that in his stead, she was to be in charge of the project.

Patience looked over her group, gauging their responses.

As usual, Mr. Tecking looked lost in thought. He had a brilliant mind but couldn't be bothered with details or planning. There was little doubt that he would hate a lead position, hate the time and energy taken from his studies. Lock him in

29

a room with Roman or Greek statuary and feed him an occasional meal and the man needn't emerge for days. No, Mr. Tecking didn't resent her status as project leader.

John was a specialist in antique weapons and, as she knew, eager to study Ashe's vast collection of medieval European and Asian weaponry. John and she had worked together on several projects and were able to help one another seamlessly on their respective tasks. She wondered if her cousin begrudged her the higher position, but if he did, it was carefully hidden behind friendly smiles and light banter.

As a recorder, Mrs. Tecking kept very detailed notes on certain aspects of the project. Without instruction from the team, she had no actual skill to research or catalog. Her position was necessary, but alas for her, she was not knowledgeable enough to assume lead position. Unfortunately for Patience, their working relationship was strained because Mrs. Tecking believed all of the negative gossip surrounding Patience and made little secret that she found her behavior objectionable.

Patience turned back to Lady Caroline. "On behalf of the British Museum, I'd like to thank you again for donating your husband's collections. A special dedication ceremony will be held during the season next year."

Lady Caroline smiled cordially, but this time it seemed somewhat strained. "George loved his antiques. He would want them to be appreciated by others in your field."

There was an undercurrent to her words, and only by the slimmest margin did Patience resist making further inquiries. Her father kept reminding her that someday her curiosity was going to land her in real trouble. After the Antleberry fiasco he had just given her a fatherly look and shake of his head and had muttered something about someday seeing her wed and saving his sanity.

She brightened. "We can begin tomorrow. It would be helpful to make an overall perusal of the collection. By doing so, we can determine where each of us will begin, and create a schedule for the work."

Patience elaborated on the different specialties of the team members.

"And what is your specialty, Miss Harrington?"

"Please call me Patience. I have some familiarity with all areas of your husband's collection, but Ancient Greece, Egypt, and the occult are my specialties."

Lady Caroline clapped her hands together. "Excellent. I would be delighted if you would call me Caroline. Tomorrow after you rise and breakfast, I will take you all on a cursory tour of the castle and grounds, then we can discuss your plans in a more detailed fashion."

"That would be wonderful," Patience replied, and even Mrs. Tecking looked interested.

"Patience, you have met my nephew, Viscount Blackfield?"

"Briefly in the hall." Patience tried not to fidget with her teacup.

"Yes, well . . ." Caroline hesitated. "Thomas is not a collector, and he is often preoccupied by estate business."

The statement was awkward. Was she being asked to forgive any rudeness on Blackfield's part? If there was one thing Patience was accustomed to, it was eccentrics.

"Giving away my secrets already, Caroline?"

All of them turned to the drawing room door, where Lord Blackfield stood, resplendent in a hunter green coat and snug brown breeches. Patience was able to examine him in real light for the first time. His hair was in better order, but it still fell with a rakish messiness. He looked powerful and masculine, with broad shoulders and strong body lines. No dandy here. She was pleased to note that if she looked closely enough she could see damp spots on his breeches where they brushed his shiny Hessians. Must not have had time to change, no, *peel off*, his breeches, as indecent as they were.

She looked back up to see him staring at her, eyebrow raised at where she'd been gazing. She colored and focused on a spot above his left shoulder.

"Lord Blackfield, may I present Miss Harrington, Mr. Fenton, and Mr. and Mrs. Tecking."

He nodded and bowed in turn. "Welcome to the castle. I hope you will enjoy your stay with us."

With his tone somewhere between cold and frigid, Patience somehow doubted his words.

The ornate gold clock that stretched across the mantel chimed. Lady Caroline gasped. "Oh, goodness, look at the hour. Where are my manners? After your exhausting ride, I should let you retire for the evening. I will have Kenfield assign someone to show you the way. The castle can be a labyrinth of twists and turns, so unless you are feeling adventurous, pull a bell cord, and the staff will guide you to the dining room in the morning."

Lord Blackfield politely chatted with John and Mrs. Tecking, who both expressed their delight in staying at the castle. Patience hung back and watched Mr. Tecking poke an elephant umbrella stand near the door, while Caroline went to speak with the butler.

Although polite, Patience would bet that Blackfield had waited until he knew they were about to retire before making his entrance. They were obviously unwanted guests as far as he was concerned.

Caroline returned with maids assigned to guide each of them. Blackfield gave Patience an unreadable glance as she followed her assigned maid from the room.

The young woman accompanying Patience seemed a bit skittish, and her behavior made Patience slightly nervous. As they separated from the others on the second staircase and headed toward rooms in the west wing of the castle, she seemed to peer anxiously into every nook and cranny and cautiously around every corner.

The wing was furbished entirely in midnight blues and blood reds. The farther they walked, the more the lighting dimmed and the shadows grew. The shadows began to take shape, and gnarled red fingers curved along the dark ceiling frescoes and walls. Statues snarled from sharp alcoves inset in the walls, and Patience edged away from the sides of the corridors. Flickering sconces shaded the features of cherubs, making them appear more like demons fallen to earth.

Suddenly, the maid skirted left, and a suit of armor on the right lurched forward, its lance falling directly toward Patience. Patience backed against the wall, her hand over her mouth to stifle a scream as the heavy pole bore down to strike her. She shut her eyes for the blow.

"Miss?"

Patience pried her eyes open. The wide-eyed servant was backed against the wall on the other side. Her shaking hands clutched her lamp as she waited for Patience to acknowledge her.

Patience glanced back at the suit of armor. There was nothing amiss or out of place. The lance was upright, its movement a trick of the moving light.

She took a deep breath. "Pardon me. I was just a bit startled."

The maid nodded apprehensively.

"How—how long have you worked here?"

Patience asked. The young woman seemed frightened out of her wits. And although Patience had a vivid imagination, she had to think that the maid's anxiety was rubbing off on her and influencing her reactions in some way. Maybe the maid was scared of the dark.

"Just this past month," the maid said in a near whisper.

Patience nodded. Perhaps her response was due to the size and shape of the castle, the expanse of hallways, the sheer magnitude of rooms, the drafts and strange noises. Lord knew that most people were not accustomed to working and living in a castle. Patience sure wasn't, and therefore she had looked upon her time here as an experience to relish.

The maid moved on, her steps edgy and awkward. The fabric of her dress swayed and rubbed across the floor as she skittered down the corridor. Patience examined the geometric designs in the railings and floors, catching glimpses of the odd feral cupid at the edges of her vision. *That's it*. She was cutting off her supply of Radcliffe novels while on this trip.

With a small sigh of relief, they finally reached her room where Tilly was waiting. The castle maid literally ran off, and Tilly raised a brow in inquiry as she shut the door.

Patience's room was beautiful. Lush and warm, done in dark greens, blues, and deep wood tones. A large oriental rug dominated the floor, and the coverlet on the bed reflected its intricate designs. Patience poked around the corners and even looked under the bed, much to Tilly's amusement.

"Did you speak with the castle staff, Tilly?"

"*Oui, ma petite*. They are nice, but cautious. I do not know if it is the storm that causes them this wariness, but they aren't terribly forthcoming."

"And Mrs. Tecking's maid?"

"As frigid as her mistress, *ma petite*."

"Tilly!"

Her maid blinked innocently. "*Oui, ma belle?*"

Patience shook her head. "You are incorrigible."

After several minutes' further discussion of the accommodations and servants, and a warm glass of milk, Patience readied for bed, then bid good night to her maid.

Walking to the window, she brushed aside the heavy emerald window covering and strained to see across the darkened expanse at the rear of the estate. A bolt of lightning flashed, and she heard a thunderous boom seconds later. And again. And again. And again. Four times in rapid succession. Patience shook her head to clear her thoughts. Bursts of thunder coming so quickly upon one another was not normal, Radcliffe novels or not.

She again peered through the glass and saw what she thought to be lamplight flickering in the distance. She listened to the steady beat of rain for a few minutes until there was another flash and multiple cracks of thunder. Three eruptions that time. The distant lamplight was extinguished with the last blast of thunder. Who or what was out there? Patience shook her head, her imagination running wild as she let the drapery slip from her hand and walked to the bed.

The candlelight flickered in the room, casting hooked fingers along the walls. When she was young her father used to tweak her nose and check under her bed to make sure nothing was hiding beneath. She smiled at the memory.

Capping the candle, she slipped under the covers, reflecting on her first few hours in the castle. It was only her first night there and already she had experienced an adventure. Whatever the rogue-turned-viscount had been doing by entering through a window, it had definitely made an already exciting trip more interesting.

She wondered if she would discover why he had suddenly turned so cold. He had been anything but cold initially. Patience ran a finger across her lip, tracing the path that the viscount's thumb had traveled.

Chapter 3

⌒⌒✦⌒⌒

Tilly woke her early, and Patience spent a peaceful moment at the window, gazing out onto the grounds. She had a beautiful view of the formal gardens, the rose garden, the lake, a number of plain outbuildings, and the small forest north of the property.

The sun was rising in the sky, and even from a distance everything appeared clean and bright after the night's downpour. Patience hoped a tour of the gardens was on the morning agenda. She loved the fresh, clean smell of the plants after a rain.

She dressed and left her room for the dining hall without pulling the bell. She was feeling adventurous, and she somehow doubted Caroline would be surprised that she had struck out on her own.

The castle appeared completely different in the morning light, and she was reminded of the dual personality of the entrance hall the night before. The shadows were soft and passive, and the gilt sparkled in the sun's early rays. The eerie, nearly oppressive, feel was missing, as if scrubbed from existence while she slept.

She shortened her strides to examine a mural depicting the story of Psyche and Cupid, and stopped to admire a Canaletto. An inlay hall table struck her fancy, and she poked underneath it, opening the drawers, feeling the undersides of the wood, and marveling at the craftsman who had shaped it. Only after she bumped into a second maid when crouching beneath a small, but beautiful drum table, did she notice the odd glances the passing servants were giving her.

Mustering some fortitude, she longingly bypassed a beautiful Greek amphora, ten Italian Renaissance paintings, five Dutch masters, an oddly shaped coat of arms that she swore had a naked man in the corner, fifteen different medieval swords, five wall tapestries, and three Chinese vases. That didn't include the countless treasures she tried to ignore completely and not identify, nor the frescoed walls, the frescoed ceilings, the priceless rugs on the floors ... good Lord.

She wondered if she would be able to concentrate on the Ashe collection and not poke around the castle's antiquities instead. What could the viscount's uncle have possibly collected that could make it additional to the treasures already inside?

Two staircases, two wrong turns, and a collision with a servant (due to Patience's tightly shut eyes to prevent her backtracking to a hall stand holding an ornate canopic jar—a rare one with the head of Anubis), and she finally entered the dining room.

Strangely enough only the viscount was present. Generally early risers, her team had either already left or run into the same dilemma as she. As she thought it over, she realized that Mr. Tecking would probably need to be dragged down. John, however, usually exerted more self-control, so his absence was especially puzzling.

Blackfield, looking much more proper but no

less appealing, with his silkily brushed dark hair and finely tailored clothes, examined her. His dark blue eyes took in every inch of her appearance. He muttered a greeting and returned to his paper.

Nonplussed, Patience walked to the walnut sideboard and selected eggs and sausage. She contemplated sitting at the far side of the grand table, but mustering her courage, took a chair near the viscount.

He sighed audibly and let the edges of the paper slip through his fingers, folding his hands on top of the pages as soon as they fluttered closed.

"Did you have a pleasant night, Miss Harrington?"

Patience blinked at his perfunctory manner, as if he only needed to iterate three more clichéd sentences and his duty would be complete.

She paused before answering. "It was interesting."

"Is that so?"

His answer was barely above the level of chronic boredom.

She pushed her eggs a bit. "Quite a storm we had."

"Yes." He peered at his nails.

"All sorts of interesting noises and lights from in and around the castle. One could take to the notion that the castle is haunted."

He made no overt moves, but there was a slight tensing in his well-tanned hands. She noticed that, while his hands were graceful and strong, they weren't smooth and perfectly manicured gentlemen's hands. No London gentleman in his right mind would be tanned or sporting calluses of any kind. And yet she could see one, just beneath the curled pinky finger on his right hand.

"Perhaps I should ask Caroline to have a maid and footman accompany you to your room at night? The castle tends to frighten those with overactive imaginations."

She thought about the near flight to her room the previous night with the maid. She had a feeling he had been informed of it. "Yes, well, nothing wrong with having imagination."

He raised a brow. "Overactive, Miss Harrington, overactive."

She really couldn't argue it at the moment. "Yes, well, I couldn't help but be captivated by all of the beautiful pieces contained in the castle. As well as the life of the castle itself."

Patience couldn't tell what the problem was, but Blackfield's expression warred between pleasure and pain. "I suppose it would take an antiquarian to recognize that about the castle. Too bad most in your field can't see past what is immediately in front of them."

"I, uh, assume that you don't care for antiquarians?"

He tapped his finger against the table. "Don't you ever get bored with it?"

Patience looked at him in surprise. "Bored with what, my lord?"

Blackfield shrugged nonchalantly. "Examining relics? Investigating the same objects, over and over again?"

She frowned. "History is fascinating. Don't you ever wonder how your ancestors lived? How they survived and discovered new techniques to improve their life, created new concepts and devices, or lack thereof?"

"But do antiquarians actually care about time periods and the way people lived?" Blackfield leaned back in his chair, his finger tapping on the wooden arm instead. "Seems to me all of you are more interested in the gilt edging on a glass or a chip in a bowl. Don't you find it repetitive? Or does it just make things easier?"

Patience narrowed her eyes. "What are you implying, Lord Blackfield?"

His gaze slid over her, washing her in a combination of coolness and heat. He waved a hand in a manner that was meant to be disarming. "It just seems to me that whenever I have met people interested in your field, they seem to be escaping from something. Burying themselves in the past or in a vase whose owners have been deceased for centuries."

The barb hit, and Patience knew it showed on her face. "That may be true for some people, as is an obsession with any hobby, not just antiquities."

"Feeling defensive, Miss Harrington?"

"Feeling offensive, Lord Blackfield?"

An unwilling smile pulled at the corners of his mouth. "Touché, Miss Harrington. I suppose I ought to be grateful my aunt has not yet graced the table. I'm sure she would be appalled at my bad manners."

"Well, my lord, one is never too old to learn manners or diplomacy. I myself have only recently learned, that one does not comment on a woman's shape, if she does not want to be clouted with a very large and ugly cane."

Patience could have happily stuck her fork through her hand. What had possessed her to disclose that?

"And what was this shape you commented

on, my dear Miss Harrington?" He sipped his black tea, seemingly interested for the first time in their conversation.

Well, it was too late now. "Whether or not Lady Shickles was breeding."

Blackfield choked on his tea and wheezed. "I will endeavor to remember your wise advice." The edges of his eyes crinkled just a tiny bit. "Did you really ask that of her? Lady Shickles? The one with the medusa-head cane and the poodles?"

"Yes." She casually forked a piece of sausage; a heady sense of freedom coursing through her at blithely repeating her blunder. "That cane is a very poor reproduction of an Italian piece on loan to the museum. Inferior workmanship. I told her I could acquire a better one if she needed assistance through her pregnancy."

She had no idea why she had told him the story. Freeing or not, it was mortifying. A social disaster. And she didn't know him at all. Wasn't even sure she liked him five quips ago. Yet, there was something about him, and when she saw the warm spark in his previously cold eyes, she felt like she, too, wanted to laugh. She wanted to laugh even though the incident had caused her to be blackballed from a number of the early-season events.

And then, of course, the Antleberry incident had taken care of the rest. Her smile vanished.

His gaze turned speculative. "I would have liked to see her face. Those mutts of hers are a menace to proper dogs everywhere."

"Been bitten, have you?" She examined his face shrewdly. "Well, take it as a compliment; they prefer only the choicest meat."

Real humor and a hint of something a touch deeper entered his eyes, and just as she was congratulating herself, John and the Teckings entered the room. Blackfield's facial expression returned to the stiff, formal one of earlier. Nodding politely, he greeted them courteously, lifted his papers, and stood to excuse himself.

He raised an eyebrow to Patience and paused contemplatively before scooping up a scone and disappearing through the archway to a room beyond. She felt a sense of loss at his departure. She had just started warming up to him, and she thought that perhaps the same had been true on his part.

As she had observed the night before, he had a dark and wild sort of beauty that made one want to tame him. No wonder she had heard women talking about him in reference to stallions. She had been confused at the time about why a man would be compared to a horse, but now it made sense.

Patience sipped her tea while John and the Teckings ate, and they discussed the wonderful art and tapestries they had spied in the halls. A light congenial conversation continued until the topic turned to the previous night.

"Quite a storm last night, even after we retired," John said.

Patience frowned. "Did you hear the massive bursts of thunder? It was striking in sudden repetition. Thrice, even four times in a row."

"I didn't hear anything strange," Mrs. Tecking said, a bit dismissively. Although she was polite enough face-to-face, Patience knew Mrs. Tecking held little love or regard for her.

"Are you sure, Patience?" John asked as he spread his scone with jam. "Could it possibly have been your imagination?"

Patience scowled. "Thank you for the support, cousin."

John smirked a bit. "Well you know it does tend to get you into trouble."

She stepped on his foot, not that her kid slippers could do much damage to his polished Hessians. "Talking tends to do that in our family."

Lady Caroline, with impeccable timing, chose

that moment to enter. "Good morning. I hope you all slept well. Are you ready to tour a portion of the estate and see the collection this morning?"

Patience looked around the group. They all looked expectant. She turned back to Caroline. "That would be wonderful."

"Excellent. Let's start with the grounds first?"

They nodded and followed her through the connecting salon and out onto the rear veranda. Trailing periwinkle clung to the neat hedgerows, and a few songbirds escaped as they neared the edge of the flagstones.

The vista took Patience's breath away. It had been incredible from her window, but the sounds, smell, and air made the view so much more. Instead of seeing the grounds from a distance, almost model-like in its perfection, here on the veranda it was magical. She suddenly felt small.

"The castle overlooks twelve thousand acres of park and woodland." Caroline kept a running commentary, and Patience kept half an ear opened while soaking in the view of the rolling meadows and lush gardens.

"We have three formal gardens, the one here

north of the castle, the other two flanking the main southern entrance. Two Greek-styled temples, one there on the other side of the lake, the other a hidden treat beyond the entrance to the woods. One of the sculpture gardens is near the hidden temple, the other is just over there, as you can see." She pointed to the west of the sparkling lake.

"The rose garden to the east . . ." She leaned toward Patience. "My favorite. It's surrounded by four separately designed fountains that lead into a number of bridle paths. One of those paths will take you to the hidden temple and sculpture garden. Please feel free to speak to our stablemaster about mounts if you enjoy riding."

Caroline led them toward the lake and formal garden. "There is a river just over the bend that meanders through the estate. A mile or two distant is an excellent location for fishing. Two other lakes can be found on the property, both larger than this one and well stocked."

They stopped near the edge of the dark blue water, and Caroline pulled some bread from her pocket and tossed it into the water. A number of ducks and swans glided toward the bank. It looked to be a ritual.

"The river runs by the ruins of Farstaff Abbey. I recommend a visit." She smiled. "I'm sure you all will enjoy the scenery and its history."

They strolled through the formal garden, and Patience trailed her hand underneath a fountain spout, a half-naked cupid pouring water from its ewer. The water was crisp and cold and as she surveyed the others investigating the hawthorn hedgerow shrubs, the primrose and yellow pimpernel, she felt a heady sense of wonder that someone could own something as magnificent as the Blackfield estate.

In the distance she could see an observatory and four brown nondescript buildings nestled near the woods. The observatory was beautiful, a domed temple in and of itself, but the brown buildings were . . . plain. Almost out of place. Two men appeared between the central buildings and disappeared inside the one on the right.

Patience spoke up. "Caroline, what are those four buildings for?"

Caroline didn't look her way, but continued to observe a primrose bush with Mrs. Tecking. "Oh, those are just some of the staff buildings. Nothing too interesting."

Patience frowned. She was sure Tilly had said the staff were all housed in the southwest wing of the castle. Granted, she had also heard there were nearly two hundred servants in residence. But those unadorned buildings were large. And one of them only had windows on the eastern half. What was in the western half that didn't require at least one window?

She stopped wondering about the buildings as soon as she entered the rose walk. No wonder Caroline said it was her favorite. The artful arrangement of flowers and statuary was enchanting, and the smell was nothing short of divine. There had to be forty different types of roses in various sizes, shapes, and colors—tall, short, large-bloomed, climbing, miniature, red, purple, yellow, white ... Roses trailing down walls, roses standing tall, roses shyly peeking from the corners. It was wonderful.

Lady Caroline led them back inside for a light noon meal, then they proceeded to explore the ground floor, with its collection of priceless tapestries, murals, and pictures.

The gallery was a highlight of the first floor. Generations of viscounts and viscountesses Blackfield peered down their noses as the five made their way through. Rich reds and golds dominated the superior room.

"The china and bronze collection down the hall are courtesy of the fifth viscountess, the lady in blue there on the right." Lady Caroline's voice trailed off as she turned the corner followed by the others. Just beyond the portrait gallery, Patience paused to examine a painting of the castle. The artist had captured the sentient nature of the building, as if the stones were waiting for the viewer to turn before taking its next breath. While searching for the artist's signature, she stumbled into a suit of armor.

Grabbing on to the arm for support, she was appalled to feel the arm and pike break off in her hand. She stared at it in shock for a moment before hastily trying to shove it back in place.

Murmurs and footsteps rounded the corner and Patience, holding the broken piece of armor in front of her, jumped into the niche between the armor and the wall. Mortified at the thought of being found holding a broken piece of antiquity, she was trapped. She could only hope that the women coming down the hall didn't glance her way.

"Did you hear it last night? Out again!"

"Shh, do you want to get us in trouble?"

"No, but I'm scared! A monster, it is! I've seen it."

"You have not."

"I have! A large, hairy beast with breath of fire and hands of steel. It will kill us all."

The other maid grabbed her and shot a quick look down the hall. "Hush, you fool. The master will have your hide if you don't stop your babbling."

The girl looked terrified. "He'll feed me to it you mean!"

The maid rolled her eyes, her face was pinched. "You're new. You'll get used to it. Just don't go near those buildings. And don't let those guests hear your nonsense, or the master won't have to, because *I'll* feed you to it."

The girl gibbered on, but the other maid dragged her down the hall, continuing to scold her.

Patience blinked. Monster? The viscount was keeping some hairy beast locked away in the plain buildings to the north? She shook her head to clear it. Next she would have him back as a vampire enthralling his victims to willingly sacrifice themselves to his pet creatures.

She shoved the gauntleted arm in place and gave a twist. It stuck at an odd angle, but it would have to do. She'd ask John to fix it later.

Walking in the direction the rest of the party had taken, she found them halfway down the hall emerging from the china room.

Caroline looked relieved. "Oh, good. I was just about to send a servant to find you."

"My apologies, Caroline, I became rather interested in one of the portraits."

Caroline smiled and led them to the stairs.

"The castle was constructed in the seventeenth century for the third Viscount Blackfield and work spanned the lives of three viscounts. They strived to create one of England's grandest country homes, an unparalleled structure that would be heralded through the ages. The finest architects and craftsmen were commissioned. Thus far, each incumbent has taken his stewardship and inheritance seriously and has enhanced the estate."

"Are renovations or restorations being done by the present viscount?" Patience asked.

"Why yes, on the interior."

"I noticed last night that the privy in the west corridor contained devices that I have never seen, even in London."

"Yes, well . . ." Caroline hesitated. "Kenfield acquired them from somewhere."

She motioned, in a somewhat flustered manner, for them to continue walking. "I'm sure you are all eager to look at my husband's collection. Anytime you want to explore further, talk to Kenfield, and he will assign someone to act as your guide. Most rooms are open for you to browse through, barring the family wings, state rooms, and Lord Blackfield's personal rooms. Please don't make the mistake of wandering through his private areas."

Caroline had looked distinctly uncomfortable when Patience mentioned the privy devices. At first Patience had thought it due to the nature of the question. But that would have caused mortification, a blush, something of that nature. Caroline's eyes had been distressed.

Patience narrowed her eyes, but followed as Caroline led them down the hall.

George Ashe's collection was everything they had hoped and more. Her father would be pleased. The museum would be thrilled.

After wiping her hands on a towel, Patience pushed a few of the escaped dark locks dancing on her forehead back toward her dangling bun.

She needed an army of clips and pins to tame it, and even without the excited motions of diving into her favorite pastime, her hair tended to stage frequent revolts.

John walked into the room looking as happy as Patience felt.

"The guns. Hakenbuchses, hackbuts, a Lansknecht Stock . . ." He shook his head. "There are a pair of Russian seventeenth-century snaphaunces that are unbelievable. And a pair of Spanish blunderbusses . . . well, I've never seen their like." John was nearly speechless.

She had briefly seen the engraved staghorn, mother-of-pearl, walnut, and pierced-iron pieces. They had looked impressive to her, and weaponry was far from her field.

"And?"

He grinned. "The collection is excellent. Your father will be pleased."

She grinned back. "It's the same with the Greek and Egyptian pieces. They're in incredible condition."

They talked, or rather gushed, about the respective collections. "It's getting late, and we need to clean up before supper," John said, finally breaking their long-winded discussion. "Do you want me to let the Teckings know?"

"Yes, better you than I. Missus dislikes me."

John grimaced. "I don't know what is worse, her obsession with propriety or his obsession with antiques. I might need you to help me get him to the table for meals."

"I thought the same this morning. He does get a bit . . . involved."

John raised a brow. "Involved? You are being kind. I think the word is *obsessed*."

Patience was reminded of the conversation with Blackfield that morning. "Yes, well, I'm sure that between you and Mrs. Tecking you can get him to the dinner table tonight. It is our first night, and she would be appalled to miss any festivities."

Patience waved before walking back to her room. Tilly was already waiting to help her wash and dress. She had packed a number of gowns and evening dresses, prepared for formal dining. She donned a sky-blue dress, which lightened her dark eyes, a gift from her French mother. She fiddled with her pearl necklace while Tilly tightened her corset and buttoned the dress. The undergarments and lines of the dress changed her average curves into fashionable ones.

Tilly finished dressing her hair, and Patience

put her wire spectacles back in place. She knew they weren't stylish, and she only needed them for reading, but she felt safer with them on. They were her battle shield.

She walked toward the dining room, stopping only three times to examine something new that had caught her attention in the halls. She was just finishing an examination of a stunning Red-Figure kylix from the fifth century B.C. when the hairs on the back of her neck stood.

She turned to see Blackfield lounging against the opposite wall, an unreadable look on his face. Pulling upright, Patience felt her face flush as she realized she had been bending in all directions to inspect the ancient Greek drinking cup, and had no idea how long he had been standing there behind her.

The ends of his mouth curved sensually upward as color climbed her cheeks. She blinked, flustered, and turned her gaze back to the kylix. Perhaps she had overestimated the quality of her shield.

"May I escort you to the dining room, Miss Harrington?" His deep voice sounded amused.

She placed an unsteady hand on his sleeve, not looking him in the eye. "Thank you, Lord

Blackfield." She was happy to note that her voice remained steady.

"I see you have taken an inordinate interest in the hall pottery."

She sniffed. "Hall pottery, indeed."

"I can find you a much nicer drinking cup in the kitchens. One without a fracture at the base."

"One made centuries ago by Euerdiges?"

"How about Wedgwood? I do believe he is a distant cousin."

A reluctant smile curved her lips as they entered the room where the others were waiting. Patience saw Mrs. Tecking give her a sharp look. She didn't want to know what images were stirring in the woman's head.

Blackfield bowed to Patience. "It was a pleasure, Miss Harrington. We must talk further about the Wedgwood family tree."

Patience smiled as he offered his arm to his aunt, the highest-ranking lady in the room, and led the group to the table. After the ladies were seated, she watched Blackfield sink into his chair like a pat of butter melting into a pan.

Caroline and John conversed freely through the first few courses. Patience had been sure Mrs. Tecking would be simpering before the viscount, but for some reason she had taken to casting speculative glances toward Patience and uttering small nearly unheard sighs.

Patience tried to ignore her glances as well as avoid looking directly at Blackfield, but she felt his gaze resting on her periodically throughout the meal. He allowed Caroline and John to drive most of the conversation, although his near silence did nothing to diminish his presence.

Patience saw John nod emphatically. "The number of pieces creating the knight's mail was a decision that could not be taken lightly. Armor was, after all, a deciding factor in determining the outcome of many medieval battles."

Caroline leaned forward. "It was a detriment at times too, yes?"

"Oh, yes. More than one knight drowned after falling into water, being unable to stand and remove his mail by himself."

Patience thought it was a great time to show Blackfield how interesting historical debates could be. "It's one of the reasons the Greeks might have had it right. There's a statue of a hoplite in the museum wearing a breastplate, helmet, greaves—which are shin guards—and nothing else. Makes one think about what is really necessary."

She had found the statue very interesting, and she and her father had discussed the advantages and disadvantages of different types of armor through the ages. She had gotten over her bashfulness at seeing the naked or nearly naked forms from the classical periods, long ago.

Patience looked up to continue the discourse and see if she could tempt the viscount into the conversation, when she suddenly noticed that the table had gone silent.

John was staring at her wide-eyed and slack-jawed. Caroline had started waving her fine linen napkin in a doomed attempt to keep the blush from her face. Mrs. Tecking's eyes were narrowed.

Oh dear Lord, she had done it again.

Mr. Tecking, oblivious as usual, just nodded to her. "Quite right, Miss Harrington. Always knew you were a smart one."

Blackfield raised a brow and drawled, "Well, nothing boring there, Miss Harrington. I stand corrected from earlier."

That seemed to break the stupor. Caroline and John hastily switched topics to conversing about the latest news occurring in London, and drew Mr. Tecking, and subsequently Mrs. Tecking, into the conversation.

Patience barely paid attention. Instead, she watched Blackfield. His smirk over her embarrassment made her itch to remove it. He returned her perusal, doing little to hide his amusement as the conversation ebbed around them.

For some absurd reason, she blamed her conversational blunder entirely on him.

She stabbed her meat, her eyes never leaving his. His smirk widened and he forked a green in response. She violently stirred her au jus, he swished his wine.

She slid her knife across her roast in a mock threatening fashion. He raised a brow and traced his wineglass in a somewhat obscene motion. Her mouth dropped in shock before she regained her wits and shot him a scathing glare.

He smirked again, as if he had known she wouldn't rise to the challenge. She refused to look away, continuing to glare at him. He retraced his glass, then lifted it to his lips. She could have sworn he did something to the edge of the glass with his tongue; but her spectacles seemed a bit foggy, and she couldn't be sure.

Dessert came too fast, and Patience had to admit momentary defeat as Blackfield seemed to be mimicking his wineglass actions with his pie and fork. Understanding just enough to make the room feel ten degrees warmer, but not skilled enough to fight back, Patience turned her gaze to the others. Apparently their conversation was so intense that no one else had observed Blackfield's behavior or the mimed interchange.

Dessert was removed from the table and, since none of the men smoked, Caroline suggested an alternative. "Is anyone interested in playing a few games of whist?"

Mr. Tecking set his napkin by his plate. "I'm going to retire for the evening and begin recording preliminary notes, if you will all excuse me for the night."

Mrs. Tecking's eyes tightened minutely. "I will retire as well. Thank you, Lady Caroline and Lord Blackfield, for a lovely dinner."

It was obvious that Mrs. Tecking wanted to stay, but deemed it proper to leave with her husband. Even though Mrs. Tecking had never been more than coldly polite to her, Patience felt a bit sorry for her.

Surprisingly, John expressed interest in retiring early as well, so Lady Caroline suggested playing whist another night, leaving Patience, Caroline, and Blackfield to their own pursuits.

* * *

As Patience readied for bed she was still thinking about dinner. She wasn't sure she was up to playing the viscount's games. For all her muddled reputation, she truly had no clue as to the games men and women played.

Not that she had never been curious, of course. And not that her curiosity wasn't being directly piqued by the viscount and his dark, teasing demeanor.

But all she needed was for another rumor to start. It would be the final nail in her coffin, and it would only be a matter of time before her soiled reputation affected her father's.

The shadows once again embraced the castle. A low, keening cry echoed in the air. Slipping out from beneath her covers, she padded to the window. Lights flickered in one of the four buildings near the woods.

Another cry, as if a banshee were wailing her distress, disturbed the air, causing the hairs on her arms to stand at full alert. Nothing more sounded, and the lights stopped flickering. Patience returned to bed and as she lay under the covers, she couldn't help but recall the maids' earlier conversation about monsters.

Visions of vampires and restless dreams about

the viscount calling forth his monster army plagued her sleep. Blackfield, with his long cape and piercing eyes, stood on top of a ridge surrounded by fiends. His eyes sought hers, and he beckoned her forth. "Join me," his voice whispered to her, caressing her even through the noisy throng of his followers. She broke from his gaze and found herself back in the castle outside of her door.

A figure turned a corner, just out of her reach. She wanted—no, needed—to get to the figure, the dark being who would wipe away her worries and shield her from broken dreams. As she turned the corner she saw the figure looking out an alcove window. Lightning flashed, but his back was to her. She approached, needing something. Abruptly the phantom turned toward her, lightning again flashed, this time illuminating his features. She froze, fear and something else clawing at her insides. Her fear smelled like peaches. Peaches? The phantom started to dissolve and she reached forward to hold him there.

The phantom reached for her, and glass shattered.

Chapter 4

Patience shot upright. Groping for her wiry spectacles, she clutched her chest with one hand, gasping for breath, then gagging as she drank in the overwhelming scent of peaches.

"Tilly!"

"*Mon Dieu!* My apologies, *ma petite*! I was preparing your clothing and toilette for when you awoke. I lost my grip again."

Patience tried to still her racing heart as she focused on the salt-and-pepper head of her maid, who was trying to clean up the mess created by the shattered perfume bottle. "It's not a disaster, Tilly. Here, let me help."

"Oh, *ma petite*, I'm so sorry. Be careful not to cut your feet."

Patience scooted off the bed and stooped to pick up the pieces. Tilly fussed, trying to prevent her from helping, but Patience ignored her attempts.

Patience dearly loved Tilly, a wise and gentle woman who had been her mother's maid. Although Tilly was getting on in years and despite the increasing mishaps, Patience would not discuss pensions until Tilly was ready to retire.

The mess was cleaned up, although the peach smell would probably remain in the room for the duration of their stay. Patience sighed as she dressed. Well, at least she wouldn't require perfume today.

Patience walked slowly to the dining room, and just as she had feared, Blackfield was its only occupant. She had no idea why she was suddenly feeling nervous.

She traded a cursory greeting with him and put scones and jam, along with slices of fruit, on her plate. She shuddered at the eggs. After the dreams of watching monsters hatch, she decided it was better to avoid her favorite morning food today. One of the footmen held out her chair, and she smiled gratefully to him as she was seated. She wondered how anyone could become accustomed to so many servants.

Patience glanced up as a hapless servant rushed to the viscount's side, knocking a full teacup right into his lap.

The viscount jumped from his seat. "What the devil?!"

The servant stuttered an apology and reached forward to blot up the spilled tea from his master's trousers.

A snort of laughter escaped her as Blackfield slapped the servant's hand away before it reached his lap and glared at the poor man. Blackfield's dark gaze then met hers, and she attempted to hide her smile by lowering her head and examining her fruit. He swore again and tried unsuccessfully to mop up the moisture from his trousers.

The flustered servant thrust an odd-looking note toward the viscount, and Patience had to take a second glance to confirm what her eyes had seen. The parchment was, well, it was *pink*. If he were one of the ton dandies she might think it was a love note or a poem composed by a female admirer, but Blackfield hardly seemed the type to exchange love notes. He seemed more suited to seduction than to courtship. The way that he held himself, the complete control hidden behind his languid air . . .

On second thought, she supposed that notes to and from a lover might be a form of seduction. Really, wasn't courtship just seduction wrapped in multiple layers of frill and chaste greetings?

Still, there wasn't much frilly or chaste about Blackfield, even if he were on a mission of courtship. And something told her that he would be successful at anything he tried. That he wouldn't allow himself to fail.

At the moment his mission seemed to be setting the paper afire merely by using his blazing eyes. He scowled at the feminine-colored paper, then motioned for one of the servants to bring a pen. He furiously scribbled something and handed the messenger the deeply creased note.

"You, out," he ordered the tea-spilling servant rooted to the spot. "Go, deliver that."

The man bobbed his head and raced off as if the hounds of hell were at his heels. Perhaps they were.

"Please, Miss Harrington, don't stop laughing

on my account. Is there any other scalding-hot liquid you'd like to see splashed across my lap?"

Released from propriety, Patience broke into peals of laughter.

"Bloody woman," he muttered, but there was a slight smile quirking his lips as he stood.

A gasp from the entryway announced Mrs. Tecking's presence. Her posture indicated she was insulted by such vulgar language and was a breath away from fainting. Blackfield cocked a brow at Patience, grabbed a couple of scones, and swept from the room in dramatic fashion.

Patience had to admire the way the man made entrances and exits. The image would be perfect if only he had a cape to snap behind him.

Mrs. Tecking made an indignant sound but loaded her plate with food and sat as far away from Patience as the table allowed.

Patience sighed. It was going to be a long day.

She was proven right a few hours later as she prepared to ride to the local village. Mrs. Tecking popped into the room.

"I'll ride along with you. I need to pick up a few things in the village as well. Wait right there."

Patience groaned as Mrs. Tecking disappeared. Her sunny afternoon trip had just taken a turn for the worse.

"Bad luck, old girl." John looked up sympathetically from his position on the floor, where he was examining a collection of scimitars.

"John, why don't you join me instead?"

His eyes were disbelieving. "And how are you going to tell her that she's not going? She's been itching to get away from dear Freddie since we arrived."

"Just say we were planning on going somewhere, doing something, anything! You know what she's like. I'll be completely at her mercy in that carriage. She'll couch some lecture about manners and propriety in pointed terms, never saying directly what she wants to, but insulting me nevertheless. And it's not like there's anything I can do or say at this point that will change her mind about me. I'm forever a fallen woman in her eyes."

"Patience—"

Mrs. Tocking strode back in. "I'm ready. Are you ready to go?"

Patience sighed. "Was there anything you needed, cousin?"

"No," John said cheerfully. "You two have a grand time."

Patience shot him a look filled with painful promises but trudged outside with Mrs. Tecking.

The trip to the village was interminable, just as she knew it would be. Mrs. Tecking wouldn't shut up about "a smart debutante's guide to manners" and how "the shelf" creeps up on a woman if she doesn't mind those manners. She also extolled the virtues of a good name, a good reputation (with a pointed look in Patience's direction), and femininity in general.

Patience looked at the scenery as the open carriage emerged from the trees and the beautiful attached stone buildings spread before them. It was a gorgeous, bustling hamlet full of greenery, life, and noise as the sun's full rays smiled overhead.

She smiled, and her spirit lifted.

"If a young lady really wants to make a good example, she will never speak until—"

A bump in the road caused the rest of the sentence to lodge in the woman's throat. Before Mrs. Tecking could recover, Patience motioned for the driver to stop. Dismounting quickly, she shouted a quick salutation to Mrs. Tecking, grabbed her supply bag, and stepped onto a footbridge at the entrance of the village. She had just broken four of Mrs. Tecking's rules of deportment in less than three seconds, and she would most likely hear about it later.

A proper lady didn't shout. A proper lady certainly wouldn't alight from a carriage without assistance. And a proper lady absolutely didn't walk off on her own.

Patience circled the livestock being sold at market, passed hawkers selling their wares, and crossed the footbridge, trying to keep ahead of her erstwhile companion. If she were lucky, perhaps Charon would deny Mrs. Tecking the crossing. She snorted. The ferryman of the mythic Greek underworld would probably be too busy plugging his ears as Mrs. Tecking lambasted him for delaying a lady.

Feeling lighter and more carefree at her musings, Patience entered the village proper and headed straight for the smithy, which was prominently marked as the second shop in the cobblestone row.

Whistling, she swung her basket and gave a jaunty little hop. The small village reminded her of their home in the Cotswolds. The yellow limestone facades were neat and beautiful. Row upon row of storefronts displayed a profusion of flowers on the cobblestone walk and flowers flowing from the second-level balconies. Plants and trailing ivy created a nice texture and color against the honey tones of the stone.

Across the street, prosperous-looking houses overlooked a large park. Children played in the square, and mothers conversed with one another over low gates and fences.

Rural life was what she missed. The camaraderie of friends and family. Life had been so much easier at home in the country before her father had taken the position at the British Museum and become involved in the politics and social whirl of London. Before Patience had been forced from the comforts of country living and into the dirty city that seemed to mock her at every step.

WHAM.

A loud crash caused the comfortable village bustling to momentarily cease, and an inhuman groan filled the air. The villagers looked about nervously, and a few sent wary, almost terrified glances her way. A minute later, the street was nearly deserted.

Patience stared in shock at the complete change in the town. The atmosphere had gone from friendly and carefree to suspicious and withdrawn in less than two minutes. What had just happened?

Whistle forgotten and feeling a bit uneasy, Patience entered the blacksmith's shop and called out, "Hello?"

A woman's head poked around the back wall and locked eyes with her. Patience stared back. The woman blinked twice and disappeared.

The day was only getting stranger.

A man hustled into the room. "Hello, ma'am, what can I do for you?"

Patience shrugged off the creepy feeling and pulled a broken tool from her bag. "I was wondering if you could fix this?"

The blacksmith took the implement and examined the two pieces in his large hands. "Not a problem. I should have it finished by the end of the week."

"Excellent. I'm staying at the castle. Would you send someone up with it when it is finished?"

His eyes were searching and shrewd. "The castle, eh? You one of the visiting folks?"

"Yes." Patience didn't know what else to say or how to react to his dissecting gaze and direct question.

He made a noncommittal noise and continued to turn the pieces in his hand in an absent fashion.

"Is that a difficulty?"

"No. Most people don't last at the castle that long, but when the work is done, I'll have it brought round to you."

The end of his sentence seemed to imply, "if you are still there." A shiver passed over her.

"Thank you."

Patience left as quickly as possible. Returning to the street did nothing to calm her. The gazes of the few villagers still in the streets seemed directed toward her. At the far edge of the village, a number of people were clustered around a building that vaguely resembled a mill. The earlier wary, frightened gazes had a sharpened edge, and Patience could still detect fear in the air. What was going on? Was it her imagination, or was something actually strange?

The delicious smell of baking bread and chocolate pastries intruded upon her musings, and she quickened her step, deciding to buy something to nibble on as she finished her tasks.

Mrs. Tecking chose that moment to intercept her. For a second Patience detected a hint of relief on the older woman's face. She wondered if Mrs. Tecking found the village as strange and unsettling as she did. Something in common with Mrs. Tecking? The oddness of the day just wouldn't end.

"There you are. I wondered where you had run off to."

Patience feigned an apologetic expression. "I finished my task and was going to stop in the bakery. Would you care to join me?"

Mrs. Tecking accepted, and the odd moment of kinship was not lost on either of them.

There were three women in the bakery—two customers and a woman chatting with them behind the counter. Their conversation abruptly stopped when they saw the newcomers.

Patience smiled nervously, uncharacteristically cowed. "Good afternoon, ladies. I was drawn to your store by the heavenly scent, and hope to purchase the chocolate croissants exuding that wonderful aroma."

The woman behind the counter stared blankly at her.

Patience's smile slipped, but she forced it back into place. "Are you selling chocolate croissants?"

No response.

Patience exchanged a look with Mrs. Tecking, who looked equally baffled.

Patience noticed a sign in French and repeated her question. "*Vendez-vous des croissants de chocolat?*"

The flat looks on the women's faces immediately changed to terror.

Patience held out a hand in appeal and switched back to English. "Bread? Chocolate?"

The women continued to stare in fright, and Patience erupted. "What the bloody hell is wrong with you people? And with this town?"

The women leaned in and began whispering to each other. Patience caught the word "French" and "trouble" before she threw her arms in the air and stalked out. Mrs. Tecking followed on her heels, the expression on her face torn between outrage at the craziness and bad manners of the townsfolk and distaste at Patience's language.

The woman shot her a look as if it was all her fault that they had not been waited on and stomped off toward the waiting carriage. Well, their accord had lasted all of thirty seconds. A record, that.

Patience sighed. The townspeople in the street continued to watch her. No more shopping. Not that it would do much good. Someone had obviously forgotten to mention that Bedlam had moved north.

Dragging her feet, Patience gave in to a small sulk. The day had not gone as planned.

First Mrs. Tecking had insisted on joining her, and after the interminable carriage ride, the village had looked like a godsend. Then that awful noise, and . . .

Patience paused. The villagers had acted completely normal until the terrible crash. And then the residents had practically fled in terror. Could there really be monsters lurking about?

But why had the villagers gone silent around her? Were they being threatened, or were they in on the "monster" scheme and although scared, trying to hide their culpability?

She shook her head and climbed into the carriage next to a huffing Mrs. Tecking. As the carriage neared the castle, Patience thought about the behavior of the castles' servants and wondered if she wasn't just going from one madhouse to another.

Chapter 5

❧

Thomas strode through the corridors, ignoring the maids who scuttled to the side or the footmen who jumped out of his way. It had been a week since the antiquarians had arrived. A week full of nothing but problems with his work and a slowly dawning horror during the evenings as he realized his growing fascination with the outspoken, bespectacled cataloger.

He could just imagine what Samuel, his business partner, would say when he returned today from his trip to London. Samuel had a caustic way of looking at a situation and would no doubt be overly amused to discover Thomas's discomfort and interest.

During the week, Thomas had created reasons for missing dinner or excusing himself from the after-dinner activities. He didn't need the distraction of company, and he certainly didn't need some fanciful female, however amusing, monopolizing his thoughts.

He had work to do. Important work. Work that did not include gazing after centuries-old dust and dirt or the pert little nose of the one examining it. He pushed aside the mental image of that appealing nose wrinkled in concentration or frowning in thought at a table or portrait or statue, unaware he was watching.

Besides, there was a problem in the Hastings Building, and it needed his complete attention. Thomas just hoped things would hold together until the final bit of testing. The archetypes were nearly ready, and if mistakes were made, it would take several weeks at the least to prepare another building. They just had to hope that the remainder of the testing progressed smoothly.

The question remained. What had happened to the workshop the previous night?

It appeared to be sabotage. They had finally created enough interest to warrant spies. Someone either in the village or in the castle must have leaked design information.

He scowled, and a maid "eeped" and flattened herself to the wall, trying to move as far from him as possible. He barely paid her any mind. He was accustomed to such a reaction from the servants, especially the new ones.

Thomas shook his head, hoping his chief investigator, Kinney, as well as Samuel, had managed to sort through the background information on the new servants. There had been a number of new hires in the past few weeks. People employed from outside the village, since the villagers were overwhelmed with projects already. It would be easy for some of the new servants to be more than they seemed . . .

A man walked out of a room and directly into his path. Paying Thomas as much heed as Thomas had paid the servants, the man muttered something to himself and walked into the gallery across the hall.

He was one of the antiquarians, the one married to the lady with the constantly pursed lips. Tucker or Tickens or something. Thomas had barely paid heed to anyone else at the table when he had actually shown up at meals, instead choosing to torment the delightfully easy-to-fluster, wild-haired Miss Harrington.

Tecking, that was it. If there was one perquisite, besides the money and power, to being a peer of the realm, it was the fact that he didn't have to remember names if he didn't choose to. The man, Tecking, had barely said twenty words the night the men had been forced to adjourn without Caroline, Patience, or Mrs. Tecking. Instead of enjoying a gentlemanly glass of port and normal conversation, the antiquarian had become enamored with an inkpot. An inkpot!

Thomas continued on, in a worse mood than before. The antiquarians were not only a new addition to the household, but another distraction. One or all of them could easily be in cahoots with a foreign power. Even Patience Harrington. Heaven knew that every country in the free world would like to get their hands on his monster models and designs. In the wrong hands it would be disastrous.

Thomas congratulated himself for having the presence of mind to send Samuel a note about getting background information on each of the antiquarians, just in case. It was more likely that the stuffy ninnies would be searching for a way to resurrect the ancients to take over the world than to deliver something of the new world into enemy hands. But everyone had his price.

Unbidden, spectacles that hid dark flashing eyes, and unrestrained hair appeared in his mind. Not much of a stuffy ninny there. He wondered what her price would be.

He continued with that thought until he reached the grounds. Heading for the outbuildings, he rounded the maze and walked swiftly alongside the rose garden. Although his sneezing and watery eyes had decreased with age, every now and again something aggravated the condition.

Stopping briefly to sift through his pocket for a handkerchief, a muffled noise met his ears. Probably the maids gossiping again. But a trill caused him to frown. Someone was conversing in French. While that was not unusual among members of the ton, it was abnormal among the servants. Leaning forward he tried to hear the conversation.

"Do you think he suspects anything?"

"No. Just handle your part. If he starts to suspect anything, we'll deal with him."

"What about the monster? How are we going

to obtain it? Might as well be dragon treasure for the way it's guarded."

"Yes, well, keep watch, and we will strike when ready."

Thomas was already running toward the break in the garden wall. It was imperative he see who was talking. Unfortunately his nose didn't agree and he sneezed. Loudly.

By the time he rounded the hedge, the speakers were gone. Thomas ran back to the side, but observed no one moving toward the castle or into the woods. He made his way briskly through the gardens, but knew he wouldn't find anything.

One thing he knew for certain, a man and a woman had engaged in the whispered conversation. And they both spoke French.

Patience watched the village boy shuffle from one foot to another as he glanced around the room.

"This is where it happens. This is it," he mumbled, his voice caught between fear and wonder as he switched his awed gaze to the ceiling.

Patience had to clear her throat before his attention finally switched back to her.

"What is your name?"

The boy's eyes went wide. "Todd Farmer, miss."

"Well, Mr. Farmer, did the smith give you any instructions for me?"

His head bobbed in quick succession. "Oh, yes. He said to oil it . . . um . . ." He shifted feet. "Oh, yes. Once a month."

She hid a smile. "Do you work for the smith, Mr. Farmer?"

Another head bob. "Oh, yes, sometimes. And sometimes I work at the Styx." This was said with pride.

"The Styx?"

"Oh, yes. Only the blightest of us."

"Brightest?"

"Blightest, yes."

"I see." She set the tool on the table. "And what is the Styx?"

"It's where we make all of the secret stuff. The secret stuff for the castle," he said, in a hushed voice.

Patience blinked. "What type of secret stuff?"

"I work on monster parts. Well, my pa does, but I sometimes help. Very interkit work."

Patience's heart sped up a few beats. Monster parts? "What type of intricate work do you do?"

The boy was avidly looking around the room.

"Oh, yes. Interkit. Very interkit. The legs mostly. My pa is teaching me so that one day I can take over his position."

Patience kept her voice even. "Have you ever seen the monster?"

The boy shook his head. "Oh, no. They keep it here at the castle, they do. I've never been here before." His voice became wistful. "I've always wanted to."

"Me too." She smiled, trying to form a connection while she formulated her next question. Unfortunately, her connection backfired.

"What do you mean?" His brows scrunched together. "You don't live here?"

"I'm a guest."

His face went white. "Uh—must be going. I must be going."

And with that he sped from the room, leaving Patience with her jaw hanging open. Yes, that settled it. She was definitely checking the village signs, if she ever returned, to see if the words *Bethlehem Hospital* adorned any of them.

The Styx? That must be the mill-type building that she had seen. An odd name for a building. Her earlier thought about Charon, the ferryman of the Greek underworld, had been right in tune with the village surroundings after all. Perhaps if one looked under Charon's hood, he would find Blackfield's sardonic gaze.

Patience had just finished telling John about the odd experience with the villager, leaving out a few of the more peculiar bits, when Mr. Tecking walked into the room Patience had claimed for organizing and cataloging her portion of the collection. He walked to the window and looked out onto the grounds. Patience and John exchanged a glance.

"Mr. Tecking?"

He waved a hand. "The servants are moving the last of the statuary and busts from the room."

Patience raised a brow. It was unlike him not to supervise the work. "I take it they are doing a fine job?"

"Yes, took me nearly two hours to instruct them on the proper procedures."

That sounded more like it. "What have you been doing in the interim?"

"Took a look at some of the rooms Lady Caroline mentioned."

"Anything of interest? Any unknown treasures?" she teased.

Mr. Tecking brushed a hair from his face.

"Yes, treasures. Although a Puckle Gun is hardly a treasure to me."

John froze, and Patience blinked. "A Puckle Gun, Mr. Tecking, are you sure?" she asked.

He waved a hand in annoyance. "Said it, didn't I? Seems like all the young people are interested in these days are swords, pistols, and swaggering. Wouldn't know a Bocca Della Verita if it bit them." He walked to the door, his short break obviously over.

Patience coughed to hide her laughter. "Yes, well, we'll see you at dinner, Mr. Tecking."

He waved carelessly as he disappeared from view.

She let loose with laughter as soon as she was sure he was far enough down the corridor. "Sometimes it is almost worth the displeasure of putting up with his wife, if only so I can hear his crotchety comments. You'd never suspect the man possessed a gram of wit by just looking at him."

When John didn't respond, she looked over. He looked as if someone had told him the earth was triangular. "John?"

He shook himself from his stupor. "Sorry, Patience. What was that?"

She thought back, trying to recall what had

been said. "Did you want to see the Puckle Gun? I thought you had already examined one."

"Well, it's not like there are very many in existence." He looked deep in thought. "It really is true," he murmured absently.

"What's true?"

The expression on his face was so distraught, it was as if he had forgotten she was there. Again. Really, she knew she was forgettable . . . but her vanity was a bit insulted anyway.

"John?" she asked, when he still hadn't answered.

"That Mr. Tecking is witty."

She rolled her eyes. "Don't stick your hand in any lion's mouth. It *would* be bitten off by a Bocca Della Verita. Listen, if you don't want to tell me, fine, just don't lie."

He gave her a weak smile. "Do you want to see the gun?"

She shrugged. "Lead the way."

They walked through the corridors until they found the room Mr. Tecking had mentioned. After a bit of searching, they found the gun. It was a mounted flintlock with a cylinder that revolved.

Patience ran her hand over the revolving cylinder. "I've never seen one up close."

"Our forces never adopted them," he said as he

examined the tripod. "Can you imagine? Shooting nine times a minute? Three times the average firing power at the time this was produced?"

A feeling of unease shot through her. "Weaponry makes me uncomfortable. It is why I don't cross into your field, John."

He gave her a small, compassionate smile. "Sorry, Patience. But you can still understand the importance of this invention."

She rubbed her arms. "Yes. But I must say that I'm glad they didn't become popular."

He narrowed his eyes. "All this model requires is some adjustment and the right investor, and it would revolutionize warfare as we know it."

A chill ran through the room. Patience backed toward the door. "Stay if you wish, but I need to return to the collection rooms. I need to go over some of my notes on the Egyptian Senet boards. You know, the boards and pieces I showed to you earlier? The games buried in the tombs? Mr. Ashe kept horrendous notes after all, and I think that I mistook one as belonging to Ramses' dynasty rather than Akhenaton's . . ." She was babbling, and she knew it.

A low, smooth voice spoke from behind her. "Akhenaton's, are you sure?"

She spun around. Blackfield lounged against the door. It seemed to be his habit. The lifted brow and smirk as well.

"Lord Blackfield," she said, as calmly as she was able. She felt as if John and she had been caught doing something illegal, rather than examining a room in an area they had been allowed entrance. John looked uncomfortable as well. "Excuse us, we were just returning upstairs."

"And here I thought you would give me an explanation on the difference between the two dynasties."

She grimaced. "I would like to think I had learned from my previous mistake with the armor."

"Going to deny me the entertainment, Miss Harrington?" he drawled.

"Hoping to save myself the embarrassment actually."

John quirked a brow, and she noticed that his gaze was focused to the right of Blackfield.

An attractive sandy-haired man who was nearly as tall as Blackfield, although stockier in build, stood next to him. He was well dressed and appeared comfortable in his fashionable attire.

Blackfield seemed to notice her gaze. "Miss Harrington." Blackfield gave her one of the bows that seemed reserved for her, full of innuendo that she couldn't comprehend. "And Mr. Fenton, may I introduce Mr. Simmons, a friend and business partner. He has just arrived from London today."

She nodded and smiled at the newcomer as John shook his hand. "A pleasure to meet you, Mr. Simmons."

He gave a friendly, disarming grin, and his light brown eyes sparkled. "Call me Samuel. I hear that you are cataloging old George's collection. Caroline has been telling me all about your progress."

She inclined her head. His reference to the others by their first names and his attire made her think that this was the friend that she had heard mentioned by Caroline and some of the servants. "I believe I have heard tale of you as well, Mr. Simmons. Will you be joining us for dinner?"

"Not tonight. I need to go over some work with Thomas. Lord knows he can't run the estate without my help." Blackfield snorted at Samuel's words. "But definitely tomorrow. Wouldn't miss seeing what you're up to," he said cheerfully. He had been shooting a couple of twinkling looks between Blackfield and her the whole time.

She and John excused themselves, as it became apparent that the two men were interested in discussing something in the room.

Blackfield barely allowed Patience room to pass through the doorway. As she brushed against him, the fine linen of his jacket caressed her arms, and the fine hairs stood on end. Catching herself before a full blush could manifest, she turned and walked quickly up the hall.

Thomas watched Patience disappear around a corner, her skirts swishing lightly across the floor.

He walked into the room and closed the door. Samuel regarded him with amusement. Thomas gave him a dark look designed to make him keep his thoughts to himself. "Did you get the materials on the antiquarians while you were in London?"

Samuel nodded, a guarded look dampening his amusement. "But after that little display, I'm not sure you will want to read it."

Thomas held out an impatient hand, and Samuel handed him the sheaf of papers he had been carrying since his arrival. "A lot to interest you."

Thomas shuffled through the pile looking for

Patience Harrington's papers first. The words *French*, *French*, and *France* popped out. "French mother? French cousin whom she still keeps in contact with? Visits to France?"

Samuel nodded, the guarded look still in place. "I realize you have some sort of fascination with her, Thomas, but you do know this is the wrong time to get interested in some chit from London. Even if the lady were as completely harmless as Miss Harrington portrays. But especially if she is a chit who just happens to be here when the monster takes its first breath. A chit who has all the connections and even a motivation for spying. Check the papers on the father."

Thomas continued flipping and reading aloud. "A recent deal with a French import/exporter. Tens of thousands of pounds. Recent bank deposits. Interest in antiquities and new machinery. Warehouses being readied, but no one with knowledge of what is being shipped."

He glanced at Samuel, who nodded, and said, "Those pieces of information have been confirmed. There are lots of rumors swirling around. You should hear the things they say about her."

Thomas tapped the pages. "Seems almost too easy."

"Some people just aren't that clever."

"From all I've heard, Arthur Harrington is exceedingly clever."

Samuel made a grudging motion. "Fine, but some people just don't make good criminals. Anyhow, it looks mighty bad. You be careful around the lady and Mr. Fenton, that cousin of hers."

Thomas looked at the gun the two had been examining. "Did you find out anything about him?"

"Not much. Seems pretty clean, cousin on the father's side, so no French blood, but he's still family, and his uncle is knee deep in French transport. Never know what someone will do in the name of family loyalty."

"Has Miss Harrington ever been linked to anyone romantically?"

Samuel gave him a strange look, but shrugged. "That's the rub of the gossip. She's linked to several men. Read the personal section. The lady has a very shady reputation."

"Yes, I figured as much from the looks the Tecking woman has given her, and the remarks from Miss Harrington's own mouth. She isn't exactly a blushing flower type. Although I can't see her in the role of a seductress either. Are you sure the information is accurate?"

Samuel affected offended dignity. "As well as it can be based on a week to discern rumor from fact. The ton seems to believe her reputation to be well based, even if you don't put much stock in their views. There are firsthand accounts of her behavior." He leaned forward. "See the Antleberry incident on the second page."

Thomas's eyebrows rose. "Antleberry can't be a day under seventy, and you are saying a twenty-year-old, unmarried woman had an affair with him?"

"Listen, the information I've gathered is all in there. Including the firsthand accounts. Just remember how Kevin McSweeney was taken in by a beautiful spy and lost all of his designs to a German firm. Let me know if you need me to dig up more information or send someone else to London. I'll help Kinney with the reports on the newer servants."

Thomas shook his head, unwilling to believe what he had just heard. "I'll read the reports. Thanks, Samuel."

Thomas flipped through the pages, wondering if he could have judged the woman so badly. But Samuel did have a point. Kevin McSweeney had lost all of his life's work because he had trusted the wrong person, thinking with his heart and lower anatomy rather than with his head. Thomas had guarded his heart for too many years to let it be his downfall.

He started carefully reading her background information from the beginning. Knowledge was power. If he was going to play a game, he was going to win. No beautiful spy was going to steal the monster.

More than a week in the mad castle and Patience already felt like throwing herself from one of the spires. Groaning, she lifted herself up and examined her stocking feet. She needed to change, get a good book, and crawl into bed.

Calling on Tilly, she took care of the first and pulled her warm nightrail around her. A quick search through her bag took care of the second. A treatise on the role of the Agora in Greek life was nestled in her lap as she curled her toes into the soft sheets and leaned against her pillows. A candle burned brightly at her bedside, and the taper was tall enough to give her the hours that she needed to finish reading. She dove in.

An hour later by the candle's measure, a series of loud cracks echoed in the night and she heard shouting outside.

Another crack sounded. She threw back the

covers and went to the window. It was hard to discern in the cloudy night, but a group of men were dragging something. Something connected by ropes or chains. Her face pressed against the glass, she squinted, trying to determine what they were doing.

She had watched men slip in and out of the estate all week. In and out of the nondescript buildings by the woods. At first her imagination had fancied them spirits drifting in and out of the fog, whereas her more rational side had figured they were probably poachers. But the men always entered and exited the same buildings, and when she had seen Blackfield talking with a few of them earlier, it had become apparent that they were part of the servants' gossip.

The clouds parted, and using the spyglass she had borrowed from the Ashe collection earlier in the day, she spotted the viscount waving his arms and directing the men. She had to admit that as irritating as he sometimes was, he made a fine sight in the moonlight. Strong, capable, and assured. Something that was lacking in many of the men of her acquaintance.

Sighing, she started to tug the drapes closed. Her breath caught and her hand froze halfway through the action. The men gave a final tug to the chains attached to the lump. A large arm rose from the lump in defiance.

The clouds shrouded the moon, effectively blocking any further view. Try as she might, she couldn't catch another glimpse. But there was no denying what she had seen. The monster was indeed real. And he was trying to break free.

Chapter 6

Patience wandered through the grounds after the noon meal thinking about the monster from the night before. And about the monster's master. The man was downright perplexing. All the way down to the pink notes, which he continued to receive each morning.

Her morning work session had been a dismal failure. She was so preoccupied by the mysterious goings-on she had witnessed in the night, she had accomplished little.

What exactly had she seen from her window hundreds of yards away? How could she report that one of the wealthiest men in England had created a monster? And to what end? What did he hope to accomplish?

Would anyone believe her allegations without substantive proof? Definitely not sweet Lady Caroline, who absolutely doted on her nephew. Nor would the townsfolk and servants be sympathetic since their welfare and livelihood depended on the lord. That left her own colleagues, and she grimaced just thinking about their reactions. Mrs. Tecking would most likely accuse her of spreading rumors to increase her own importance or some such tripe. Mr. Tecking's reaction would probably be a distracted nod and mutterings about accurately recording her observations. And her cousin . . . he would just say she was being fanciful. No, there was no help from that quarter.

Perhaps she should write a letter to her father detailing her suspicions and misgivings. But no, he was too caught up in museum and Parliament business and would worry needlessly. She would hold her own counsel for the time being and observe Blackfield's actions and the monster's more closely.

As a youngster it used to upset her when the village children asked her to prove that fairies and unicorns existed. Of course, she had been unable to do so. It was one of the reasons she was so demanding when verifying antiquities. So rigid in making sure that all the facts were gathered and all her evidence was in order before rendering a judgment on a date or crediting an artisan. Her social reputation might be in tatters, but she was determined that her professional reputation would not be tainted.

It just so happened that she was her own worst enemy when it came to social contact. Perhaps she should just avoid societal gatherings in general. She kicked a stone, then winced as her toe made contact through her kid slipper. Her brain just seemed to shut off in social situations. Work-related things came out of her mouth naturally, then the next thing she knew, her audience was staring at her in consternation, ridicule, or horror.

Strange that she felt at ease when speaking in Blackfield's company. He appeared amused, but not in a critical manner, at least not after that first morning.

A voice carried on the wind. Speak of the devil. She rounded a corner and saw him conversing with two men. The shorter of the two was gesturing wildly and wearing a smock smeared with dark red-and-brown streaks. Like blood. She squinted, trying to take a closer look. The man's plump hands were dirty, and they, too, appeared covered in blood. The taller man was nodding in agreement. Blackfield looked enraged.

"Impossible. How could it have worked itself loose on its own? Someone must have tampered with it." Blackfield ran an angry hand through his hair. "Do you think it was one of the servants?"

The bloodied man waved his arms. "I don't know, but we were nearly killed." His high-pitched voice was in direct contrast to his squat, round figure.

Patience watched in morbid curiosity. Had the monster been set free? And nearly killed them? Judging by the amount of blood on the man, it had to be.

"I know, Jones. There are spies."

The second man, tall and thin, looked nervous. "We aren't shutting down the project, are we?"

Blackfield shook his head. "No, we are too close. Instruct the men to be more vigilant. Make certain the doors are locked at all times. I'll alert the necessary villagers and arrange for everyone to meet at midnight." As he lifted his head, Patience ducked quickly behind a hedgerow.

She fully intended on spying on that meeting. She needed to see the monsters firsthand before alerting the authorities.

Thomas watched Patience Harrington duck into the maze. If she was a spy, she was a darn poor one.

Yet Samuel's investigation had been thorough and damning. And if all was true, all he needed to do was let Miss Harrington and her coconspirators hang themselves.

The project was too important to let a group of bumbling spies wreak havoc. He needed to cut off the serpent's head before it struck again. If the knowledge of what they were doing, and even worse, if the actual model was found or stolen . . . no, he didn't want to think of the consequences. They would just have to increase security. And make certain that any spies were . . . taken care of. No matter how fascinating they were.

Patience trudged to supper as one might walk to Madame Guillotine. She had passed the viscount hours after overhearing his conversation with the duo outside. The look he had given her bode ill. She wondered if he suspected she had discovered his secret. Or if he just thought she had unwittingly decapitated a prized hydrangea somewhere in the garden.

Samuel Simmons joined them at dinner, and the dynamics at the table changed dramatically in their dysfunctional little group. Mrs. Tecking perked up at having a gentleman at the table who was both amusing and attentive. A gentleman who seemed to be on "her" side. How she had obtained that impression, Patience wasn't sure. It might have been Samuel's careless, perpetually amused air, or his interest in gossip. He seemed to find everything entertaining, especially Blackfield's silence.

Patience watched Mrs. Tecking revel in one of Samuel's compliments, making her appear more youthful, a visage of the debutante that she had been seventeen years earlier rather than the dragon she had become. The change smoothed some of the frown lines from her face and made her attractive. Judging from the transformation, the woman had probably been quite a sensation before she had allowed herself to become permanently pinched.

The new seating arrangement had placed Patience minutely closer to Blackfield, and she felt every inch of the lost table space.

Blackfield leaned toward her. "Do you like English fare, Miss Harrington?" It was the first thing he had said to her all night, his voice low.

Patience frowned at the undercurrent in his voice, unsure what his game was. "Yes." There was a slight question in her response.

"What about French cuisine?"

She warmed to the question. "I love it. Actually, I find French sauces far superior to most found in England."

Kenfield entered the room and approached the table. "Excuse me, my lord, but one of the 'landscape designers' says it's imperative that he speak with you. He's standing just outside the doorway."

"Thank you, Kenfield."

At that moment servants opened the door to bring in another food course, and Patience spotted a scuffed and rumpled figure wringing his hands. Blackfield looked at Samuel, who nodded and excused himself from the table to join the scruffy man in the hall.

Not missing a beat, and offering no explanation for the man's unusual appearance or their verbal exchange, Blackfield leaned back in his chair and trapped her gaze again. "So you love French food and find it superior to English fare?"

"Is there something wrong with enjoying cuisine from France, my lord?"

"No. Are there any other things from France you love?"

Her frown pulled tighter. "Is there something you wish to imply, Lord Blackfield?"

He shrugged. "Some people love the countryside. The fashions. The wine. The politics. Some love frolicking with young Frenchmen."

A hiss spewed from Mrs. Tecking. She had obviously been listening to the conversation since her preferred dinner partner had left. Her expression seemed torn between outrage and elation. As if frolicking with Frenchmen was exactly what she thought of women of Patience's "ilk." Patience ignored her.

"There is nothing wrong with loving French culture. However, that has nothing to do with having affairs with members of that culture."

"Now really—"

"I can't believe—"

"What would you expect—"

"Excellent pheasant."

John, Caroline, Mrs. and Mr. Tecking were talking over one another, the first three paying rapt attention to the conversation between Patience and Blackfield. Blackfield merely examined Patience and sipped his wine.

He waited for a pause in the chaos before saying, "And yet you claim to be 'enamored' of the culture."

The others halted and looked at Patience. "There is nothing wrong with enjoying another country, its traditions and its people," she replied.

"Dangerous to make claims like that these days."

Patience nearly dropped her wineglass. The viscount was leaning back in his chair, the very picture of insouciant innocence.

"Are you implying that I would side with France against England if it came to that?"

Mrs. Tecking's fork clattered to her plate, and even Caroline looked as if she had a less than steady grip on her silverware.

The viscount looked amused for the first time that evening. "Not one to dance around an issue, are you, Miss Harrington?"

"No, my lord. I find plain speaking to be far more effective and efficient."

"Patience—"

"No, John. I'm anxious to hear what Lord Blackfield has to say. He seems intent on besmirching my honor."

John looked resigned, but he turned his attention to the viscount.

"Are you sympathetic to the French, Miss Harrington?"

"Of course I am, Lord Blackfield."

A gasp came from Mrs. Tecking's direction, and John even raised a brow.

"They are people just like you and I." She cast a critical gaze over his person. "Well, the rest of us, at any rate."

Blackfield smiled, but his eyes were cold. "You and your father exchange goods on the Continent, do you not?"

"Of course."

"What manner of goods?"

"I don't see what business it is of yours, but to answer your question, we mostly deal with antiquities. What do you think we trade?"

He leaned toward her, ignoring her question. "It is my business to know the character of people I allow to stay under my roof."

She leaned toward him as well. "That can be rectified."

"Yes, it can."

"Thomas, please." Caroline nervously fingered her napkin. "There must be a misunderstanding. There is nothing wrong here. Miss Harrington and her father come highly recommended. The best in their field. And furthermore they are friends. Friends that I invited here. You insult me as well."

Thomas leaned back. "My apologies, Caroline. That was not my intention. I just thought it best to warn Miss Harrington. One's political sympathies can be called into question. Gossip can be rather damaging to one's reputation."

Patience balled her fists in her lap. John sent her an imploring glance to remain silent. But she couldn't resist saying, "Thank you for your consideration, Lord Blackfield. It is people like you who destroy good reputations."

Blackfield stared at her, and she felt sure that he would retort, but he surprised her by merely lifting his fork and stabbing his fowl.

Samuel rejoined the meal several minutes later, much to the relief of the diners. He looked on, his amused face firmly back in place. "Did I miss anything exciting?"

"No, nothing," Caroline said, quickly forestalling any retort Mrs. Tecking might make. Mrs.

Tecking closed her mouth with a click, looking like a child whose toy had been snatched away.

The conversation returned to the amiable state it had been in prior to Samuel's departure. John and Caroline drew Mr. Tecking and Patience into conversation, Mrs. Tecking flirted unabashedly with Samuel, and Blackfield sipped his wine, his narrowed eyes watching them all.

Dessert was finally served and Patience nearly sighed in relief. The slight rustle of fabric was the only sound in the room as everyone savored the heavenly strawberry torte.

If she could just make it out of the dining room without being burned to a crisp by Blackfield's gaze, she would count herself lucky. No matter what topic of conversation she had been pulled into, she could feel his eyes on her, dissecting and questioning. Once again she marveled at his sheer presence. Annoying as it had become. He said nothing, and yet she was cognizant of his every move.

After dinner, Caroline nervously suggested a game of whist, and, to no one's surprise, Mr. Tecking declined. However, Mrs. Tecking voiced her intention to stay, the first time during the week she had not retired with her husband. And John's announcement that he needed to continue with his research tonight also proved surprising, since he was an avid cardplayer.

Retiring to the game room, the players drew lots for partners. Much to her chagrin Patience ended up with Blackfield. Caroline and Samuel partnered, and Mrs. Tecking sat out the first game.

Play began and Patience shot a wary glance across the table as Blackfield read her hand correctly, and they won the first point. On two previous evenings she and John had been partnered against Blackfield and Caroline. She found Blackfield an infuriating opponent. She was of the mind that she'd find him an infuriating partner as well, but as the match progressed she was surprised to find their bidding and playing styles complemented one another. He had a brilliant head for strategy, and she had occasional moments of intuitive brilliance. Conversely, she had moments of intuitive disaster, but his steadiness balanced her mistakes.

To her further surprise she found that she and Caroline were swept up into a cutthroat rivalry between Blackfield and Samuel. The boasting, glaring, and braying continued unabated until they reached the deciding game of the rubber—and then silent concentration reigned supreme.

Luck was with them on the last hand as she and Blackfield held all four honors, giving them an extra four points and the rubber.

"Maybe next time, Samuel old boy."

Samuel glared good-naturedly and scooped the cards up, shuffling fiercely. Lots were drawn, and Caroline sat the next one out. Lady Fate was having a good time at their expense, because Blackfield ended up as Patience's partner again.

Play resumed. Mrs. Tecking broke the silence as she leaned toward Samuel in a conspiratorial manner, her cards dipping forward the slightest bit. "Any news in London during our absence?"

"It's been a dreadful bore these last few weeks." He played his card, the humor on his face briefly extinguished. "All the talk concerns Napoleon Bonaparte, France, Italy, and what he might crown himself king of next."

Blackfield appeared thoughtful. "Once he turned the Italian Republic into the Kingdom of Italy, it was only a matter of time really before he crowned himself King of Italy. I'm surprised he waited two months."

Patience could only nod in agreement as she scooped their trick.

Samuel scoffed, but maintained his good-natured facade. "France can't even keep itself together to have a government longer than five years. The Directory, the Consulate, and now this 'Empire.' This 'Emperor' upstart will be gone soon, mark my words. King of Italy." He snorted.

Patience held her cards to her chest, not amused. "I think you underestimate him. Look at the people with whom he surrounds himself. And I hear that his very presence demands obedience. Men rally to his side." She looked around the table. "That's a dangerous man. Look at how easily Cambacérès and Lebrun were pushed aside."

Blackfield idly tapped the back of his cards. "A man who grows bloated by others' praise is a man who grows complacent in his failings. His ego will be his downfall."

She sent him a sharp look. "Quite possibly the wisest thing you've said all night, Lord Blackfield."

He raised a brow, but Samuel cut in. "You think Bonaparte will grow stronger, Miss Harrington?"

"I do. But at the same time, I agree with Lord Blackfield." She grimaced. "Strong leaders only remain as strong as those they surround themselves with, and if Bonaparte's ego continues to grow, he most likely will begin punishing those who do not fall to his will. And that will lead to his downfall. He will poison his own council and follow it to its sweet death. The ultimate failing of those with extreme power."

She glanced at Blackfield and was surprised by the guarded respect she saw in his eyes. Unwilling respect, but respect nonetheless. She turned her gaze back to Samuel, who was looking at her in contemplation.

"You are interested in France, Miss Harrington?"

"My mother was French."

"An émigrée?"

"Yes."

"Do you feel loyalty toward France?"

She inhaled and willed her hackles down, reminding herself that he had been absent during that part of the conversation. "Let me be frank, Mr. Simmons, I am an Englishwoman first and foremost. That doesn't mean I do not sympathize with the French struggles. The people are confused. They are looking for leadership and a way to rebuild their economy. I may not like the way Bonaparte is handling things or care for the man, but I can understand how easy it is for the common folk to be swayed. They are only human, and, just like our fellow countrymen in England, all they want is a better life. They believe Bonaparte will give it to them."

"Do you?"

"No, I do not."

Samuel gave her a searching glance and played his card, allowing the game to continue. Blackfield maintained an unreadable expression for the rest of the game.

The card games had left her restless, and Patience decided to work a bit before sleuthing. Work generally focused her mind. She walked from her chambers, head down as she tried to decipher George Ashe's notes on the Egyptian mask. For a man so serious about his collection, George had really taken haphazard and shoddy notes. The rumor that he had a fabulous memory and had been able to remember every detail about his collections, no matter how small, seemed to have merit. She'd ask Caroline in the morning.

She read over the last sentence in his work

journal. Osiris? Anubis? That sure looked like a round letter at the beginning and an "is" at the end. She squinted, pulled the paper closer, and plowed straight into someone.

Looking up, she met the dark eyes of Anubis himself and gave a small squeak.

Anubis lifted a brow. A familiar one. "Miss Harrington?"

"Er, Lord Blackfield. Fancy meeting you here." She tried to steady her heartbeat.

"I do live here."

"So you do." She moved to skirt around him and consequently hide her cheeks, which were flaming from embarrassment. "Good night."

"Off so soon?"

His words had a challenging bite, and she stopped and met his eyes.

"Was there something you wished to discuss?" she asked evenly.

"Interesting conversation tonight."

"I'm sure that you found it so. I'm left either to my initial impression that you wish all antiquarians ill, or that you've just targeted me."

He leaned against the wall, and a painting, a Tintoretto, if she identified it correctly, shifted behind his back. He didn't seem too concerned that the priceless piece might come crashing down. She wondered if he treated all his possessions in such a careless manner. Perhaps they burned priceless objects and antiques in a huge bonfire each new moon, as a sacrifice to whatever monster they were raising. Perhaps they were even now devising which pieces would see their devastating end in a week.

"Miss Harrington?"

"What?" she snapped, still picturing the antique burning monster in her head.

"I asked if you had everything you needed?"

Her eyes narrowed. "For what? Burning portraits?"

He looked stunned for about two seconds, before his sarcastic mien appeared. "Is that what you are doing in there? I'm not sure that is what Caroline had in mind when she donated the collection. But please, have at it, no loss to me."

He shrugged, and the picture on his other side, a Raphael, shifted as well. Her ire increased, even as part of her brain screamed that she must have had way too much tea that day.

"Of course you wouldn't," she muttered. "Anyone with monsters, minions, vampires—"

His eyes narrowed to slits. "What did you say about monsters?"

She snorted, not the least impressed by his

obvious anger. "They are all over the place here."

He took two steps forward and pinned her to the wall. "Be careful what you say, Miss Harrington. Monsters come in various shapes and sizes."

She shivered, whether from his words or his body so close to hers, she didn't know. As much as she should feel nervous pinned in place, with not a servant in sight, Blackfield didn't scare her. Oh, he made her feel many emotions—anger, irritation, confusion. He caused her stomach to clench and her chest to feel as if someone were sitting on it. She didn't know what any of those things meant, but she knew they weren't evidences of fright.

She wondered how she knew that. There was just something about him, something unidentifiable that spoke to her, something that would override all else, even if she found out he *was* a vampire after all.

"Are you a monster, Lord Blackfield?"

He released her, but didn't step back. "What do you fear, Miss Harrington?"

She looked into his eyes. Loneliness, the loss of her family, the loss of her freedom, proving to be unlovable, other nameless things.

She didn't answer and he leaned in close, only

a breath away from her lips. "That is where you will find your monsters." And with that he was gone, his coat snapping behind him as he turned the corner.

Patience leaned against the wall, the forgotten journal lying on the floor next to her, dropped without thought minutes before. Her heart raced, her breath caught.

She was going to that meeting tonight if it was the last thing she did.

Chapter 7

Patience sighed as she changed into darker clothes and settled into a comfortable chair to read. Blackfield was turning out to be one of the most aggravating men she knew. One moment hot and the next cold. She'd give a pretty penny to know what went on inside his head.

It wasn't that she hadn't dealt with people making insinuating comments. Especially men. But there was something about Blackfield that made it harder to deflect his barbs. She wondered if it was something about the man himself, or perhaps it was the way they had met, before they had known each other's identities. Or perhaps how she reveled when she coaxed a smile from him, something rare and to be treasured if his normal behavior were anything to go by—if being a sarcastic beast in darkened hallways counted as normal behavior for anyone.

The candle had burned down to a stub by the time Patience closed her book, a fascinating look at the ancient influence on seventeenth-century life. She had discovered it in Mr. Ashe's collection. She checked the time. Half past eleven. Nearly time for the viscount's meeting. After that night's experience, Patience was more than ready to discover what was going on.

Throwing on her dark dressing gown and shoes, she slipped into the hall. The shadows swirled, but Patience threw her shoulders back and strode forward with purpose. She was on a mission.

Said mission ground to an abrupt halt as a man turned the corner. Just in time she ducked into a darkened doorway. The man marched past, thankfully without looking her way. It was the thin man she had observed talking to the viscount and bloodstained man earlier in the day. Unlike the leashed control of Blackfield, or the wild-eyed fervor of the bloodstained man, this man was nondescript. A slight twitch to his step and face gave him a nervous appearance. He didn't seem to be paying attention to anything but where he was going and moved along steadily.

Patience stepped into the hall and followed him, sticking to the shadows. Trailing him was her best chance. If she waited, and the meeting didn't occur in that outlying building, she might never find the meeting place.

If caught indoors, she could say she was going to the library and got lost. It wouldn't be a total fabrication. With over two hundred rooms in the castle, Patience wasn't sure she could make it to the library without guidance, having only set foot in the room once. And she *did* want to revisit. She just hadn't had time yet.

Her first challenge while trailing the man came at the main staircase. She waited for him to descend and turn the corner before following. Hurrying after him, she was able to catch up as he exited the castle. She noticed others heading in the same direction—toward the plain buildings at the edge of the woods. She continued on, sticking close to the gardens, then finally ducking into a hedge. The others were all entering the mysterious building farthest northeast.

Patience counted to one hundred and sprinted to the building. She rounded the corner looking for an open window or another entrance. No such luck. Changing tack, she returned to the entrance and pried the door open a crack. No one was present.

She walked nervously through the vestibule, checking behind her every few seconds. Her plan had seemed like a good one when she had first devised it, but the more she thought about it, the more dangerous it appeared. If she admitted it to herself, she was a little deprived of excitement. Spending most of her life in libraries and archives really didn't do much for her sense of physical adventure. But having an adventure was one thing, being stupid was something else.

The entrance door opened with a bang. Eyes wide, Patience threw herself into action and scurried around a corner and down the hall. Muffled voices came from a door ahead. She could hear the door to the building opening again and two men in conversation. Patience opened the first door on the right and leapt inside. A closet. Just her luck.

The decision to return to the castle evaporated.

The voices passed by, and she breathed a sigh of relief. The muffled voices were a little louder from inside the closet, as the rooms appeared to share a common wall.

She could only catch snatches of the conversation.

". . . we need them ready in time . . ."

". . . watch for anything out of the ordinary . . ."

". . . need guards at all times . . ."

". . . Fool! Send someone to the front now . . ."

Heavy footsteps trudged past. Patience sucked in a breath. She put her head in her hands as the discussion resumed. Perhaps she had opened a cursed burial artifact.

". . . the government would be against it . . ."

". . . prototypes . . ."

". . . dangerous . . ."

". . . destructive . . ."

". . . if this gets out . . . entire forces destroyed . . ."

". . . do it . . ."

". . . use all means necessary . . ."

Patience started chewing her nails. What were they doing? From the snippets of conversation it could not be good. The discussion grew muffled as voices broke into groups, and conversations layered on top of each other, becoming indistinguishable. This continued for what seemed like hours, and Patience grew increasingly uncomfortable and tired. She was wedged between shelves and the door, and something was poking the small of her back. She reminded herself that contrary to popular belief, not all aspects of an adventure were filled with boundless excitement.

Finally, the voices ceased and feet tromped passed the cramped closet. It took another fifteen to twenty minutes until she was sure that she was as alone as she was going to be. She carefully opened the door and peered out. She could hear two people talking near the entrance. *Guards. Great.*

Heading toward the meeting room, she slowly pushed open the door. The room was dark. No one was in sight.

She let out a sigh of relief.

Her eyes had adjusted to the dark hours ago and she could see the faint outlines of machines and hanging objects. She walked farther into the room. The windows were too high to escape from, but they let in enough moonlight to allow her to look around. Walking over to a work-bench, she picked up an object lying there.

Manacles. The dark shadows shifted. She dropped the manacles and inched toward the door. Perhaps it was time to leave.

Scurrying back to the hall, she headed into one of the other rooms and was pleased to see a Patience-sized window. She unlatched it and edged it up slowly before slipping through and pulling it back down. Satisfied, she headed back toward the castle, staying away from the open paths that might allow the guards to see her.

She released another breath when she was in-side the castle and moving toward the stairs. A noise to her right alerted her, and she ducked into the hall on her left. Unfortunately, the person turned left as well.

Just when she despaired that luck had com-pletely deserted her, she spotted an open door. An open door that led to the library. She scooted inside and stood stock-still behind the door.

The footsteps neared, then stopped. Patience closed her eyes, praying for deliverance. The pendulum of the library clock swung in mea-sure with her racing heart. Time seemed suspended. Eventually, the person moved on, and she exhaled the breath she had been holding.

A hand shot out and grasped her arm, pulling her against a hard body.

"And what do we have here?"

Nerves gripped her as she recognized the viscount's voice. "I was just picking up a book. I couldn't sleep."

"It's late to be out. People could get the wrong impression." His breath tickled her neck, and she involuntarily moved back against him. "Or have the wrong intentions."

Her muscles tightened. She stepped away and twisted to face him. "That they could. You should heed your own advice, my lord."

She was pleased to note that her voice was cool and calm, in direct contrast to the rest of her body.

The viscount let go of her and leaned negligently against the doorframe. "And why would I do that? Of what do I need to take heed?" He leaned forward, his lips inches from hers. "This is my domain, and I can take what I want."

She forced herself to remain still, not wanting to give an inch.

His expression was both smirking and triumphant, and it was mixed with something she

131

couldn't identify. "I have never claimed Patience; perhaps I should work on that besetting sin." And the last inch of space between them was lost.

Chapter 8

Thomas had been halfheartedly walking toward his study to work after the meeting, his mind wrapped up in other matters. Female matters. Matters concerning a particular female.

He needed to discover if she was really a spy. She didn't seem the type, but then neither had the woman who had spied on Kevin Mc-Sweeney. From all accounts she had been considered a pleasant, somewhat meek woman. Patience Harrington wasn't meek, she was spontaneous and . . . seemingly naive. A cultivated naïveté, if the rumors were true.

She always had a quip to add, no matter the appropriateness. He needed to figure out how to twist her tongue to his bidding. He stopped. Now there was an image. The woman threw herself into everything, be it an inappropriate conversation or her antiquities. He wondered what it would feel like to have that passion directed at him.

Actually . . . that wasn't a bad idea. Not bad at all. Get her to confess her secrets between the sheets and gain a, what looked to be, fierce lover in the process.

It wasn't like she wasn't experienced. The other antiquarian woman had made sure to show her disapproval of Patience and a fast reputation, all couched in seemingly concerned tones and sentences, of course. Samuel's report had only confirmed, and worsened, her reputation.

Thomas had no desire to bed the servants or villagers, women that he would interact with on a daily or weekly basis. So he went months between his major trips to London in forced celibacy. Yes, the seduction of Patience Harrington was a great idea.

He started a general plan in his head and walked into the library to find the book that he knew was directly on the left shelf. He was only two feet into the room when sudden movement drew his attention. A spy! He reached out, and the next thing he knew he had an armful of warm, wiggling woman.

Just the spy he was looking for. Lord knew there was no time like the present to put a plan into action.

Patience gasped as Blackfield's lips touched hers. His mouth was soft and warm, and searching, so unlike the man himself. The contrast held her spellbound for a moment before she tentatively moved her lips against his, little tingles traveling through her body at the sensation. At the apparent invitation, he deepened the kiss, applying more pressure. His fingers tangled into her hair at the base of her head, pulling her closer.

She melted into him as he ran his tongue along her bottom lip. She felt hot and flustered, and somewhat dreamy.

His tongue caressed hers lightly.

The brief caress caused her to tense and pull away, wresting control back from the romantic innocent portion of her brain. What was she doing letting Blackfield kiss her? The man had been dreadful to her just hours before.

She backed into the wall. "Wh—what are you doing?"

He put a hand against the wall near her head and leaned close. "Just having a taste." He twirled one of her unruly strands between his fingers and brought it to his lips. Her breath caught, and a funny feeling bloomed in her stomach.

"Well, I hope you enjoyed it."

Dammit. Her mouth was doing that thing again where it ceased listening to her brain.

He smiled. A slow, feral smile as he dragged the captured strands across her lower lip, similar to what he had done with his thumb that first night and in her dreams every night thereafter. "Oh, I did. Your beautiful mouth is put to much better use this way."

Outrage warred with the funny feeling, which she was starting to suspect was that desire thing the maids talked about. Fortunately, outrage won.

She reclaimed her curl and pushed at his chest. He moved back, but in a lazy motion that suggested he was "allowing" the move.

She couldn't think of what to say, outrage or not, she *had* kissed him back, however briefly. So she kept her response simple. "Good night, Lord Blackfield."

He gave her a mocking little bow, his eyes never leaving hers. "Good night, Miss Harrington."

Patience stepped from the library, head held high and hoping to leave before he noticed her damp and muddy slippers.

"Oh, Miss Harrington?"

She stopped, expecting the worse. "Yes?"

"Weren't you looking for reading material?"

She turned around in time to catch the book he tossed her way. Glancing at the title she gave him a measured look.

"*Famous Spies and Thieves?* How droll. Good night again, Lord Blackfield. May your nightmares come true."

She headed back to her room, his laughter following.

Patience scooped some eggs onto her plate and sat down next to John.

"Good morning."

She mumbled a reply, and he gave her a concerned look.

"Good morning," she enunciated. She had only caught a few hours' sleep between her nighttime wanderings and trying to figure out why the viscount had kissed her.

"Maybe you should return to bed, Patience. You look terrible."

She glowered. "Thank you, John. However, I need to work on the papyrus collection."

"It can wait."

"No it cannot. I want to complete it and leave this madhouse." The last part was mumbled into her teacup.

"Perhaps you should just try and ignore Blackfield."

She snorted and continued blowing on the liquid.

"Seriously, Patience, I haven't seen you react to someone like this in a long time."

She paused, then continued blowing across the surface to cool her tea. The viscount did seem to have a rather perverse effect on her.

She sighed. "Perhaps the viscount has that special quality that makes people want to jam his tongue down his throat."

John looked at her strangely, and she fought the blush rising in her cheeks. Her mouth was doing that thing again.

Patience hastily took a sip of tea, burning her tongue in the process. She made a squawking noise and jerked the cup away. So much for appearing calm and collected.

Blackfield chose that moment to enter, and Patience examined her plate.

No sooner had the viscount filled his plate and sat in his chair than a servant handed him a pink note. Another pink note. Patience watched him open it. She absently drank her tea, burning her tongue at the tip again. She swore, attracting the attention of both men. The viscount looked amused before returning his attention to the feminine stationery. His face grew dark and he left the room, his plate remaining full on the table.

She caught John looking pensively at the door. She really wanted to confide in him about last night's activities, but couldn't. Not only would he be appalled that she had slipped out to spy, but he would lecture her on her curiosity, and she would be stuck listening to him for hours. Furthermore, she had no doubt that he would interrogate her and at some point she would blurt out that Blackfield had kissed her. And then he'd tell her father.

No, confiding in John was definitely out. But that didn't mean that giving round hints and vague allusions were forbidden.

She pushed her fork casually around her plate. "How have you been sleeping? Is everything comfortable in your rooms?"

His brow knit in confusion. "What do you mean?"

"Just what I said. Have you been sleeping well here?"

Something must have registered, because his gaze grew shrewd. "Are you finished eating? Would you like to walk?"

Patience looked at the servants, who were waiting to take their dishes. Servants with two perfectly working ears. She nodded and grabbed a roll.

As soon as they were on the grounds, John steered her toward one of the open topiary gardens.

"You've heard the noises, too," he said in a low tone.

She nearly sighed in relief. She wasn't going to have to admit to spying or be unnecessarily coy. "Yes, and felt the tremors and seen the lights. Do you know what is going on?"

He hesitated. "No. Do you?"

Something in his manner, the reticent but shrewd look in his eyes, gave her pause. "The maids whisper about monsters, and the villagers act extremely odd. Men walk the grounds at all hours. And I saw something from my window the other night . . ."

His eyes tightened, and suddenly Patience felt uneasy. This was her cousin and good friend, but she had never seen that look in his eye. Something cold and calculating. A shiver passed through her.

John laughed, but it was a far cry from his normal warmth. He looked her in the eye. "Patience, some things are even too much for your imagination."

"No, honestly, John, haven't you heard the servants talk? Hasn't your valet said anything? Tilly has heard strange things as well."

His eyes narrowed. "Wait a moment, did you say something about men walking the grounds? Have you been following your nose for trouble?"

"No, of course not," she said hastily. "I saw them from my window."

"Patience," he said, with a large amount of exasperation.

"What?" she asked, a bit defensively. "I'm not allowed to look through my window?"

"You know that isn't what I meant."

"Then there is no reason for you to sound so crotchety. In fact, I was thinking that if there were a reasonable explanation, perhaps if we were to—"

"No."

"But—"

"No."

She harrumphed and poked a toe at one of the topiaries. "It was just a suggestion."

"Patience, some things are better left alone." John's tone was dark.

She tried to hide her unease. "Oh, John, next thing I know you will be spouting off about mummy curses."

He grabbed her hand. "I want you to be careful. You aren't to go walking around the grounds at night. Nor about the castle for that matter."

Patience withdrew her hand. "I can look after myself, as you well know. But thank you for your concern."

"Yes, we all know how well you take care of yourself."

Hurt lanced through her. John saw it, and his expression turned apologetic, but lost none of its firmness.

"Will I never have a clean slate?" She asked it softly.

His lips tightened. "It's not fair, Patience, but it

is the way of the ton. You need to learn to control yourself more in conversation. And in your actions. You know that."

She didn't respond.

"If I see or hear of your being out after you retire for the night, I will write to your father. You have no idea what you are dealing with."

Her eyes narrowed, anger replacing the hurt. "I see. Well, if there is nothing further, Mr. Fenton, I have some scrolls to catalog. Good day."

John looked as if he were going to respond, but he just nodded, his lips white with tension. He had been acting strangely lately. Agitated and stressed. And he had been missing on more than one occasion, offering only a vague excuse as to where he had been.

As she turned to leave, she noticed John's gaze centered on the building where the meeting had occurred the night before.

Patience entered her workroom, the smell of lemon oil so overwhelming she could nearly taste it. She suspected the new maid, Jenny, had tried to clean the armor again. She'd have to say something to Caroline. She had told Jenny twice to leave everything be, but she always seemed to be lurking about with her cleaning supplies and a feather duster. And she barely knew one end of the duster from the other, always staring at something else in the room, or out the window.

Patience snorted. And people thought she was a daydreamer. At least she could concentrate on a task.

It took a few hours for her to get over her pique with John. A number of good scrubbings to clean her instruments had gone a long way to relieving her irritation. Even as shifty as John was being, she knew her cousin was just looking out for her best interests.

Patience unconsciously waited for Blackfield to show up as she sorted through the papyrus and scrolls. She didn't know why, but it felt inevitable somehow. He hadn't grilled her last night when she had been caught in the library. He had given her the book, yes, but still, she half expected that he would cart her off to the constable and ask questions later.

Labeling the last sixth century B.C. krater, she wondered how Blackfield would act at dinner. Would he treat her any differently? Would he have told anyone? She could already envision Samuel's amusement and Mrs. Tecking's gossip.

She set the bowl with the others and absently

gazed at the pieces. Tomorrow her father would be sending a padded cart to ship some of the pieces they had finished. That had been the plan at least.

Mrs. Tecking sauntered into the room, disturbing her musings. "Freddie has finished the smallest of the Roman statuary."

"Good. I have the Greek pottery ready for you to record, along with the Egyptian papyrus." Patience handed her a sheaf of notes.

Mrs. Tecking took them with a sniff. "Mr. Fenton is nowhere to be found, and he hasn't given me his yet."

Patience realized she hadn't seen John since their tiff. "I will have him bring them to you as soon as I see him. The first load should be ready for tomorrow. Will you be able to finish compiling everything?"

She sniffed again. "Of course I will."

Mrs. Tecking departed, and Patience was left to wonder how the woman had survived to the age of thirty-five without a permanent crick in her neck.

She put Mrs. Tecking out of her mind and began wrapping and loading the bowls, drinking vessels, urns, and jars into the crates they had brought with them. They would get replacement crates tomorrow, trading them for the ones they'd fill tonight.

Patience smoothed and packed another crate. Her task would at least give her an excuse to be out of her room that night if she wanted to take another look within the building she had hidden in the night before. Or take a look through Blackfield's rooms. She remembered Caroline mentioning where they were during their tour. And she was pretty sure she had been in a personal study of some sorts the night the viscount had come through the window.

Making a decision to go through with it later, John's warning be damned, she continued packing.

It was late in the afternoon when she finished packing the pieces. She decided to rest and explore the rose garden. The late-afternoon sun kissed her skin as she strolled across the grounds. A gentle breeze blew across the tips of the grass and whistled in the lone tree that stood in the middle of the English gardens. She had noticed the small maple before and wondered why it was planted there. Out of place in the formal rows, it nevertheless proudly stood its ground. The tree couldn't be more than twenty years old, and she wondered if as a child Blackfield had had something to do with its planting.

Stepping forward to examine it more closely, she was thrown to the ground as one of the buildings she had planned to investigate exploded.

Chapter 9

"**Y**ou are wearing a path across the floor, my lord."

Thomas recalled an image of a caged lion pacing back and forth at a spectacle in London. He had sympathized with the beast. "It has to be one of the antiquarians."

Richards, the man in charge of the Hastings Building, nodded. "Maybe more than one. We found a message about their shipment tomorrow. There has to be a contact outside of their group, too."

They had been going over this ad nauseam for

the last hour, since the Hastings Building explosion. Even though Thomas had thought Patience might be the spy, the reality of it made him furious. He didn't know what he was more furious with; that it was she, or that he had to acknowledge that fact. The thought just made him angrier. He couldn't let her get to him. It was a one-sided seduction. He wasn't interested in any type of commitment, especially not with a false woman.

With difficulty he refrained from snarling. "Thanks for putting the traps in place so quickly. Excellent thinking, by the way."

Richards nodded. "Keeps the boys busy."

"Yes, well after this they are going to be plenty busy. Our hand has been tipped. The spies know we're onto them. We can't expect them to make the same mistake twice. Are the new measures in place?"

"Being put in as we speak."

Thomas watched through the study window as the last of the flames was quenched. The building was completely intact, thanks to the way the trap had been set. The blast had been designed more for show than to do damage. A very large warning signal, of sorts. If only they had captured the person who had triggered it.

"Did we get a tally of who was missing during the time of the blast?"

"The Teckings were in their rooms. Not sure the man ever leaves them, to be honest. The younger man and woman were out. The woman was found on the grounds, and the man appeared roughly fifteen minutes after the blast. Apparently he walked to the abbey ruins and had no idea anything had happened. Said he did hear the blast though. Not surprising with the amount of gunpowder we used. Would have been more suspicious if he *hadn't* heard it."

"And the servants?"

"Much harder. The kitchens were accounted for, as the cooks and scullery maids were preparing dinner. Although it's possible that one of them could have slipped out. That's really the crux of the matter. We either need to interview the whole lot, or just watch them more closely in the future. If it is an outsider, then we are wasting our time."

"Bait another trap. Have the council meet tonight to discuss it. I'll speak with Samuel."

"Yes, my lord."

Thomas watched as Patience Harrington and John Fenton whispered to each other as they, too, watched the last of the flames die away. Plotting, no doubt.

It had been pure genius for the men to put traps on and around the buildings that morning. It was now going to take the spies more than just a saunter through the door if they wanted to steal the designs.

Patience Harrington was going to have to work quite hard now if she was going to steal anything other than a one-way ticket to Newgate.

After the earlier explosion, dinner was a relatively quiet affair. Blackfield gave a minimal explanation about the gamekeeper's store of power exploding, then kept silent and didn't antagonize Patience. Mrs. Tecking kept silent and didn't antagonize Patience. John and Caroline picked at their meals, and Samuel had cried off, citing a previous engagement. Although where he had to go was a mystery. The coward probably didn't want to sit amidst the doom that had seemed to embrace the castle and its inhabitants.

But the tension was high, and even Mr. Tecking shifted uncomfortably in his seat at the thick air and darting glances.

After dinner Patience continued packing artifacts. She had lost an hour after the explosion in recovering from the blast and talking to John. A bit shocked, but thankfully not hurt, she had watched the servants scramble to clear the smoke and extinguish the flames. Flames that miraculously never reached the structure, even though they had seemed to engulf it previously.

Maybe the monster was a dragon. She snorted and picked up her tools. The only dragon she was likely to meet was Mrs. Tecking or Black-field. But a part of her couldn't forget the lifted arm she had seen from the window the other night.

It was well into the evening when she stopped working and decided to put into action her plans to poke through Blackfield's study. She just needed to make sure to stay out of sight, or John would give her an earful if he found out.

Hiding in a hallway alcove, Patience waited as servant after servant hurried past. They must have been on a task, because there were at least ten of them that had rushed past her hiding spot in the last five minutes. She waited an additional two minutes until she heard no more footsteps before venturing forth.

Suppressing a yawn, she slipped down the hall and stairs. She was still in her day clothes, having stayed up to finish packing, and her skirts whispered across the floors and oriental rugs. She tried to retrace her steps from the first night, but still managed to get disoriented twice. Finally, she found the study where Blackfield had entered through the window.

Thankfully, it was unlocked, and she was able to slip inside. She had never learned how to pick a lock. Although she had always wanted to learn, she had quickly discovered picking locks wasn't a skill for her temperament. Five minutes into fiddling with a hairpin had seen her frustrated and bored.

She held up her lamp and moved forward, taking stock of the room in a way that she hadn't been able to when the viscount had been present.

Bookcases and a large desk dominated one part of the room, while the other was centered around a cozy set of chairs in front of the fireplace. The area where she had sat with Blackfield on the first night.

Complementary furniture surrounded the chairs, and the lacquered liquor cabinet sat innocuously to the side.

Patience moved to the desk. Inkpot, a lamp, several books. It was clear of papers. Either this was not Blackfield's main study, or he was obsessively clean about his work spaces. She opened one drawer after another, lifting and replacing papers, but they, too, were neatly filed, and nothing looked very exciting.

Fragments of conversation she had heard the night before echoed in her mind . . . the government would be against it . . . destructive . . . if this gets out . . . entire forces obliterated . . .

Ominous, dangerous words. But still, she had no idea what she was looking for, and, furthermore, the whole idea of searching for clues had seemed much more exciting and fruitful in her mind when she had devised it. Much like her trip the previous night to the Hastings Building, as she had heard some of the servants call it while cleaning up the debris. She grimaced. A pattern was developing.

She poked around a bit more, looked at the shelves, and even opened the liquor cabinet. While she could honestly say that he had an impressive collection of spirits, she couldn't find much other personal information in the room.

It reminded her of how little she knew about Blackfield. She had heard the rumors, of course. But as a victim of gossip herself, she had paid little attention. However, he definitely fit the picture of the dark, mysterious eccentric he was painted. And the eligible bachelor as well. Patience could grudgingly admit the busybodies hadn't exaggerated his physical appeal. Nor had his sarcastic nature been terribly exaggerated. Although it was couched in more fashionable terms such as *rapier wit*, he nevertheless could probably skin a bear with his tongue if he tried.

Patience moved from the room and entered the hall, cupping her hands around her light to keep the shadows close. A low boom rumbled in the distance. The statues and art along the walls regained their menacing cast, and she had to decide consciously to ignore them as she continued. The flickering light gave the shadows movement, and her racing heart increased its pace without her consent. Tamping down on breathlessness turned panic, she decided that searching one more room was plenty of sleuthing for the night. It was late, and she had to rise early to greet her father's movers. Frankly, she had reached the end of her bravado.

Footsteps echoed down the hall. Thankfully her slippers made no sound, and the whisper of fabric could be taken for the occasional castle draft. She ducked into an alcove and blew out her lamp. Darkness engulfed her.

The footsteps clinked down the hall like the rattle of chains, and she felt a pressure against her chest. A low moan escaped from someone, and she stopped breathing altogether.

The footsteps paused for a second, then resumed, drawing ever nearer to her hiding spot. She pressed into the wall, her skirts a barely noticeable murmur upon the floor.

But it was enough. A break in the footsteps alerted her. But before she could run or scream, someone had pinned her to the wall.

Chapter 10

⁓◯◯⁓

The hard planes of a man's body pressed into her back.

"What have we here?" a low voice questioned.

She didn't answer, but as the man's hands ran down her sides as if to identify her by touch, she squeaked. The hands didn't still, and she started to fight.

She was quickly turned around, the body now pressed into her front in a lascivious manner that would have made her blush if she weren't scared out of her wits.

"My dear Miss Harrington. Fancy seeing you out so late in the evening."

She knew that low, mocking voice. The panic immediately disappeared, and she pushed against Blackfield's chest.

"Let me go, you cad!"

"No, I don't think I will."

She mutinously glared at him through the shadows, trying to project her displeasure. "Let go of me, this is quite unseemly."

He leaned forward, his lips inches from hers, just as they had been in the library. "Too bad."

The nature of their pose, in the middle of a hallway no less, renewed her struggles.

He let her struggle, not letting up on the pressure, which, while not harming her was making her increasingly unsettled. And the normally cold and drafty hall seemed to have grown much warmer.

"What do you want?"

She could practically hear his smirk. "A dangerous question, don't you think, Patience?"

"Don't call me that," she groused.

"Oh, but after all we've *shared*, surely you don't expect me to call you Miss Harrington?"

"Shared? Dinner conversation? Word wars? I hardly think that—"

"—an intimate acquaintance?" He drawled the interruption. "No, but this definitely is."

And he pressed his lips to hers. Warm and soft and needy, just as they had been in the library. And she found her body had the same traitorous desire to give in. And he was doing that thing with his tongue along her bottom lip. She hadn't known kissing could make one feel captured and free at the same time. She pulled her head back, but he simply followed, pulling her hips hard against his and bending her ever so slightly back as if to devour her like the vampire she had first thought him.

He took his time exploring her mouth, and she let him, enjoying the sensation and forgetting about the Patience-eating shadows in the hall.

Sucking slowly on her bottom lip he let it go with a pop and looked down at her in the dark. She couldn't read his expression in the nearly pitch-black hall. And somewhere along the way her eyelids had refused to stay open, so she was looking at him through bare slits.

She felt wanton and wondered what she looked like.

"So, Patience, what are you doing down here at this time of night?"

Her brain wasn't quite steady yet. "Searching

for . . ." Her brain caught up quickly enough not to complete the statement.

"Searching for what?" he prompted, although there was a hard edge to his tone.

"Searching for you, actually. And then the kitchens. I've been up all night working and decided to request a cup of tea."

"Mmmmm." It was obvious he didn't believe her. "And what did you need with me?"

"I was sent to tell you of our plans tomorrow."

He lifted a brow. "You had to come all the way down here by yourself to tell me your plans?"

"Yes, well, we drew lots, and I ended up with the shortest stick."

He leaned back against the wall, his features shadowed. "And what are your plans?"

"Men will arrive in the morning and the first shipment will leave with them." She was a poor liar. It probably showed.

"Couldn't you have sent a note with a servant?"

"You left dinner, and the servants have all been scuttling around, and we weren't sure . . . oh, bloody deal with it. There, message delivered."

She turned to go, and he shot out of his relaxed pose and blocked her way before she could leave.

She was forced to look up as he loomed over

her. Suspicion warred with excitement inside her as he ran a finger down her cheek. "Maybe you just missed me at dinner? Wanted to deliver the message personally?"

"You flatter yourself, Lord Blackfield."

"Call me Thomas."

"No."

Damn but she amused him. "No? Why not?"

"I don't want to."

"But *I* want you to."

She gave him a look like one would give a recalcitrant child.

"Please?"

"Fine, Thomas. Carts will leave tomorrow at daybreak, Thomas. Have a good evening, Thomas."

"Thank you, Patience."

She pressed her lips together. "Fine, but only in private."

He could see her underlying excitement and latched on to it. The night before she had kissed him like a woman first experiencing passion and drowning in it. There was an innocence in her reactions that was as exciting as her sensual response.

He was hard just thinking about it.

Furthering his plot, he leaned in just a bit.

He could smell the lightest hint of peaches surrounding her. Fresh and innocent and full of life. He needed to experience again what she tasted like.

"Mmmm . . . only in private then."

And with that he gently touched her chin and kissed her. Strawberries and cream with a hint of peach. Delicious.

She responded, just as she had the night before, with curiosity and an innocent passion. Her approach might feel innocent, but she kissed like she wanted to drown in him. Her kisses didn't imply games. The rest of her might, but she was unfettered in her physical response.

He wanted to know what she tasted like everywhere.

She broke the embrace, her breath coming in gasps. He tipped her chin up again. "Why did you come down here?"

"To find . . ." She caught herself again, just in time. "To find you and deliver the message."

Any lingering doubts to the plan were discarded. Twice she had nearly revealed herself in her postkiss daze.

She was remarkably quick to recover though.

"Why did you feel the need to ask me again, Lord Blackfield?"

"Thomas," he corrected, trying to size up her reaction. Intelligence and suspicion shone from her large hazel eyes. "Just making sure that it wasn't for me," he said lightly.

"Hmmm . . ."

"My leaving from dinner and servants scuttling or not, next time you might want to try the bellpull. Or to summon your maid. It gets cold at night." He rubbed her arms. "And dangerous if you were to . . . stumble on something."

She shivered, and he used the motion to rub her arms again. "See, you are already shivering."

Not from the cold, she thought.

"I'll escort you to the kitchen to get your tea, then to your room."

"No, that is quite all right, Lord B—, Thomas. I think I will just go back to my room."

A boom rumbled in the distance, and Patience felt Blackfield stiffen.

"Nonsense. Let us get you that tea."

Not waiting for an answer he steered her toward the kitchen, of whose location she made note. A servant quickly made tea while Blackfield leaned against a counter, watching her.

She grabbed the cup, thanked the servant, and made to exit as quickly as dignity allowed. Unfortunately, Blackfield appeared in front of her before she made it into the hall.

"Can't have the guests losing their way, can I? Perhaps I should assign myself your personal guard. After all, this is the second time this has happened."

Patience chuckled nervously. "That isn't necessary, Lord Blackfield."

"You don't plan on leaving your room at night then?"

"No, that isn't what I meant."

He gave a small smile at her disgruntled look. "What did you mean then, Miss Harrington?"

"That I do not plan on getting lost again."

He leaned forward, brushing her arm lightly. "Not all things require planning."

Patience might be innocent, but she wasn't stupid. "Exactly. So you need not plan on being my guard."

He shook his head at her twisted logic but continued to stare into her eyes, as if he could decipher something in their depths.

Feeling warm despite the draft of the kitchen, Patience checked to see what the servant thought of their banter and physical proximity. But there was no trace of the servant. They were all alone.

She again laughed nervously. "Well, I should really be getting to bed now that I have my tea." She motioned with her cup, placing it between them.

There was a lazy humor in his eyes, as if he knew exactly what she was thinking.

"Excellent idea. I'll join you."

"What?" she screeched.

"I'll join you on your trip to your room. It is on my way."

"No, really—"

He took hold of her arm and steered her to the door, cutting off the rest of her objection.

His fingers were warm on the thin fabric of her gown, and she could feel the heat on her skin. He grabbed a lit lamp with his free hand, keeping possession of her arm with the other.

They reached the top of the steps and Patience felt it was a sufficient distance. She tugged her arm from his grasp, surprised when he let her. Surprise was replaced with shock a second later as he slipped his arm around her shoulder and pulled her up against his side.

"You're cold."

She sputtered and tugged back, feeling a

spark of irritation at the obvious humor in his eyes. Blasted man.

She stepped in front of him and poked him in the chest. "You go to your room, I'll go to mine."

"So suspicious, my dear Patience. I believe I am wounded."

She gave him a disbelieving look. "I'm sure."

"Miss Harrington, I believe we have started off on the wrong foot."

"And whose fault was that?"

"Far be it from me to suggest it be a lady's."

"Excellent. You are giving this a real go."

"And you are making it so easy, I see."

She waved a hand at his raised brow. "Sorry. Do go on. I believe you were at the part that goes, 'My dear Miss Harrington, I can't believe I was such a brute, can you ever forgive me?'"

"Yes, of course, something like that."

"Well, in that case, yes," she agreed magnanimously, a spark in her beautiful eyes.

He felt lightened at her look. Something in her response chipped away at his long-held bitterness.

Yes, this had been the best plan he had ever devised.

* * *

Patience examined Blackfield's compelling features in the low light. There was a teasing cast that had been missing during all of their previous encounters, except possibly the first night.

And he kissed her like she was the only woman alive. Like some tasty treat he *had* to finish.

She shivered, but not from the cold. He had sparred with her again, but this time there was something else in his gaze. Something that pulled her toward him. A blind woman would feel his magnetism.

She wondered if it was an inbred talent. He didn't seem to be part of the social ton, and neither had he gone out of his way to talk to his guests. In fact, the opposite had occurred. And despite his at times rude and boorish behavior, there was something about him, something that caused people to vie for his attention even as he cut them to shreds. She had even caught Mrs. Tecking, as restrained as she had been over the past week, casting more than one glance his way.

No, it was not odd that she found him irritating yet immensely attractive. She blamed it on being a normal human, as susceptible as the next person to a siren's song.

And that last exchange had been almost . . . friendly.

The physical part of relationships had always intrigued her. Her undeserved reputation as fast had enlightened her to some of the aspects, as people didn't take care with their verbal taunts. Studying ancient statuary and art hadn't left her in the dark about the male form or other elements of the dance between men and women.

All in all, her body's responses were overruling her brain. Patience looked up at Blackfield—Thomas. His gentle taunt about her reason for bearding him herself, that it had been to search for him rather than to deliver her message replayed itself. Perhaps it had been, in part, her reason to search.

Mind, she would still do her best to discover what was going on, but at the same time perhaps she could figure out Thomas, too.

He was fiddling with the cuff of her dress. A burst of heat started in her stomach and uncoiled outward.

Kissing Thomas was quite nice. She was perfectly willing to experience more, while keeping an eye on him at the same time.

Yes, that was a good plan.

"Excellent," she repeated. Thomas didn't look concerned by her silence; in fact, he appeared amused.

He held out his arm. "In the newfound spirit of friendship, may I escort you down the hall? Just as far as the first corridor, of course."

Her lips quirked. "That would be wonderful, thank you."

She laid her hand lightly on his arm, and they maintained a comfortable silence. When they reached the corridor he lifted her hand and pressed a warm kiss onto her knuckles. Breathing a little more heavily, she tried to extract her hand, but he twisted it and placed a kiss, hotter than the last, on her wrist. Liquid heat pooled in the lower part of her body, and her knees threatened to buckle.

His dark eyes were piercing and filled with something she couldn't name. They pinned her in place.

"Good night, Patience," he murmured. The husky tone sent pleasant shivers down her spine.

"Good night, my lord."

He smiled, a slow, sensual smile, and released her hand, his fingers trailing from her wrist, across her palm, and along the underside of her fingertips, his thumb caressing the other side of her hand as his fingers worked their way.

With the last touch of his fingers to hers, her breath returned in a whoosh and she curtsied and walked back to her room. A few steps from her door she turned, not knowing if she expected him still to be standing there or not. He was, his sensual smile in place. Tipping his head in farewell, he disappeared into the dark shadows.

Chapter 11

~~∞∞~~

Tilly's bustling awakened Patience. Her maid had been busy lately. She wondered where Tilly had been spending her time.

"Good morning, Tilly."

"*Bon jour, ma petite.*" Tilly retrieved a lilac morning gown and the corresponding accessories. "Will Mr. Arthur's men be here this morning?"

"Yes." Patience stretched and yawned. "Isn't it just like my father to have the men here early and awaken me at daybreak?"

"Well, it will be good to see them."

Patience nodded, not awake enough for conversation. She quickly dressed and readied for the day. She could take a nap after the men left if she still needed it.

Tilly hustled her out the door with a cheerful wave and the promise to see her downstairs. If Patience didn't know better, she would suspect her maid of having an affair with one of the workmen who were coming to collect the first batch of artifacts from the Ashe collection.

Shaking her head, she walked down the stairs and into the dining room. Preoccupied with thoughts of Tilly and plans for the day, she bumped into someone.

Looking up, she saw Thomas's amused eyes. The man was intriguing when he brooded and devastating when in good humor.

"Good morning, Miss Harrington." His tongue caressed her last name.

She shivered. She was just glad he hadn't called her Patience in public.

"Good morning, Lord Blackfield."

He motioned to the room. "I would hardly be a gentleman if I entered before you."

She snorted and entered the room. Thomas and she had been the last to arrive.

He followed her across the room. "Miss Harrington, have you tried the scones? They are excellent."

As they approached the sideboard, Patience narrowed her eyes at Thomas. What was going on? Sure, they had declared a truce, but—

"Buttery, warm, fragrant." His voice dropped. "You hold them in your hand and marvel at how soft they feel. Once you savor the delights, you yearn to make the experience last longer. They slide right across your tongue."

He held a scone to his mouth. Patience stared openmouthed and checked behind them, thankful for the large room, as no one at the table seemed to have heard or witnessed his dramatics.

"Lord Blackfield, please keep your food fetishes to yourself."

He breathed into her ear. "As long as I can keep my Patience fetish . . ."

She blushed, quickly piled a few items on her plate, and managed to move to the table and seat herself without dropping anything.

There was companionable silence while everyone ate and read the papers, but Thomas spoke up soon afterward.

"How many men is your father sending today?"

All heads turned toward him. He had not shown one ounce of curiosity about their activities the entire time they had been there. Suddenly he was asking a question delivered in a fairly good-natured manner. Patience looked at the reactions around the table. John's brows were knit, Caroline's were raised in surprise, Mrs. Tecking's were suspicious, and Samuel seemed amused. Mr. Tecking, well, he seemed oblivious. Probably didn't even hear the statement, too busy thinking about the collection.

"With the size of the collection, probably five or six men."

"How did you know the number of pieces in the collection?"

"Caroline provided the approximate information before we arrived. I also posted a note to my father the day after we began."

Thomas glanced at Caroline. "I didn't know you had gone through George's collections."

Caroline looked at her plate. "How could I not know its contents? It was all George talked about."

A cloud passed momentarily over Thomas's face before the scowl smoothed into his prior pleasant facade. "Of course."

A servant entered the dining hall and paused

next to Patience. "Miss Harrington, the carts have arrived."

Patience thanked him and rose. Surprisingly, everyone else at the table rose to leave as well, including Thomas.

They trooped out to the drive to see two carts and six men. Patience was delighted to see Jeremy White unlatching the back of one cart.

"Jeremy!"

He turned and grinned. "Miss Harrington. Good to see you."

She walked to him, barely refraining from skipping. She had known Jeremy a long time. He was like a member of the family.

"Ready to work?" she teased. "We arranged the pieces to give you the maximum amount of weight and size."

He grinned. "I'm sure you did."

Patience turned to introduce the men and noticed that Thomas's eyes were narrowed on Jeremy. Jeremy seemed to be sizing up Thomas as well, and when they shook hands, both hands turned white. She shook her head.

Patience directed the men to the boxes, and one by one they began carefully hauling artifacts to the carts. The painstaking task of carting the heavy crates took a few hours, and by the time everything was loaded and secured, they were all tired.

Patience was happy to hear from Jeremy that her father was doing well and progress was being made with Parliament. The men finally bid farewell, thanking Thomas's staff for the lunches that had been packed after the men had announced they would not be staying.

Patience gave Jeremy a message for her father and waved as the carts lumbered down the drive. The men would return in a week to gather the second load, and a week after that, if all things went well, to take the last. Two weeks more, and the job should be finished.

Throwing off a sudden strange burst of melancholy, Patience turned to see Thomas leaning against the door, a basket clasped in his hands. She sent him an inquiring gaze, and he lifted the basket.

"Picnic lunch. The kitchen staff made an extra one, and I thought you might wish to join me down by the lake. I have a few questions about the collection."

She brushed the hair from her eyes. "Fine. Would you like me to invite the others?"

He smirked. "No."

She quirked an eyebrow.

"You are the head of the venture, I only wish to ask you. Besides, I have some questions about your team that I would rather not discuss in their presence."

She nodded and stepped past him and into the entrance hall. "When shall we meet?"

"An hour? I know you have things to finish. I will fetch you from your cataloging room."

She checked the stately clock in the entrance hall and nodded.

Fifty-five minutes later she was chewing the nails on her right hand and checking the small mantel clock for the twentieth time.

"Patience! I've asked you three times now how you want these blunderbusses labeled."

She spun around and sent John, who was looking exasperated, an apologetic glance.

"Let's just do them the same way as the bayonets, yes?"

"Fine. But you could have told me that when I asked ten minutes ago."

"My apologies, John. My mind was elsewhere."

He cocked a brow. "Or on someone else?"

"Lord Blackfield wants to discuss our plans for the next two weeks. We are having lunch together."

His eyes narrowed. "Do you wish me to join you?"

"No, I will be fine."

"Patience—"

"John, it's fine. Really."

A voice interrupted their conversation. "Glad to hear it."

Patience spun to see Thomas lounging in the doorway. She wondered if he practiced the gesture.

"Lord Blackfield."

"Miss Harrington. Mr. Fenton."

She wrung her hands, a bit flustered. "Right. I will see you later, John. Cataloging the blunderbusses the same way as the bayonets sounds like the best plan."

John nodded, not taking his eyes off Thomas.

Patience slipped between Thomas and the door, forcing him to follow as she strode down the hall. He caught up to her.

"Eager to be alone with me?"

She snorted. "Of course I am, my lord."

"I thought you were going to call me 'Thomas'?"

"Yes, well I thought you would like 'my lord' better than the alternative that just came to mind."

"My dear Patience, what vulgar thoughts circulate in that head of yours?"

He chuckled at her scowl as they descended the stairs. A servant was waiting for them with a basket. The day was sunny and warm, and Patience could see a blanket spread beneath a willow near the edge of the lake. Two other baskets were open beside the blanket, and place settings were already laid out.

Patience looked pointedly at the basket in Thomas's hands. He gave her a cheeky grin. "Appearances. Can't let you go thinking I didn't do this myself."

She couldn't restrain an answering smile, and the mood was sufficiently light as they arranged themselves on the blanket and loaded their plates. Cold chicken, fruit, bread, and cheese were the main fare, and what looked like apple tortes were hiding in the bottom of one of the baskets.

Thomas uncorked the wine and poured it into two goblets. "I heard you say something about rifles to Mr. Fenton. Is he your firearms expert?"

"Weapons expert."

"Ah, so he handles other weapons as well."

She nodded. "His specialty is firearms, but he also has an interest in blades, especially medieval daggers. They comprise the most extensive part of your uncle's weaponry collection; John deals mostly with those, although he has waxed poetic over a number of your uncle's firearms as well."

"Does Mr. Fenton have interest in modern and experimental firearms also? I know many collectors have both."

Patience thought for a second. "I don't know. Perhaps. Weaponry is not on my list of interests, so John and I don't discuss them much."

Thomas appeared to consider her response. "What about the other two?"

"Mrs. Tecking is our scribe. Mr. Tecking is obsessed by anything Roman."

"Ah yes, obsession, the mainstay of a collector."

Patience took a bite of her chicken, determined to ignore his taunts. It was too nice a day.

"And Mr. White? What part does he play in your father's business?"

"Jeremy is in charge of shipping."

Thomas's eyes gleamed. "Busy with shipping lately?"

She sent him a withering glance, not wanting to repeat the French discussion. "I would hope so."

"What does the museum plan to do with Uncle George's collection?"

She looked at Thomas as if he had asked why the grass was green. "Put it on display."

He shrugged. "Are there people other than collectors who would care to view his collections?"

"Of course! This is history. We want to make the items available for everyone to see."

"Most people would be concerned with making money."

She frowned. "Yes, well, there is nothing wrong with making money, but educating the public will, I hope, make our society better."

He cast her a disparaging look. His eyebrows looked ready to disappear into his hairline. "You think that displaying a collection of dusty artifacts will make our society better?"

Her back straightened. "I know it will. You have to give people access to resources, or else society will always be about those who already have the power."

"Good for the people in power," he pointed out.

"Yes, but society becomes stagnant and dull in that case. Revolution is inevitable."

Thomas smiled, a real smile. "You are a veritable bluestocking, Patience."

She bristled. "I know that my position is not welcome in most drawing rooms, although it may have taken me a few conversations to realize that."

His eyes sparkled, and he leaned forward to refill her glass. "Well, don't stop on behalf of mine. My drawing room hasn't seen such spirited discourse in a long time."

She swirled her glass and looked across the water. "Why do you hate antiquarians?"

His smile slipped, but the abrasive shield he had been erecting was not present. "My uncle was obsessed, and so were his friends. His obsession led to unforgivable actions."

Before she could ask more, he switched the focus back to her. "How did you get into antiquities?"

Let him keep his secrets for now. "My father. My mother died when I was very young, and my father cared for me. We lived a pretty solitary existence in the country, and I devoured books, manuscripts, and anything else I could get my hands on." She shrugged. "I was enchanted by the tales of ages past. It was both a blessing and a curse when I went to London. I thought everyone had similar interests."

She couldn't keep away the chill of loneliness,

and had a bad feeling it showed on her face. She quickly replaced it with determination.

"Society wasn't what I expected. And neither was I what *they* expected. I quickly discovered the men and women in society look in disfavor on those who are different."

Thomas laid his hand over hers and rubbed it in a soothing motion.

She smiled at him, warmed by the gesture. "It's all right. I love my dusty tomes more than I care what they think. And my father's opinion means more to me than any hundred of theirs."

His gesture appeared unfeigned, and although she was surprised by its gift, she appreciated his silent support. Something made her look back toward the castle, and she saw a drape pulled back. It was dropped as soon as she looked.

Patience tried counting windows to determine the room, but there were too many. It could have been anyone from John or one of the Teckings to a random servant cleaning a room. Still, a shiver passed over her.

Thomas pulled her hand into his lap and rubbed it with both hands, lightly pulling each finger from root to tip. She nearly sighed in pleasure, it felt so heavenly. A light breeze rippled through the tree, making the contentment complete.

And then he yanked his hands away, leaving her bereft of contact and wondering what she had done wrong. She wasn't left wondering long when he sneezed. Loudly.

A string of curses emerged from his mouth, and her chin dropped when he started looking around the tree. The man had gone mad. Maybe he really did keep monsters.

He started muttering and she heard the words "damn" and "weedy flowers."

"Are you bothered by the flowers?"

He pointed at an offending stalk that was innocently resting against the far side of the tree. Some of its fluffy heads had been blown onto their blanket with the breeze.

She smiled at his offended expression. "Would you like me to remove it?"

He sneezed again. "No." Sneeze. "Too late."

She hid a smile and started placing the food into the baskets. He stopped her, a mutinous glance on his face. His eyes were a bit puffy.

She took sympathy on him. "Is there anything I can do?"

A shout in the distance shifted their attention

to the buildings along the tree line. A man was frantically motioning to Thomas.

Thomas's mouth pulled tight, but he stood. "Forgive me. Can you—"

"I'll be fine, go ahead."

He nodded and started walking toward the man. She stopped him.

"Thank you for lunch."

He held her gaze for a long second, and a small smile graced his features. "See you tonight."

And with that he was off. Two servants popped out of nowhere to clean up, and Patience had to wonder where they had been hidden.

She took a final glance toward the outbuildings as she trekked back toward the castle. Both Thomas and the man were staring at her while they talked. A shiver similar to the one she had felt when looking at the castle window traversed her spine.

She didn't relax until she was safely inside the castle.

Chapter 12

Thomas watched Patience disappear into the castle, and turned back to his worker. "What is wrong, Kenneth?"

Kenneth pulled a shaky hand through his thinning hair. "We had another attempt."

Thomas fought to stay calm. "Where?"

"The Hastings Building again."

"New traps were set, I assume? And no one but those needing entrance today were told what they were?"

He nodded. "Yes, and the attempt was thwarted again."

"Good. Walk with me." Thomas headed toward the brown buildings. "The spy will gain entrance eventually. Are the other precautions in place?"

"Yes, my lord. Escape routes have been set up, as well as decoy materials."

"I'm sure that has made experimenting more difficult."

"A bit, but we all agree it is well worth it."

"The Monster Project will be ready on schedule?"

"Yes, even with the delays we built in enough time."

Thomas grimaced. "If the other governments catch wind, it may be more than just the French we have to deal with."

"We had word from our contact in the Foreign Office. He is setting it up so that when we are ready to loose the monster our government will be first in line. He even mentioned funding."

Thomas frowned and picked up his pace. "We don't need blasted funding. We need reassurances as to what they will do with it. I've had my reservations about this project since its inception."

"I know." Kenneth tried for a soothing tone, but it just wasn't a trait that sat well on the heavy and gruff man. "But it's as well that you let the mad surgeon have his pet project. He will continue to be an asset afterward. If you hadn't let him . . ."

Kenneth let the sentence drag, and Thomas gave an answering nod. Joseph, the man whom the other workers dubbed the mad surgeon, likely would have gone elsewhere to see his dream completed. And the monster in the wrong hands . . .

Secretly, Thomas didn't think there was such a thing as the right hands for this project; but as a scientist himself, he understood the desire for innovation. As a leader he had a responsibility to make sure that the innovation did no harm. The latter was what kept him awake at night.

"Your handling of this problem continues to impress me, Kenneth. Be sure to set up something for the men soon. Talk to Meg or Caroline if you need anything."

He had full faith in his housekeeper and his aunt's ability to take care of anything.

"I will. We've all been under a lot of pressure. It will be good for the men to relax and celebrate."

They entered the Hastings Building, and a number of men stepped forward to make their reports. Thomas motioned them to the meeting room and turned to Kenneth and Keith, who had just joined them.

"I only have time for a brief meeting. Can we complete it in half an hour?"

Both men nodded.

"Keith, any news on the intruder?"

"No, but we did find a piece of fabric in one of the closets. Looks like a piece of silk from a dress."

Thomas sighed. He thought of how the conversation would go. "Patience, what were you doing in the closet?" "Looking for antique dresses, Lord Blackfield."

He sighed again. "Anything else?"

"Just some footprints outside. The men are working on them. How about you? How is the investigation going?"

Thomas restrained another sigh. "I hope to have something by the end of the week. Keep working on the servants."

Keith and Kenneth both nodded. They were courting maids in the castle who kept them informed of the latest news.

Thomas tapped his foot. If only the lady he was "courting" would do the same. He might even be able to forgive her spying if she would.

* * *

Patience put down her tools and sighed. It had taken her twice as long as usual to complete her work. Her mind kept straying to Thomas, the strange men wandering the estate, the buildings, the explosion, and the picnic. Thomas had taken her on a picnic. *A picnic.* It just didn't fit.

Of course, he had said it was to discuss the future of the Ashe collection, but Thomas had seemed more interested in other things. If she harbored the secret fantasies of the silly young debutantes, she would almost think he was courting her.

Pink stained her cheeks. So she wasn't exempt from secret fantasies. But she wasn't a slave to her fantasies. All right, so she wasn't *always* a slave to her fantasies.

Patience stood and began clearing the clutter she had spread across the floor. She needed to get her mind out of the clouds and back in the real world.

There were no monsters, the castle was not haunted, and Lord Blackfield was not courting her. She nodded. Perfect.

"Patience? You look like you are preparing for war."

She smiled at John, who was standing in the doorway looking quite bemused.

"Finished with the medieval pieces already?"

He entered the room, nodding. "Yes. I'll begin with the Eastern pieces tomorrow. I was wondering if you needed assistance."

"Nothing you can help with, unfortunately. Mr. Tecking might need some assistance though."

John shuddered. "Are you sure there is nothing I can help *you* with?"

Amused, she shook her head. "Why don't you take the night off. We're ahead of schedule, so go do whatever it is men enjoy doing. I heard there is a lively tavern in the village, or perhaps you can challenge Blackfield to evil overlord chess."

John smiled and turned. "I think I will have a look at the village. Thanks. See you at dinner."

Patience waved him off. Throwing back her shoulders, she commanded herself to focus on her work.

Two hours later it was time to wash and dress for dinner, and her command had only partially worked. But at least she was through the Egyptian household items. The next day she could start on the burial artifacts, one of her favorite areas.

Patience entered the terrace where the others were already gathered. Lanterns were strung from posts. The atmosphere was light and festive. The staff had prepared a splendid dinner to celebrate the new month. The guests sat and immediately were presented with the first course.

As she sipped her soup, she caught Thomas's eye. There was a twinkle in their depths, and she again wondered what type of changeling he was to so abruptly alter his demeanor.

"Miss Harrington, how did your cataloging go this afternoon? Must have been a relief to ship a third of the collection this morning."

Mrs. Tecking's spoon was frozen halfway to her mouth. John blinked at the cordial tone. Caroline was trying to act as if nothing were out of the ordinary, but her eyes had gone a bit wide. Samuel looked perpetually amused. Mr. Tecking kept eating, blithely unaware as usual.

"Oh, it was a productive afternoon. I start on burial artifacts tomorrow, and am quite looking forward to it."

"Really? What about them sparks your interest?"

"The importance of the afterlife and the heart as the house of the soul. The types of things that were considered important in the afterlife. Common things and extraordinary things. And I have quite a fondness for canopic jars."

Samuel raised a brow. "What exactly is a canopic jar?"

"Those are the ornate jars where they put the body parts the person would need. Imset, depicted as a human, housed the liver, Hapi, the baboon took care of the lungs, Duamutef the jackal for the stomach, and Kebechsenef the falcon for the intestines."

Everyone's eyes except Mr. Tecking's and Thomas's were wide.

Thomas smirked at Samuel's expression. "And what about the brain, Miss Harrington?"

"Oh, they pulled it out through the nose and discarded it."

She paused as soon as the words left her mouth. She really needed to stop doing this. She peeked upward. Thomas seemed to be taking perverse delight in the green shade of Samuel's face, and it reminded her again how fiercely competitive they were.

Thomas gestured toward her before the others could regain their ability to speak. "Have some oysters, Miss Harrington. They are Cook's specialty."

"Thank you, Lord Blackfield." She was grateful for the topic change.

Mrs. Tecking's mouth pursed in displeasure.

She grabbed an oyster before Patience could reach one.

She had barely tasted it before she was simpering. "Oh, those are truly delightful, my lord."

It was Patience's turn to blink. She had been shocked when Mrs. Tecking had restrained from simpering to Thomas. That she had suddenly regained the ability seemed equally startling.

"Miss Harrington is not used to such rich foods, but I'm sure that even she will enjoy it."

Ah, so that was the reason. Now that Thomas seemed to find amusement in Patience's gaffes, Mrs. Tecking was determined to pick up the slack.

"Patience has never been fond of oysters," John said.

Well, that was unexpected. What was John up to? And why did everyone suddenly have an opinion for her?

"They are quite good." Caroline smiled, although there was a guarded look to her eyes as if she was trying to figure out what was going on with her guests.

Patience looked at Thomas, whose eyes were narrowed in Mrs. Tecking's direction. He glanced at Patience, and the twinkle returned.

"Oysters, a subject worthy of debate."

She couldn't stop her smile.

"By the by, Miss Harrington. I was wondering if you would like to travel to the abbey ruins on the edge of the property. I believe they are medieval."

If the twinkle in his eye was anything to go by, he knew perfectly well what they were.

Mrs. Tecking jumped in before Patience could reply. "Oh, may we make a group outing of it?"

Patience wasn't surprised by the request. Mrs. Tecking was a social creature, even if Mr. Tecking was not.

Thomas didn't lose the twinkle. "Alas, I'm afraid that won't be possible this time. I spoke with your husband earlier, and he assured me that he needed to stay in the castle tomorrow and needed you to help him, isn't that true Mr. Tecking?"

Mr. Tecking perked up for a second. "Quite right. Quite right."

Mrs. Tecking was displeased. Patience wasn't sure that the woman's lips could pull any tighter.

John spoke up. "Well, I'm free and can go with you two."

Thomas sipped his wine and somehow managed to look apologetic. "No, we couldn't ask it of you, Mr. Fenton."

"It would be no trouble. I would enjoy seeing the ruins."

"Enjoy seeing them again? Surely not. I wouldn't subject you to something you no doubt scoured thoroughly the other day." Thomas said it smoothly, nothing in his tone to suggest malice although his eyes read otherwise.

John shifted in his chair. If Patience hadn't known John as well as she did, she wouldn't have caught the slip in his composure. But he looked as if he was berating himself. He had said he was looking at the ruins when part of the Hastings Building had exploded. What else had John been doing?

"I don't mind. I quite enjoyed them."

Mrs. Tecking saw an opportunity. "And you two can't go by yourselves. I know that *some* people don't believe in propriety, but really, there is skirting the line, and there is dancing right over it."

Thomas swirled his wine. "Amazing how some have no sense of where that line is."

A warm feeling spread through Patience at his words. She immediately tried to rein in the emotions that took flight. She had the love and support of her father and friends. She didn't need someone to defend her. But, darn it felt *good*.

She caught Thomas looking at her and gave him a genuine smile. His eyes crinkled in response, and she again felt a warm surge. She had to be on guard, or she would fall victim to this man who had suddenly begun to appeal to all her secret womanly fantasies—even with their inauspicious start and his somewhat rough edges. Somehow that made his recent attentions all the more special.

Patience shook her head and sipped her wine. She had never before understood some of the tendencies of her gender. She had a bad feeling that she was about to start understanding them.

A bit of color entered Mrs. Tecking's cheeks, the only sign that she had understood his comment.

Thomas nonchalantly continued to swirl his wine. "Caroline, you expressed interest in going to the ruins tomorrow."

Caroline didn't miss a beat, seeing her chance to guide the conversation back to safe ground. "Yes, that would be pleasant. Mr. Tecking, share with us what you have been working on?"

Mr. Tecking blinked owlishly from his place, then launched into a dissertation on ancient Roman politics. He had become somewhat of a dinner scapegoat for Caroline. One could always rely on the man to drone on endlessly.

Dessert was quickly consumed, and everyone retired to their own pursuits.

After doing some research for her work the next day, Patience decided to walk down to the library. She hadn't actually had the opportunity to peruse the considerable stacks.

Navigating the halls, she passed numerous servants who were cleaning up for the night. Maybe it was the presence of others in the halls that diminished the eerie glow usually present. Or maybe it was the leftover warmth from dinner. Whatever it was, the hall lamps sparkled cheerfully as she walked.

The library was open and lit, as if someone had been there and just stepped out. She headed to the first stack on the left. Historical novels and fiction. Excellent.

Patience bypassed the Gothics. There was enough atmosphere in the castle already. Instead, she skimmed until she found an old copy of *Edmund*. Pulling it out, she thought it the perfect reading material to take her mind off of everything going on at the castle.

Love, pride, heroes, villains . . . love . . . all right, maybe it wasn't the best choice, but it was one of her favorites. Although she had always thought Heloise a better heroine. Who could measure up to the ideal of Isolda?

Patience waffled on her choice. Perhaps she should go with Locke or Wollstonecraft (much to her delight she had seen copies peeking from the corner). A treatise or something else.

Patience shook her head. No, she'd made her choice, and she was keeping it. Satisfied that she had beaten herself into shape, she turned.

A warm hand caressed hers and plucked the book from her hands. The touch sparked a path directly to her brain, and she immediately recognized Thomas's smiling features.

"*Edmund*? I always thought he should have ended up with Heloise."

He might as well have said that Copernicus was wrong and the sun really did rotate around the Earth.

"What?"

He tapped the cover. "Heloise. Smart and lively." He looked at her. No, *leered* at her. "My favorite kind of woman."

The weird feeling in her stomach returned along with the annoying racing heart it caused.

"Really?" *Stupid, stupid, stupid!* What had she said that for?

He leaned forward, his lips near her ear. "Most definitely." His breath caressed her ear and cheek, causing her to shiver.

His lips trailed from her ear, brushing her cheek and traveling ever nearer. The journey seemed to take hours as Patience focused completely on the sensation of his lips as they barely touched her skin. She could smell his cologne, a clean scent like the air after a storm.

His hands slipped around her waist, and he pulled her closer. His lips, still just brushing her skin, trailed down to her jaw, and she involuntarily tilted her head back to allow him access as he continued his exploration down her neck. Soft breaths sent caresses through her entire body. Warm lips fired her blood.

And then his lips caressed a point just below her jaw. The beat of her heart steadily increased, and the feeling coalesced under his lips as he gently nibbled and kissed the skin there.

Patience melted. In fact, she wouldn't have been surprised to have found herself boneless at his feet. But his arms just tightened around her, as if he understood perfectly the reaction he was coaxing from her. The thought that he was deliberately coaxing a response barely registered before she discarded it. Her annoying thoughts were intruding in the pleasure of whatever it was he was doing to her.

His lips trailed back up her jaw and captured her own. He tasted faintly of brandy and mint, and she found herself gripping his shirtfront as he kissed and licked and nibbled her senseless. She tried to respond, but her senses had left her three kisses back, and she just clutched on and reveled in the ride of sensations.

Thomas pulled away, regret showing clearly on his face. She must have looked as befuddled as she felt, because he explained, "The servants will be closing this wing."

Her non-Thomas senses returned, and she could hear voices and echoing footsteps. She let go of her iron grip on his shirt, unsure whether it was embarrassment or disappointment that left her unwilling to meet his eyes.

He tipped her chin up and caught her eye before briefly pressing his lips to hers. "I will see you in the morning, and we will ride to the ruins in the afternoon."

Patience nodded, not knowing what to say, her brain unable to deal with the new situation between them.

He handed her the copy of *Edmund* and winked. "Sweet dreams, my smart and savvy lady."

Dazed, Patience took the book and walked to the door. She risked a glance back as she walked into the hall. He was still observing her, an amused look on his face. And she forgave herself for hoping that perhaps she saw a hint of tenderness there as well.

Chapter 13

⁓◦◦◦⁓

Patience changed into her riding habit an hour before necessary, trying to ignore Tilly's sly questions as to what had her so excited. Her maid had been demonstrating a cunning side never before revealed. Patience wasn't sure she was very happy about Tilly's cunning side showing up to torment her at that particular moment.

John had sent a few inquiring glances her way, but had said nothing more after his comments at dinner the previous night. He had been acting strangely since they had arrived at the castle. Perhaps as he had said, he was just concerned for her. Or perhaps there was something more. Blackfield's pointed comment about John's absence during the explosion had obviously registered with John. Patience didn't know what was going on there. Perhaps John was trying to investigate the monster project, too. He had made enough sharp remarks the other day.

Determined to ask him about it later, she focused on her last burial mask. She had saved the canopic jars, her favorite, for later.

The funerary mask was cataloged and set aside. Most of the work she had scheduled for today was completed. Breathing a satisfied sigh of relief, Patience was startled to hear a soft chuckle from the door. She turned to see Blackfield lounging against the frame, an irresistible grin curving his lips. His shirt set off his broad shoulders and his riding trousers fit him snugly.

"Finished?"

Patience nodded and bent to fiddle with the crate, trying to hide her blush behind the hair that had loosened from its bun to hang around her face. She straightened, still a bit flustered. "Are you ready?"

"Of course. Picnic items are packed, and I've requested two servants to chaperone."

"What about Caroline?"

"Something came up. But don't worry, your virtue is safe."

He smirked at the light stain that had once again risen to her cheeks, and she gave him a disgruntled look. "I'm ready."

He offered his arm, and they descended to the ground floor and walked to the stables. It was a good walk, and she was further flustered as he pulled her close, leaning over to point out different features of the gardens and castle walls.

His closeness was playing havoc with her emotions. She tried to calm her scattered wits as they approached the stables.

"Good afternoon, my lord, Miss Harrington," a smooth, male voice intoned. Patience turned to the stablehand who stepped from the building.

"Good afternoon, Henry. Are the horses ready?"

"Yes, my lord."

Thomas nodded and briefly disappeared into the stables.

Henry smiled at Patience.

"We have an especially nice mount for you,

Miss Harrington. Jasmine is a fine mare for a lovely lady."

Patience's eyes widened at the stablehand's words and leering eyes. She had been flirted with before, but even for a servant, the man was a bit too attractive to give her much notice. Then again, Thomas was definitely too attractive, and he had kissed her. More than once. Maybe that new facial cream that Tilly had concocted for her to keep from burning in the sun, really *was* a miracle cream.

The stablehand swept a bow, a bit on the rakish side. "Henry Spent, my lady."

A charmer. She had seen his type before. Tended to go through all the maids and other women within a ten-kilometer radius. Still, he was pleasant, and she could take care of herself. "It's a pleasure to meet you, Henry."

"The pleasure is all mine, Miss Harrington." He sent her another too-wide smile, just as Thomas reappeared.

Thomas winked at her. "Ready, Miss Harrington?"

The warmth in his eyes caused Patience to hum a bit, more pleased than she would like to admit. Darn Tilly and her sly suggestions. "How long is the ride?"

"Depending on how hard one rides, around twenty minutes."

"I like to ride hard. I've missed my daily rides and the feel of all that power beneath me."

Thomas sent her a strange look, but Patience couldn't figure out what could have earned it. She had always enjoyed horses and riding, the faster the better. Patience cooed over her mare and allowed Thomas to help her mount.

They began a slow walk from the stables, which quickly turned into a trot, then a canter. Patience laughed. Riding in the city was so restrained. It had been a while since she had felt the wind in her face.

The ride to the abbey was joyful and unrestrained, the meadows and hills covered in buttercups, pansies, and thistle. By the time the large stone gatehouse came into view she was flushed and breathless, her hair in loosely tangled strands around her face. As she called back to him, Thomas had an odd glimmer in his eye. Feeling more flushed at his look, she turned her attention to the gatehouse. It was fully standing, fierce, yet lonely, as it proudly secured the way to the abbey.

"We can stop here on the way back if you'd like."

She nodded. "Absolutely. I'd love to explore."

They rode at a more sedate pace along the winding country lane sprinkled with encroaching grass. A break in the hills allowed her a first glance of the abbey, and she saw a view that caused her breath to catch.

Verdant sloping hills and the gentle flow of the river gave the area a romantic feel. The abbey ruins were enveloped by the greenery, yet strangely removed from the peaceful scene. The walls of the abbey stood as sentinels on the hill. Lonely and forgotten. The slight rustling of the wind against the tall grass and infrequent caws of crows were the only sounds that broke the stillness. The sentinels stood silently in their wait.

The building had once been a mighty fortress. A fortress of study and God and political corruption.

It was a shame that the abbey had been allowed to fall to ruin. But there was something tragically beautiful and wild about the crumbling walls, the fallen rocks, and the lichens that nestled in the cracks.

Thomas's low, soothing tones broke through her reverie. "Welcome to Farstaff Abbey, founded by King John in the thirteenth century, dissolved by Henry VIII in the sixteenth, along with every other monastery in Britain."

She smiled. "I thought you didn't know anything about the abbey?"

His feigned innocence couldn't hide his smirk. "I don't?"

They dismounted, and Thomas took her hand and led her toward the gutted structure. She peered back to see the guards disappear from view over the southern hill. They were alone, but Thomas didn't seem concerned about the lack of chaperones as he pulled her along. She wondered why she felt no concern either.

"The most unique thing about this abbey is the way in which the builders used the land and river and compensated in their designs to structure it. The cloisters were not square, the dormitory was on the southwest, rather than the southeast, the infirmary was on the north side."

He pointed to the crumbled walls and foundation stones that traced the building's pattern across the earth, walls that were now merely stone paths among the grass. Two bands of columns holding a great arch stood proudly, covered in carvings. Arched recesses were still standing in some of the walls.

"The main problem was drainage. Unable to redirect the river, the engineers and masons had to conform to the land and flow of the river."

She noticed an admiring tone to his voice. Thomas liked something that was considered an antiquity? She kept quiet, determined not to provoke an argument. At least not yet.

They walked through the ruins and discussed the layout. The cloister, infirmary, stables, storehouses, cellar workshops, refectory, abbot's private rooms, record room, scriptorium. They poked at the standing fireplace and chimney. Patience smiled as two rabbits hopped through the rooms, one seeming to give chase to the other.

The entire trip was enjoyable, and Patience was surprised by Thomas's knowledge, though more scientific in nature than aesthetic.

"You seem very knowledgeable about the abbey and the life of an ascetic. Something you are interested in?" Patience rested against one of the pillars and raised a brow in mock challenge.

Thomas placed an arm against her pillar, his body moving close to hers. "The ascetic life?"

"Yes."

"No," he whispered as he came closer. "That's not at all the life for me."

The sun was on a downward path, and Thomas was backlit by its rays. They caressed the sides of his face and hair as his mouth descended upon hers, and she was momentarily covered in darkness. His hands moved to her neck and lightly ran fingers across her cheeks and into her hair. The caress was almost sweet. Not demanding as she had thought it would be. More coaxing and questioning.

Patience watched him lean forward, once more feeling as if she were in his thrall. And she found herself responding to the question and kissing him back. The moment was pure bliss. The sun's rays hit her face again as he gently pulled back and again trailed his fingers through her hair and across her cheeks.

"It's getting late, we should return to the castle," he murmured. "Another day we will come back and explore the gatehouse."

She knew he was right, but all she really felt like doing was continuing to receive those melting kisses. The romantic feel of the area had for a time overridden the lonely and proud ruins.

Hand in hand, they walked back to the ridge where they had last seen the two accompanying servants. They reappeared, and Patience felt as if time had been compressed. As if she had only arrived five minutes before and now was being told to leave. She smiled. If she didn't know better, she would think she was being seduced.

The ride back was silent but comfortable. Henry, the stablehand, met them at the front gate, helped her dismount, and led her horse down the cobblestones toward the stables. She and Thomas were alone once again.

"I will see you at dinner?"

Her cheeks felt heated. "Yes. Thank you, Thomas, for taking me to the abbey. It was lovely."

"Lovely things are always a pleasure to see. And it was my pleasure today," he said, with a roguish grin as he walked backward. He gave her a faux bow and wink before riding off toward the stables.

Patience stood watching his retreating form, trying to regain her bearings, cool her cheeks and stop her heart from beating right out of her chest.

"Patience!"

Patience whirled to see John rushing across the courtyard toward her. "John?"

He finally reached her and rested his hands on his knees, attempting to catch his breath.

"John?"

"Mr. Tecking had an attack."

Patience immediately started toward the castle. "Was it bad?"

John was still breathing heavily, but he kept pace with her. "Not as bad as his last. We don't know what brought this one on. He was looking out the window, you know, as is his wont." John took a breath. "And something that he saw sent him into a fit."

Patience felt a chill despite her dismay for her colleague. "Do you know what he was looking at?"

John shook his head.

"Has a doctor been called?"

"Yes, Lady Caroline sent for one. Meanwhile, Mrs. Tecking is trying to calm him."

They rushed through the halls, dodging servants. Patience caught her breath at the landing of one flight of stairs. She turned to John. "Which room was he in?" "

John's expression was grim. "He was in the gallery facing north."

Toward the buildings lining the woods. Toward the Hastings Building and the monster.

Patience nodded before hurrying up another flight of stairs. They ran into the room to find Mr. Tecking still flailing his arms and fighting to sit upright. He didn't seem able to talk, but his gaze was caught between panic and rage.

Patience looked to his wife. "How long has he been like this?"

Mrs. Tecking's face was more pinched than normal. "The servants said twenty minutes."

Mr. Tecking was prone to fits, but to Patience's knowledge, he had never experienced one for any length of time. She noticed a half-full glass and liquid spilled over the disheveled bedcovers.

"How did you manage to move him in here?"

Mrs. Tecking gave her a nasty look, but answered anyway. "It took two footmen and Mr. Fenton to move him."

"But why did you move him?"

Mrs. Tecking's eyes narrowed. "What did you expect, for us to leave him there?"

Patience refused to rise to the bait. "Frankly, yes, since that is what you have done before."

If Mrs. Tecking were a dragon, Patience would have been burned to a crisp. "I'll have you know that he was in the midst of a roomful of weaponry. Would you rather have had him thrashing around cutting himself?"

Patience ignored the barb, but not her words. A prior doctor had said not to move him while he was convulsing. And he had been in the middle of a roomful of broadswords last time. They had been told to move the swords, not the man.

The next fifteen minutes were a mad confusion of rushing servants, shouting, and seizures. Mr. Tecking went limp just minutes before the doctor arrived. The doctor promptly began removing what he called the "ill humors" from Mr. Tecking, and everyone but Mrs. Tecking filed from the room.

John leaned his head back against the wall and sighed. Patience nudged him.

"Tilly is sending for tea. Would you care to join me?"

He nodded, and they walked to her workroom. John plopped into a chair just as Tilly brought in the tea. Tilly sat in a chair as well and propped her feet up. John raised his brow, but Tilly closed her eyes and began humming to herself, totally oblivious.

He turned his gaze on Patience who, accustomed to Tilly's eccentricities, just shrugged and sipped her tea.

John cleared his throat. "Did you like the abbey?"

She withheld a blush. Barely. "It was wonderful."

"Nothing untoward happened?"

"What, like a pillar falling on me?"

He looked disgruntled. "No, you know that's not what I meant. With Blackfield. Did he do anything inappropriate?"

She continued to keep tight rein on her impending blush. "There were two servants with us." Well, they had been there on the ride to and from the ruins. She hadn't actually seen them while they were *at* the ruins.

John frowned. "Patience, I want you to be careful."

"For goodness sake, I can take care of myself, John."

He held up a hand in a conciliatory fashion. "There are other things going on here. Things you don't know about."

He shot a look at Tilly that Patience could only describe as furtive.

"So why don't you enlighten me?"

There was that look again. Definitely furtive. "Just be careful."

Patience let out a sigh. "That isn't very helpful or specific, you know. Perhaps you have some other warnings you'd like to be vague about?"

"I'm serious, Patience."

"Well, then give me something tangible."

He threw up his hands. "Fine, fine. There was

a lot of talk in town about Blackfield selling secrets to the French."

Surprise didn't begin to describe her state. "Blackfield? The same man who basically accused *me* of selling secrets to the French?"

She could almost hear John's teeth grinding. "I'm just letting you know what I heard. Interesting personal tidbits have cropped up about Blackfield. Rumor has it that on the rare occasions when Blackfield is in London, women throw themselves at him. And that he delights in taking them up on the offers. Seems a bit strange that he was antagonizing you one day and flattering you the next."

Patience bristled at his implication. "I'm not an idiot, nor a country bumpkin. At least not anymore. And I also don't put much stock in rumors, you know that."

His face softened a fraction, but she plowed on. "Of course, I have heard some rather outrageous rumors about him myself. Like his selling monsters. Or his soul."

John's gaze turned to frost. The room felt a few degrees cooler. "What have you heard?"

Patience again experienced the wariness she had felt the day of the explosion. She attempted a laugh, although it sounded forced at best, and even Tilly opened an eye to peer at her. "Every castle has dungeons and monsters, don't you know?"

John's eyes remained narrowed. "Patience, if you know something, I insist that you tell me."

And, just like that, her cousin and childhood friend was gone, replaced by the cold, demanding stranger seated across from her.

She leaned forward and refilled her cup, refusing to let her unease control her. "If I see any monsters, I'll be sure to let you know, John."

She finished her tea and wondered when her world had turned topsy-turvy. Instead of being open and forthright, she was being evasive with her cousin while protecting a man that she had met only two weeks ago. A man who vacillated between tormenting and charming her.

She was startled when she felt John's hand cover hers. "I'm just worried, Patience. Forgive me?"

"Of course, John. It *has* been strange here. Even with my normal flights of fancy I have found myself jumping at shadows. It's just the castle. And too many gothic novels."

John smiled, although his manner still seemed strained.

Throughout dinner and the evening John's

words and actions stayed with her. When night claimed the sky, she pulled the drape back from her window, as she had done every night since arriving at Blackfield Castle. And once again she observed the unnatural mists circling the grounds, the figures disappearing into its jaws, the pearly arms sucking the unwary into its grasp. A flash. A boom. A howl.

She wasn't just sticking close to Thomas because she was beginning to like him. She was still trying to discover what was amiss. She added John to the list. She needed to figure out what, beyond familial concern, was wrong with him as well.

BOOM. CRASH.

She padded to her bed and tucked herself in, as unsure as ever where her day ended and dreams began.

Chapter 14

Patience wiped her forehead with the back of her hand and directed the men to move the last sarcophagus to the other side of the room. The four men had been drafted earlier when Thomas had passed by the room and seen her trying to maneuver a small, stone sarcophagus onto the wheeled platform she had built for such occasions. He had immediately volunteered the four men walking with him, then left them to their fate.

Disgruntled to say the least, they had been sending her suspicious looks the entire time she had been telling them where to move the heavy items.

She was finished with the burial items. The canopic jars were labeled and loaded in straw-lined crates. The ceremonial masks and jewelry were neatly wrapped, packed, and ready for shipping. Two sarcophagi were tied on their wheeled platforms, waiting for the third and final one to join them against the far wall.

The men fidgeted, obviously growing impatient. Patience was curious about them. These men were not servants, and she wanted to know their roles on the estate.

She had seen Jim and Theodore talking to Thomas before the mysterious evening meeting; Richards, an arrogant-looking man, regularly walked the grounds at night; the fourth man, Peter, was unknown to her. It was Jim, the slightly rotund man with the perpetual frown, who intrigued her the most. He was the one who had been covered in blood when she last saw him.

With a final heave they lifted the sarcophagus, but unlike their experience with the larger two sarcophagi, this lift was wobbly and poorly coordinated.

Thwack.

Patience winced as Theodore, the tall, thin man, dropped his corner of the sarcophagus on his toe. He squealed like a cat whose tail had been stepped on, and began hopping in a circle, holding his injured foot and swearing in what sounded like Welsh. Patience stepped forward to offer assistance. Unfortunately, the small, rotund man, Jim, who had been helping with the same side chose that moment to step backward to balance the heavy weight. His foot connected with Patience's, and she stumbled into him, causing him to lose his grip on the sarcophagus.

Which landed on his right foot.

Jim, obviously Cornish, began swearing, too. And with the one end of the sarcophagus down, the weight dragged Peter and Richards forward, and they lost their grip as well. The twenty-stone sarcophagus promptly fell on the foot of the hard-looking, Richards, who bellowed. The fall shook the lid off the sarcophagus, and it hit the floor with a ground-shaking thud. Peter, who had escaped a flattened foot breathed a sigh of relief.

A very short sigh of relief.

The elbow of the hopping, rotund Jim jabbed

him in the back, sending Peter into a headfirst plunge. Right into the open sarcophagus.

An earsplitting shriek ripped through the room as Peter moved body and soul to extricate himself from the coffin and the dead body inside. He managed to snag a loose piece of wrapping as he struggled to free himself.

Patience ran to help, but before she reached him, Peter succeeded in disentangling himself. Unfortunately, he disentangled a portion of the mummy, too. The force of his tug tore a finger from the mummy, which snapped upward, hitting him straight between the eyes.

He went cross-eyed for a split second, his eyes rolled backward in his head, and, as he passed out, he finally caught a piece of good luck—his fall was cushioned by a rug.

The whole incident took less than ten seconds. Patience took stock of the situation. Three men were swearing, their combined voices creating a cacophony of language. The fourth man was peacefully slumped on the rug, so she left him for last. She grabbed the nearest man to her, Jim, and pushed him toward a chair. She had just gotten him seated before two maids, the butler, John, and the Teckings jammed in the doorway, all vying to enter at the same time.

"We need some bandages," she called to no one in particular, heading toward Richards, who held up his hands to fend her off.

Kenfield backed out of the doorway and disappeared. The jostling allowed the others to enter, and the maids immediately went to help the remaining two men. Patience slumped in a chair and rubbed her eyes. She knew that staying in bed that morning would have been a good idea.

"I never liked the floor in here either."

The low, warm voice melted over her. She grunted, unsurprised that the noise had attracted him, too, and looked at the disaster area. The sarcophagus looked remarkably intact. It hadn't fallen far. She'd still have to check it over for damage. The wood floor, however, had at least two large dents.

"What happened to Yensen?" Thomas was pointing to Peter, who was passed out on the floor.

"Beaten by the mummy."

"Ramses Jr. puts up a good fight, eh?"

"Harrumph." A smile threatened to ruin the good sulk she was planning.

"Well, do you want that thing moved?"

She peered up at the viscount. "Yes. But do you think anyone will be willing to assist me now?"

He smirked. "Perquisites of being the lord of the castle." His smooth voice was deliberately haughty.

Swearing, this time in English, came from the corner. "Woman, leave me be." Jim swatted a maid's hand from poking at his foot.

"Quite the colorful linguists you employ."

A lift of his lips was the only acknowledgment to her comment. He called the maid over. "Jenny, please ask four footmen to assist us up here."

The maid hurried off. Thomas cast a speculative glance at his injured men. "This will give me something to threaten them with—helping you move these sarcophagi downstairs when you ship them to London."

Patience shook her head. The new laborers appeared quickly and before long the disturbed mummy and his sarcophagus had joined the others, and everyone except the maids had disappeared.

Patience stepped forward to clean the mess, but Thomas's hand on her arm stopped her.

"You need a break. You are ahead of schedule, aren't you?"

She nodded, a bit bemused.

"Let them clean up. Come, we are going fishing."

Confused, Patience allowed him to lead her downstairs. She wondered where they were going to fish. She had been to the lake on the grounds more than once during her visit, and although picturesque and pristine, it seemed devoid of activity. She had seen geese and ducks but no critters or fish. Caroline had said there were frogs in late summer, but Patience had her doubts.

Thomas picked up a picnic basket and guided her outside. He seemed inordinately fond of picnics, and Patience was perfectly pleased he wanted to share them with her. She loved picnics, but wasn't able to indulge in London, and since her father had started working at the museum they had been bound to the city.

Thomas veered right as soon as they stepped outside, and Patience realized they were heading toward the stables. The horse she had ridden to the ruins was saddled, and something was bundled on Thomas's stallion.

"Where are we going?"

"To the river. Good fishing there."

Patience nodded, remembering that Caroline had shared that information on their tour.

Thomas hooked the basket to his horse, then walked around and lifted Patience onto her mare. His eyes met hers and a look resembling possession flitted across his face, so fleetingly that Patience could have imagined it.

The river wound past the abbey, on the north side of the estate. Less than a ten-minute ride. Their route took them past the outlying buildings, including the Hastings Building. Patience had tried surreptitiously to peer inside, but Thomas had been talking to her at the time, his eyes never leaving hers, and she'd been unable to get a good look.

They trotted through the woods and when they emerged Patience felt her breath catch. It was beautiful. A variety of trees and wildflowers flanked the wide river, purple loosestrife clinging to the edges, reeds and pussy willows clumped at its sides. Submerged plants swayed with the water and a Fritillary butterfly fluttered just above the surface. The water looked surprisingly deep in parts. A stream parted from the river and ran to the north, and Thomas explained that it turned into another river farther up.

"A perfectly good spot to fish farther north, but it takes another thirty minutes of trekking to get there."

She looked at him, wide-eyed. "Fish? You weren't joking?"

"Haven't you ever fished?"

She bit her lip and shook her head.

"I thought you lived in the country?"

"I did. And I've always wanted to fish." A wistful note entered her voice, unbidden. Her father had enjoyed fishing with her mother, and he had given it up after her death. He had said that he couldn't bring himself to do it without her. Patience had thought it might allow her father to feel closer to her mother's spirit, but it was the one thing he was adamant about. He chose to bury himself within the museum's walls. A very rational man, he had admitted it was an irrational act but could not be budged.

Thomas untied the straps on his mount and handed her a bundle. The two men who had accompanied them dismounted and removed two blankets, a lamp, and other assorted gear, then disappeared into the woods.

"I see we've lost our chaperones again."

He smiled without looking up. "Have we?"

She shook her head in bemusement and bent to help him unravel his bundles. Inside were two fishing rods and several small boxes. He explained that the boxes contained flies.

"Who makes them?"

"My gamesman makes the flies and rods. We have maure flies, tandy flies, and wasp flies here. All are made from mallard breasts and buzzard quills. These rods are hazel and aspen. Sometimes he uses willow."

Thomas explained the principles of tying a fly to the line. After their poles were pressed together, he walked to the water, Patience eagerly behind.

He demonstrated how to cast, and his fly sailed through the air, pulling the long line behind, and landing the fly with a small plop some twenty feet into the river.

"Think of casting the line like slinging a long Spanish whip through the air. You pull line with your left hand, and pretend there's a clock above your head. Cast your rod backward to one o'clock in one smooth, steady lift. Pause while the line extends itself, then thrust it forward with even and continuous power to an eleven o'clock position. When the loop forms in front of your rod, stop the rod, let go of the line in your left hand, and allow the looped line to unroll off the tip."

It looked easy enough. Patience pulled her arm back and threw it forward. She barely kept her grip, almost chucking the pole in the river. The line that she had let loose puddled three feet in front of her.

Thomas coughed, and she shot him a disgruntled look.

"Even, continuous power."

"Fine, fine."

She managed to mimic Thomas's earlier cast, and the line puddled six feet in front of her. His Haughtiness somehow managed to keep back a grin.

"Just keep pulling it back and throwing it out. Like this." He pulled the line back and tossed it out, tugging at the loose line near the reel. With every pull and toss, the line sailed farther into the river, and the fly plopped on the surface.

Patience tried casting a few more times, but she couldn't get the feel of what her muscles were supposed to be doing. Thomas put his rod down and walked behind her. He leaned against her back and put his right hand over hers.

"Feel the motion."

He put his other arm around her and gripped the line. He pulled the rod back, her hand under his, and flicked it out, letting the line loose at the same time. The action flattened her back to his chest, then her lower half to his. She barely noticed the fly's landing in the water.

"You just keep pulling back and thrusting the bait farther in."

The words caressed her left ear, causing her to shiver. Their bodies were pressed together, so that she was leaning back against him.

"Spread your legs apart and balance your weight. Relax. You're too tense."

Tense? He had no idea.

He repeated the motions, pulling the line back and flicking it out, his body rocking against hers with each movement. Again and again until Patience thought she might puddle to the ground in imitation of her first cast.

"Can you feel it?" he whispered into her ear.

"Yes." Her voice cracked a bit, and she cleared her throat. "I think so."

He pulled away, his fingers perhaps straying a bit up her arm as he did so. It was hard to tell if they had actually made contact or if the hair on her arm had reacted on its own after everything else.

Patience took a deep breath and cast. Ten feet. She pulled the line back and did it again.

It took another fifteen minutes of practice and Thomas's heavily lidded smile asking if she needed more instruction before she felt comfortable with the motions.

And then they were fishing. She was really fishing! And it was wonderful. Thomas had caught a few fish while she was getting the hang of things, and had released them all. Patience was eager to catch her first.

She let out her line, saw the fly disappear, and felt a tug.

"I have one!"

"Well, reel it in."

It took several minutes for Patience to pull the pint-size fish in. It flopped on the ground as she admired her prize.

"Nice minnow."

"Hey! Leave him alone." Patience smiled at her fish, before looking up. "What now?"

"Take the minn—, er, small perch off like I showed you and toss him back in."

Patience eyed the fish dubiously, but gamely

reached for it. It flopped a bit, and she shifted her hand around trying to find the best angle to grip it. It finally settled in one spot, and she reached the last few inches to grip it.

She was concentrating so intently on the fish that when she touched it and felt Thomas's finger poke in her side, she jerked in surprise. The fish jumped and she shrieked, yanking her hand back. She had forgotten Thomas was next to her and perfectly within finger-poking range.

He laughed, clutching at his sides, oblivious to the calculating looks she sent him. Finally, she unhooked the fish and set it in the water. Thomas was still laughing at her. Putting her hands on her hips just increased his laughter.

Patience did the only thing that she could. She pushed him in.

The look on his face was worth every bit of being laughed at, and it sent her into her own gales of laughter. Unfortunately, she missed *his* calculating stare in her moment of victory, and hence was completely shocked to find herself on land one moment and flying through the air the next. Really, she shouldn't have been surprised.

She surfaced, still laughing, and he pulled her to him, kissing her soundly. She wrapped herself in his embrace, kissing him back. There was nothing like it really, this kissing thing. Or at least, this kissing thing with Thomas.

The water was cold, but with his hands tracing the garments that had molded to her body and his mouth tracing hers, she might as well have been swimming in the warm springs at Bath.

Thomas pressed his forehead to hers, then pulled back. The look in his eyes was lazy and sensual, with a good amount of heat beneath. She unconsciously shivered. They both seemed to realize that they were in the middle of a river at the same time, and also how they had gotten there. They shared a smile and helped each other onto the bank.

The sun was on a downward path, but the air was warm. Patience wrung out her skirt and hair, as Thomas stripped off his shirt. She blinked as he casually tossed it to the ground and lifted one of the blankets to dry off. He stood there without a care in the world, half-naked, drying himself. She couldn't look away. He caught her gaze and winked. Heat suffused her cheeks, and she pretended interest in wringing more water from her skirt.

The next thing she knew a blanket was wrapped around her, and she was being rumpled dry.

"Wh—" The blanket was gently swiped across her face and some of the linen caught on her tongue. She freed one of her hands to wipe her tongue, and he fluffed her hair.

Patience pulled away, hands on hips, to glare at him. He smirked, and she realized she probably looked like a wet cat, hair in every direction, a thoroughly disgruntled look on her face.

"Remove your dress."

Her arms dropped to her sides, and she blinked. "Excuse me?"

He motioned to her garments. "Take off your clothes. They need to dry."

All her befuddled brain could come up with was, "But the buttons are in the back."

She caught a glimpse of another smirk before she was turned and his fingers ran nimbly down her back, unhooking buttons and peeling her dress down her body, leaving her in her shift and corset.

He whistled appreciatively, and she wished herself anywhere else. In fact, she figured the hole that was supposed to open up under her feet so that she could slip through should have been appearing anytime.

"Step out."

It was more the realization of how close he

was to her nearly naked body than his command that forced her into taking a step backward. Thankfully she did not trip over her clothes. He would likely have caught her, and that would really have been too embarrassing, what with the near nakedness and the kissing and the stroking hands, and the—

"Patience?"

"Yes?" she squeaked.

He smiled. A real smile, not his normal smirk. "Let's hang these up and continue fishing."

"Like this?" she said, pointing to her state of undress.

"Exactly like that." He winked. "You can try and beat my fish count while my rakish eyes are too busy."

She blushed, but a pleased thrum coursed through her body.

They found a small tree and hung their clothes to dry and resumed fishing, to her utter relief and the slight disappointment that she firmly repressed.

They fished for two more hours, and Patience wasn't sure whether it was the motion of fishing that she found so relaxing, or their shared smiles and being near Thomas. They caught a lot of fish, but since they released each one Patience was sure they just kept catching the same daft bugger over and over again. She said so to Thomas, and he laughed for at least half a minute.

"The sun is going down. Let's feast on cheese and crackers and watch the sunset, shall we?"

As the sun dipped lower in the sky, the temperature slowly dropped. Thomas wrapped them both in one of the blankets as they pawed through the food basket. He pulled her securely against his chest as he leaned against a tree trunk. The sun sank into a small break in the trees, but it was just enough to reflect warm pink, yellow, and orange across the water and onto them as it disappeared from view.

She felt fingers pulling through her hair and massaging the back of her neck.

"We should be getting back." He tipped her head and gave her a mock critical look. "And perhaps some tidying would not be amiss."

Patience leaned into him again, soaking up the safety and heat. She couldn't imagine what would happen if Mrs. Tecking were to see her in this condition, dress on or not. Part of her didn't care what the dragon had to say. She felt happier than she had since they had moved to London. She felt safe with Thomas, despite his monsters, secrets, and curious explosions. But the other part of her was still sensitive to what others said, no matter how long and hard she had tried to convince herself otherwise.

She nodded and started to move. Thomas stood and hauled her up, planting a soft kiss on the top of her head before wrapping the blanket around her and retrieving his shirt and her dress. He helped her into her dress, redoing all of the buttons, and even helped put her hair back up. Her glasses had been placed to the side earlier, and she slipped them back on her nose. Shield back in place.

Placing two fingers to his mouth, he gave a shrill whistle, and the two men who had accompanied them appeared less than five minutes later. Patience had nearly forgotten them. After fishing in her shift for two hours, she had lost a bit of her modesty, but still hoped they had been well out of view.

One of the men lit a lantern as Thomas helped Patience mount. The short trip to the castle was made in silence, and Patience was caught between happiness and dread. Thomas had resumed the mask he seemed to wear most of the time.

It wasn't reassuring. The river had been a world away, a retreat. And this Thomas riding next to her wasn't the same one with whom she had shared the outing. Even through his swift personality changes, he kept giving glimpses of other facets. But what did it mean that he hid those facets from the world? What secrets did he bear that caused him to act this way?

She was still trying to puzzle out the answers when she entered the castle. Her motion came to an abrupt halt as someone blocked her path.

Mrs. Tecking stood in front of her, a malicious glint in her eyes.

Chapter 15

~~~OO~~~

"**G**ood evening, Mrs. Tecking." Patience tried to pass around the woman, but she stood firmly in place.

"And what have *you* been up to?" Mrs. Tecking demanded as she took in Patience's appearance.

Patience attempted to sidestep her again, but was blocked. "I've been out. If you don't mind, I'd like to rest and change before dinner."

"Oh, but I do mind. An unmarried woman gallivanting about the countryside without a chaperone in the company of a confirmed bachelor is unseemly."

Patience pressed her lips together.

"But the rules don't apply to you, do they, Miss Harrington? They never do. The rest of us mortals must bend to society's dictates and slave to keep a good name, but not you." Mrs. Tecking's voice grew increasingly bitter until her final words dripped like acid. "No, never you."

Patience had no idea what she had done to earn such enmity, but it made her tired. "Yes, Mrs. Tecking. Could you let me pass now?"

"No. It's time someone took you to task about these things."

"Took me to task?" Patience voice rose. "What do you think happens every time I enter a ballroom? And for what? Not knowing how to converse? Not knowing the etiquette well enough? Trusting people too easily? I think I get taken to task plenty well enough, thank you." Patience had had enough. Before Mrs. Tecking could respond, she pushed her aside and walked to her room.

A knock sounded on her door minutes later. She had been prepared for Mrs. Tecking's confrontation—it had simply been a matter of time. But it didn't mean she enjoyed it. She wasn't in the mood for company.

"Come back later."

"Patience?"

She groaned and buried her face in her pillow. "I'll talk with you at dinner, John."

"May I come in?"

"No. I'll see you at dinner."

She heard footsteps moving down the hall and turned onto her side. She didn't want anyone else to see her bedraggled state. Mrs. Tecking was sure to inform everyone as it was. No need to confirm it.

Dratted righteous, moth-eaten harpies who thought they had an obligation to make life miserable for anyone who didn't agree with them or follow their dictates. And the funny thing, if she had been in a laughing mood, was that she hadn't even *earned* half the derision. If they had just made sport of her for being a country simpleton, she would have been embarrassed and thought it cruel, but it would have at least been somewhat understandable.

But she had been labeled fast. She had an idea that a few of the debutantes had encouraged the label to ensure their own places and increase their reputations. She even thought that perhaps the well-timed entrance into the room where Antleberry had taken her might have been planned. Not that it was planned for Antleberry to take her to the room (an action no doubt instigated *because* of her reputation), but the entrance itself. It was just a little suspicious that four busybodies, all in one group, decided to open a random door . . . No doubt one had seen her leave with Antleberry and had called the other three to follow.

Her father blamed himself for not preparing her for the rigors of the ton, and for not hiring a chaperone who could stay awake for more than two hours at a time. Patience blamed the people who had perpetrated the rumors and those who believed them without question. Her plight was sport for their ennui. Who cared if the rumors about a society peon were true or not? All that she was good for was relieving their boredom now and again.

She sighed. She was going to become a bitter woman if she maintained this train of thought. And she wasn't going to give anyone the power or satisfaction to do that.

One thing that her tainted reputation had allowed her was a certain degree of freedom that others her age, station, and gender did not possess. She had a feeling that this perceived freedom had caused the bitterness she had heard in Mrs. Tecking's voice. Patience didn't have nearly the power that a man had, but she was somewhere near the "widow" category. Maybe the wicked-widow category.

The freedom, ironically enough, gave her the ability to pursue things with Thomas and finally fulfill some of her rumored exploits. An additional boon manifested in that she was able to forego regular society functions, which she hated. Her reputation provided the excuse. It did limit her pool of friends, however, and loneliness sometimes set in when her father and their immediate acquaintances were away. But still, she had a lot to be thankful for, and she wasn't going to languish over other people's opinions—no matter how hurtful.

Feeling better, she rang for Tilly. Her maid came in chattering in French, about some goings-on down in the servants' quarters. Patience let it wash over her as she bathed. She kept remembering the feel of Thomas. His warmth, his hands, his lips, his actions, the picnics and rides, his smile . . .

He enraptured her.

Whereas, contrary to her reputation, she might have been a little nervous about having a man pursue her so blatantly, with Thomas she felt a delicious sense of inevitability. She *liked*

Thomas. Liked him in a way that she hadn't liked any of the previous men she had met, whether at parties or any of the scientific functions she attended with her father. Of course, she had entertained a fantasy or two about some handsome male, but after a few conversations those fantasies had dissipated into either friendly respect or complete disillusionment. Her feelings for Thomas had only grown stronger since she had met him, even when they had been arguing.

He was almost courting her. And if she were being honest with herself, she didn't mind. She didn't mind one bit.

Whist that night was an odd affair.

The silence seemed to stretch on and on during the dinner courses, no one having the temerity or inclination to break it. Thomas looked amused and seemed happy enough to send smoldering glances Patience's way. Patience was quite happy to sit quietly and let those glances warm her.

Even Caroline, who usually made a valiant attempt at being a good hostess, was reserved and made little effort at conversation. Since they were Samuel-free for the evening, there was no devil's advocate either.

Therefore, when John finally spoke up during whist, there was a visible reaction from everyone except Thomas, who continued to drink and look pleased with himself.

"Lady Caroline, how was your trip to the village? Did you find the man you were looking for?"

Caroline startled and nearly dropped her card. "Oh, yes, thank you, John."

Patience was curious as to whom they were talking about, but felt it was none of her business to ask. Mrs. Tecking, who had been knitting while they played, had no such problem.

"Whom did you meet, Lady Caroline?"

Caroline looked distinctly uncomfortable. "Oh, just a servant asking for a position."

Thomas frowned. "Why would you go to the village for that?"

Caroline studied her cards. "I was in town anyway. It seemed easier."

Thomas's eyes narrowed, but John jumped in before he could say anything. "Caroline was kind enough to pick up a tool from the blacksmith. Thank you again, Caroline. I am in your debt."

Patience blinked. She knew for a fact that John's tool had been delivered from the village yesterday by the same lad who had delivered hers the week before.

Caroline sent him a grateful smile. "Think nothing of it, John. I was glad to help."

Thomas looked irritated. "Caroline, if you could join me in my study later tonight, I have something to discuss with you."

Patience couldn't help but feel a twinge at the panicked expression that crossed Caroline's face. She didn't know why John and Caroline were lying, but the woman had been nothing but nice to her since their arrival.

"Of course I will," Caroline said, every bit the lady.

It wasn't until after they retired that Patience thought of trying to determine what Thomas wanted to talk to Caroline about. She also wanted another book from the library. It was as good an excuse as any, not that Thomas would believe it any more than he had the last time she had used it.

Stepping into the hall with her lamp, she ignored the shadows and noises and headed straight to her first destination, hoping that John really had intended to turn in for the night, as he had vaguely mentioned when they retired.

Patience passed the closed study door on the way to the library. It was a quick trip through the library, as she knew exactly what book she wanted to take. With the book securely tucked under her arm and her lamp in hand she walked back down the hall at a turtle's pace.

The hall was quiet, the voices not penetrating through the study door. Just as she was deciding whether to press her ear to the door or cap her curiosity and return to her bedroom, the door opened. Instinct caused her to jump behind a statue next to the study door. She cursed her foolishness. If someone were to see her, there would be no explaining away her guilt.

Caroline emerged from the room. "Thank you, Thomas."

Thomas leaned against the archway of the door, hands in his pockets. "Just don't do it again, Caroline. I can't afford not to trust you, too."

Caroline bit her lip and nodded. "Good night."

"Good night, Aunt."

Caroline walked down the hall, and Patience held her breath. If he would just turn back around—

"Examining the castle statuary, Patience?" He stepped forward, his eyes locked with hers.

"How did you know I was here?"

"I would recognize you anywhere."

She stepped out into the hall, feeling sheepish and uneasy. "I was getting a book from the library." She held out the book. "And the door opened as I was walking by. It startled me, and I jumped behind the statue." It all came out in a rush. It was mostly the truth, too, come to think of it.

One side of Thomas's mouth lifted. "Well, come in. Let me still your racing heart."

He turned and disappeared into the room. She hesitated. It was late . . . but her thoughts kept going back to the afternoon . . .

She followed him inside.

Chapter 16

The atmosphere inside the study was heavy with the smell of cleaning solution and anticipation. A fire crackled merrily in the hearth. The room's shadows were warm and mysterious in the firelight. Thomas swirled a drink, the amber liquid clinging to the sides of the glass before sliding back to the base.

Patience walked around the room, absently inspecting the books on the shelves and a fresco on the wall that she hadn't yet had a chance to study. It was of a man holding the world in his hands. The man bore a passing resemblance to Thomas.

"The second viscount. He had quite a good opinion of himself," Thomas said.

An influx of cherubs sprawled across a fresco on another wall, much different in nature to the herocentric designs of the second viscount's. Thomas caught her gaze. "The third viscount fancied himself in love. Those were created for his bride Mary—"

"How lovely."

"—who went on to have a lusty affair with their neighbor, Lord Pillenhurst."

Patience blinked. "Well, the cherubs and turtle doves are still lovely."

Thomas smirked, and Patience turned away from the frescoes. She watched his gaze turn pensive, his face half in the illumination of the firelight.

"Do you miss your mother?"

The question startled her. "Yes."

"You never knew her."

It wasn't a question, and Patience wasn't sure how to respond to so personal a comment. She walked toward him. "How do you know of my mother?"

His shoulders lifted. "I listen when people gossip."

She ran her hand along the brocade back of a chair. "My father speaks of her all the time. I feel as if I knew her. I miss her every day."

Thomas swirled his glass again and looked into the flames on the hearth. "I never knew my mother. I wonder if I would miss her if Father had ever spoken of her."

Her heart gave a tug at the wistful undertone in his voice. "Do you miss your father?"

He sipped his drink, almost as if fortifying himself. "He was authoritarian. Everything was his way or no way. I'm not sure he ever gave one word of praise. I certainly do not recall one."

She felt another sympathetic twinge. Her father had always been her primary supporter. "You didn't answer the question."

He smiled, a slightly wicked smile of up-turned lips and creased eyes. Eyes brimming with secrets that dared her to pick up their challenge. "No, I didn't."

Patience continued her saunter, running her fingers along the arm of a plush leather chair in front of the fire before sinking down. "What are you drinking?"

"Scotch. Would you like some?"

She shook her head, and he sat in the chair next to hers.

His hand dangled near hers, and acting on instinct she reached over and picked it up. "Shall I read your palm? Researching the occult was one of my more intriguing areas of study. It has some of the most bizarre and interesting artifacts."

His eyes were heavy as he took a sip of his scotch and set it on the table. "Read my palm? Only if you give me a good fortune."

She traced the lines on his palm, her hand sliding across his. His hand was warm and inviting, with just enough roughened areas to make it interesting. Not idle hands. He didn't fritter his days away on a lord's fancies. They were strong hands. Hands used to command but still able to dirty themselves.

"I find it fascinating to learn how different people live and in what they believe. One reason I enjoy ancient cultures so much. You can discover the most interesting information from finding out how someone lives."

Her finger followed the lines and light calluses on his palm, the feel of his large hand captured between her smaller ones sent a strange thrill through her. His strong lifeline, the heart line that appeared to grow stronger under her ministrations. As she drew her finger across his palm and onto the softer skin at his wrist, his pulse seemed to quicken. She smiled, pleased that she could affect him as he affected her.

"You will live long and have a prosperous life," she reported.

"That's it?" His voice was even huskier than normal.

"You will live long and have a prosperous life with a well-hipped woman and many children nipping at your heels."

"Mmmm." He leaned forward, his free hand brushing across the side of her throat, around and under her chin. Feather light touches, almost a breeze against her skin that inflamed rather than cooled. The light touch continued a path around her jaw until gently tilting her chin upward.

Their eyes met, and something tightened in her chest, making her breath come faster and her eyelids heavier. The firelight danced across his features, but it was his eyes that held her immobile. They were dark and fierce, and just the slightest bit tentative. The tightness in her chest rippled out, and she reached forward and placed a hand against his cheek.

Slowly she leaned into him until they were

nose to nose. She could smell his cologne, the scent of fresh rain mixed with mint. She leaned forward a bit more, and their lips touched. Softly, smoothly. Her eyes slid shut, but not before she detected a hint of triumph in his. The thought was pushed from her mind as he deepened the kiss. She had never realized how many pleasurable tingles could be generated from the lips until he kissed her. And every tingle in her lips appeared to be attached to tingles throughout her body. It was as if a fuse had lit them all.

His lips moved over hers, and she responded with the same eagerness. His tongue traced her lip, and she gasped at the remarkable sensation, her lips parting beneath his. His tongue darted inside, and he groaned as if the taste of her was more than he remembered. The sound sent a shudder through her body, and she immediately returned the gesture, wanting to know what he tasted like as well. She tentatively returned his caress, tasting the fresh, minty rain of his scent.

It was intoxicating, and when he tipped her head back and traced his lips down her jaw and over her throat she felt as if she had indulged in too many glasses of wine. He sucked on the spot just below her jaw and her body automatically arched upward. His hands were buried in her hair, rubbing gently on the nape of her neck, but as she arched, they moved down her neck, down her arms, and then up and over the bodice of her dress.

She hadn't thought that anything could feel better, but the slow, steady circles he traced over her breasts forced her to reconsider. He continued to suckle her neck, and the fleeting image of a vampire crossed her mind before his thumbs pressed and circled the fabric right above her nipples, causing all rational thoughts to disappear and a low sound to escape from her throat, her breaths still coming in short pants. He caught the end of the sound in his mouth and hands reached around to undo the back of her gown. It slipped from her shoulders, and he continued to ease it down, all the while doing sinful things to her mouth with his.

He broke away for a second to lift her hips and slide her gown off, the satiny fabric slipping across her skin in a way that she had never been aware of before. And then he was kissing her again, nearly crawling into her lap as he pressed her into the back of the chair. His hand slid down her shift and around her stomach and sides, mapping the area and causing the pleasure to spread.

The strong fingers lifted her garter and ghosted across her thigh. The muddled, pleasure-ridden center of her brain cleared for a second, the beginnings of a warning sounded as his fingers slid up her thigh and curled between her legs. She opened her mouth beneath his to say something—

—and promptly forgot everything as he crooked a finger and a noise somewhere between a moan and shriek fell from her lips to his. His mouth curved against hers, and he moved his finger again. Her body moved without conscious consent, and she broke away from his kiss as he stroked her again and again. Her head lolled onto the back of the chair while the rest of her body arched into his. One knee was on the chair next to her as he leaned forward, his free hand returning to her nape, disappearing to stroke under her hair, just as his fingers were stroking under her shift.

His eyes maintained contact with hers, and the fire inside of them, the intensity, burned her as much as his fingers. His shields were down. She was looking at Thomas. Thomas, the man, who didn't have ulterior motives or secret plans. Just a man with a ready wit, quirky personality, devastating smile, and a hurt deep in his eyes that begged to be healed. A man she didn't fully understand, but he was showing her anyway. And she fell in love.

Hard.

The feelings shot through her, his eyes clasped to hers, his hands urging the heat higher, and she cried out as the heat exploded within.

His eyes never left hers, seeming to drink in and claim the reaction. Intense, possessive, and dark. And as the waves of heat traveled through her, he kissed her again. A kiss full of need, desire, and possession, echoing his eyes and branding her.

And Patience had never felt more complete, or more frightened.

Chapter 17

⌒⦅⦆⌒

Patience dragged a crate forward, ducking her head as she attempted to ignore John's searching look.

"You look different today."

"The air this morning is invigorating."

John frowned at her third evasion in as many minutes.

Servants bustled in to carry more of the crates downstairs, interrupting further attempts to pry. Patience followed them, calling out directions. She needed to put distance between herself and John. His too-perceptive gaze made her nervous.

Had he observed her sneaking back into her room? Or had he somehow been witness to the dreamy smile that graced her face as she fell asleep?

Thomas hadn't said much after their interlude. Words had been unnecessary. And the passionate kiss he had given her as they said good night had pasted the foolish grin on her face. It had still been present when Tilly walked in that morning.

The carts were nearly loaded, and Jeremy gave her a farewell hug and a letter from her father. Another week, and she would be home. A pang shot through her. She missed her father, but the thought of leaving Thomas . . . well, she wouldn't think about that yet.

A higher power seemed to disagree, as Patience caught sight of Thomas disappearing into one of the perimeter buildings. She didn't know what she was going to say to him, but the urge to see him was too powerful to ignore. She stowed her father's letter in her pocket, walked to the building, and knocked on the door.

"Hello? Thomas?"

Her voice echoed off the walls, and she found herself in an open foyer connected to three halls in each direction. She chewed her lower lip and shifted her weight. Perhaps she should try and catch him later.

As she turned to depart, she heard a pop. A stinging bittersweet odor assailed her nose, and she knew no more.

Patience awoke to voices arguing.

"Tried to kill her!"

"He did not. He was the one who carried her all the way here. If he had wanted to kill her, he would have left her there."

"But did you see his face?"

"Like the devil, he was. I ain't never seen him so angry."

"Upset he didn't do the job right, I tell you."

"Yes, like his sister."

"Shhh!"

"Shut your trap, Jenny."

"You don't know nothing about what happened. All you new 'uns care about is mystery and rumor."

"But—"

"No! Now, off with you, before I give you something real to worry about, like a stripe on your backside."

There was a shuffling of feet, and the door slammed closed.

Patience opened an eye and yelped as two watery blue eyes stared back, no more than three inches away.

"Good, you're up. The doctor will be here soon."

"Doctor?"

John's face appeared in her vision. "You were poisoned."

"Poisoned?"

"Chemical fumes. Someone drugged you. Do you remember anything?"

She furrowed her brow. "I was following T—, Blackfield. I wanted to speak with him about the second shipment," she improvised. "When I entered the building and didn't see him, I turned to leave."

"And?"

"I smelled something strange." She tried to remember. "And there was a noise I think, like a jar popping open."

The door opened, and a freckled maid's face appeared. "The physician is here, ma'am."

The maid disappeared, and John sat pensively, staring after her.

"How did I get here?"

John turned back to her. "Blackfield carried

you. Said he found you in one of the buildings. He terrified nearly all of the maids, at least the younger ones." He looked closely at her. "He was angry. Very angry. Furious, in fact."

Patience shivered. "Was he angry with me?"

John looked torn, as if debating with himself as to what to say. He sighed. "No. He didn't look angry with you. He appeared angry because of you. After he brought you here, he stormed out, raising holy hell." The words were dragged from John, as if he would have been happier to say Thomas was furious with her.

"What was all that talk about Blackfield's sister or was I imagining it?"

"His sister died under some very unusual conditions. She was very young. The senior staff is secretive about it, but I overheard one of the younger maids say that rumors are that Blackfield murdered her."

Patience scoffed. "And I heard the head maid say otherwise."

John leaned forward. "But she didn't actually explain anything, did she? Why is that, do you think?"

She chewed her lip, surprised that it wasn't already chapped, what with all the worrying she had done to it over the past few weeks.

"I don't know." She leaned back. "Leave it for now."

The door opened, and a gaunt man carrying a satchel popped in.

"Oh, and if that doctor tries to bleed me, I'll sock him."

The doctor stopped his forward momentum. Thomas entered after him, the fury still lurking behind his eyes belying the slow smile curving his lips. She could see why the maids had been terrified if that unholy light in his eyes had been present before.

"And if he tries to bleed you, I'll hold him down for you."

The doctor's eyes widened, and he blinked nervously at the leeches in his bag. Fortunately, or unfortunately, for him, a weathered woman bustled in and brushed the doctor aside.

The gaunt man bristled. "Now, hold right there madam—"

Thomas steered the doctor back toward the door. "Terribly sorry to have inconvenienced you, Doctor. Please accept our apologies. Kenfield will reimburse you for your time."

The man seemed somewhat mollified, but

shot the woman a scalding look before leaving.

"Here now, dearie," the kind, but plain-spoken woman said. "What seems to be the problem?"

Patience took stock. She had a blazing headache, which she seemed to have forgotten in the initial excitement of waking up. "Headache, and I'm a bit dizzy."

The woman nodded. "That's what his lordship thought you might be feeling. Drink this."

She handed Patience a vial of something. Patience gave it a doubtful glance and looked at Thomas, who gave her an encouraging nod. She drank it.

It tasted like chalk and bark mixed with something long dead. The cure was worse than the symptoms. Hacking a bit, she shoved the vial back to the woman and resisted the urge to scrub her tongue. But the offending brew worked, and Patience felt some of the tension in her head ease.

She reached for a water glass on the bedside table, hoping to rinse away the horrid taste. She shot Thomas a deadly glare. He had obviously known what it would taste like since he had recommended it.

Speaking of which, how had he known what

her symptoms would be? "What was that?"

He gave a careless shrug, but amusement showed in his eyes. "A restorative. You should feel better soon."

"I do," she said, with an acerbic edge. "How did you know what to give me?"

"It should counteract the chemicals you inhaled." He ignored her question and knelt next to her. "Why were you in the building?"

"I saw you enter and followed. I wanted to talk to you."

His face was unreadable. She had no idea if he believed her or not.

"Did you see anyone else?"

"No. The building was empty. I called out and turned to exit. That was when the smell overpowered me. The next thing I knew I was listening to the maids arguing."

His expression turned amused for a second before becoming serious once again. "Please don't go into those buildings unless I accompany you."

She weighed her words. "Thomas, what happens in those buildings?"

"Nothing too exciting." He sounded nonchalant, but the atmosphere was anything but.

"I'll bet," she muttered.

The weathered woman retreated to the back of the room to talk to John about something. Thomas pushed a loose tress of hair behind Patience's ear and stroked her cheek.

"Promise you won't enter the perimeter buildings. I don't want anything to happen to you."

She gave him a somewhat wobbly smile. "I am curious though. What is so secret?"

He looked away from her. "Perhaps someday I'll show you."

Patience wasn't going to count on it. But even the revelation that she had fallen in love with Thomas didn't stem her curiosity or uncertainty.

They talked a bit more before he left. An hour later she was itching to leave her room. She walked to her workroom and halfheartedly went through the motions of cataloging a collection of Greek coins. It wasn't until nearly dinnertime that Mrs. Tecking entered the room.

"Heard you fainted while trailing after the viscount."

Patience refused to look up. "I'm feeling much better, thank you."

"Dangerous business you are getting yourself into."

Patience narrowed her eyes. "What do you mean?"

"Throwing yourself at Blackfield."

"I am *not* throwing myself at Blackfield."

Mrs. Tecking hummed a bit. "Nasty rumors surrounding him."

"Yes, well, I don't listen to rumors."

"The reality is worse, is it?"

Patience sighed. "What do you want, Mrs. Tecking? This is becoming rather irksome."

"Just a friendly warning, Miss Harrington."

"Friendly, ha," she muttered under her breath, picking up another coin to distract herself from her guest and signal her disinterest in further conversation.

Mrs. Tecking leaned forward conspiratorially. "They say everyone who gets close to the viscount dies."

Patience looked at the pinched face of the woman, the unhappy crease lines making her look old before her time. "That is rather an absurd comment. Even you would have to admit that Lord Blackfield is quite fond of Lady Caroline, who appears remarkably healthy."

Mrs. Tecking's eyes narrowed for a second, before gleaming. "I heard tell that maybe she was in on the murder."

"Is this in regards to that tripe about his sister's death?"

Mrs. Tecking's brows rose in surprise. "Heard of it already, have you? Hoping to escape the curse?"

"One person's death, though tragic, does not a curse make."

"That's not what your Egyptian fairy tales say." She hummed a bit more.

"Yes, well, as hard as it was for me to separate fairy tale from the reality of the beau monde, I found myself turning over a new leaf after living in London. At the present, fairy tales seem much tamer in comparison."

Well, it looked as if she hadn't *quite* conquered the bitterness yet. But there was always a bump or two in a work in progress.

"Now, if you have finished your *friendly* warnings?" Patience didn't wait for an answer. "I have work to do. Good afternoon, Mrs. Tecking."

The woman surprisingly left without further word.

* * *

"She's not a spy, Samuel."

Samuel raised a brow. "And what now makes you so sure?"

Thomas looked at him incredulously. "She was attacked."

"Perhaps there was a falling-out amongst thieves."

Thomas gave him a dry look. "That is stretching things a bit far, don't you think?"

Samuel waved a distracted hand. "We are so close. We must catch the spies. We can't allow them to ruin things. It's all there, right in front of you. She. Is. A. Spy."

Samuel was passionate about their projects, but in his zealousness to catch the fiends he wasn't being realistic.

"No, she isn't."

"Just because she was attacked?"

Thomas ran his fingers through his hair. "No, not just because she was attacked. It just doesn't feel right. She is innocent."

Samuel snorted. "She is anything but innocent, Thomas."

Thomas sent him a searing look. "You aren't helping, Samuel."

"And you aren't thinking with the correct

portion of your anatomy! Seduce her, fine! Play with her body, entice yourself with her *innocence* and *strange appeal*. I thought your idea to seduce her was splendid, but somehow you are the one who is ending up seduced! By some mousy nobody who can barely string together two sentences in public."

Thomas narrowed his eyes as Samuel continued ranting.

"Goodness, man, I'm not even sure what you see in her. She's a mousy thing, always wearing those spectacles about, her figure barely average. And that barbaric mane of hair." He shuddered for effect.

"That's enough, Samuel." Thomas clenched his fists. He had never been more furious with his friend.

Samuel made a placating gesture. "Fine, Thomas, my apologies to Miss Harrington. But look at the evidence. You know better than to trust some random emotion, especially one resembling adoration. The evidence says it all. She has the connections, the motive, and the opportunity. She speaks French. Her maid *is* French. Her mother *was* French. Our spies *are* French."

"She is not a spy!"

271

"She is not innocent! She is a terrific actress—she should be treading the boards in Covent Garden! She will betray you. Just like what happened to Kevin McSweeney, mark my words."

"Fine, consider them marked."

Samuel sighed. "Just be careful."

"Thank you for your concern," Thomas said, in a clipped voice.

Samuel held up his hands. "You are the one that was always griping about Letty's death and guarding your heart so that it couldn't happen again."

Thomas considered strangling his friend. But then he would have to hide the body, and it would be just his luck to run into Patience as he was carrying some musty, old oriental rug wrapped around Samuel's dead form. No doubt Patience would *have* to examine the rug. And then she'd yell at him for bloodying a priceless antique.

"Listen, Thomas. It was wrong of me to bring up Letty. I just don't want to see you hurt." Samuel worried his lip just like Patience would in the situation.

Thomas sighed. "It's fine, Samuel. I know Patience isn't 'innocent' innocent. But I still don't think she is a spy."

Samuel smiled in relief. "Then you will stick to the plan? And if she's not a spy, perhaps you will gain a fine mistress out of her."

Thomas considered the different rugs lying around the castle. Surely he could find one that Patience wouldn't care about?

Patience decided to seek Thomas out after everyone had turned in for the night, having missed him at dinner. She needed to talk to him, find out more about what had happened to her earlier, and maybe ask a few questions that had been raised since then. And frankly, she just wanted to be with *him*, the man she had fallen in love with.

She was unsurprised to find him in his study. He seemed equally unsurprised to see her, even going so far as to hand her an already poured glass of wine as if he had been expecting her.

"Would you care to stroll through the gardens?"

She took a sip of the Madeira. It was sweet and slid easily over her tongue. The gardens would be dark, but the moon was nearly full, bright enough to lead the way and perhaps lead to other delightful things. "I would love to."

He held out his arm and they strolled

through a back door that led directly to the formal gardens. Thomas didn't linger. He headed for the maze, his fingers caressing her hand as it lay on top of his arm.

"You weren't at dinner," she said casually, as they entered the maze. The air was still but for a nightingale who was singing his little heart out in one of the hedges. She had a feeling they were headed toward the garden at the center. It was well hidden from prying eyes and was hard to hear through the high hedgerows.

"Something came up." He grimaced briefly, then looked through the fringe of hair that fell into his eyes. "Did you miss me, Patience?"

A thrill coursed through her at the tenor of his words. They were deep and hot and dark, just like the rest of him.

"Oh, of course I missed you. Who else can dampen an entire meal by raising one sardonic eyebrow and expressing one cutting comment?"

"Your colleague, Mrs. Tecking, seems to handle that in my stead."

Delighted laughter escaped from her, and she leaned into his body. Taking another sip of her Madeira as they walked, she murmured, "Poor Mrs. Tecking, unable to defend herself whilst we talk of her."

"I'd much rather talk about you anyway," he said, his breath caressing her ear.

They turned into the maze garden, the atmosphere inside as heavy with anticipation as with the brilliant smell of clematis and hydrangeas.

"Let's discuss you instead," she said. "And what you do in those buildings during the day and all hours of the night."

"Tut, tut, Patience. You are not living up to your name. I said *someday*, not today."

"Someday could be twenty years from now."

He led her to one of the stone benches and lifted a heavy blanket from the ground, laying it over the stone. He had obviously planned their walk. He pulled her down next to him on the bench. "Will you still be talking to me in twenty years?"

"That depends."

"On what?"

He scooted a bit closer, and her body hummed in awareness. It seemed that after last night's activities, it didn't take much for her body to remember exactly what it had felt like to have him so close. Her body moved toward him of its own accord.

"On you."

"Mmmmm." He reached out and stroked a

275

lock of her hair, rubbing it between his forefinger and thumb.

His fingers moved to the nape of her neck, just as they had the night before, and he stroked one finger down. His other hand plucked her glass and set it on the ground. He did the same with the glasses on her nose.

A firm tug had her sprawled on the bench, her legs dangling over the side. As he leaned over her, she registered that he hadn't answered her unspoken question. A vague sense of unease stole over her. She looked into his eyes, the deep, possessive tint from the night before was still present, but it was overlaid by real fondness. She relaxed, breathing in the lush scents of the surrounding flowers and the night air. She hadn't read him wrong after all. Her skills at reading others had failed her in London, but she liked to think she had honed her ability.

He covered her lips with his, and she stopped thinking.

His deft fingers worked at the buttons on the back of her dress, as he subtly pushed against her with his hips. A surge of some feeling centered where his body touched hers. A need for something she couldn't name unfurled in her body and mind. His hands moved across her skin as

276

he pulled her dress down her arms. She startled as she had been so caught up in the feel of him against her that she hadn't realized he had finished unbuttoning her dress. Each touch of his fingers blazed a trail of heat across her skin.

Her corset was duly unlaced, her shift, garters, and stockings summarily removed. Somewhere along the line he lost his shirt, all the while his lips and tongue stroked hers, his hands caressed each new area he laid bare until she was lying naked before him.

He drew back slightly to look at her. The soft glow of the moonlight and relaxing scent of beeswax and flowers were lulling, but falling in love with him or not, she was self-conscious enough to attempt to put her hands in front of her.

He circled her wrists and drew them up and over her head with one hand, laying her completely open for his view. His eyes were dark. Dark with passion, power, and something she couldn't name. He ran his free hand down the center of her body, curling around her breasts, her navel and the curls at the base, around her thighs and back up. His eyes captured hers as his fingers continued their exploration. Like a dark panther stalking its prey. That she was perfectly happy being the prey should have surprised her, but instead only caused the pool of heat at her center to rise a few degrees and for her to forget to be self-conscious as she reveled in the look in his eyes and the feel of his hands.

She loved this man.

He took his time examining and lightly mapping her skin. He ran his thumb over her breast, and her breath hitched audibly as she fought a moan. He leaned back down, bringing their bodies closer together.

"Beautiful," he whispered against her neck as he sucked gently at her pulse point.

Her breath caught again, and she tipped her head back to allow him freer access. He continued the exploration of her neck, as if she were a seven-course meal, and he wanted to savor each taste. His free hand ghosted down to stroke her. His fingers curled into her, and her hips involuntarily bucked at his ministrations. Her eyelids felt heavy, her skin so warm. And he was doing that thing again, the thing that had caused her to burst the night before.

He kissed her, harder than before and crooked his fingers. She felt as if she were reaching toward something, toward that same burst. It were as if she were climbing a hill, and with each step the journey became more intense.

He pulled back and divested himself of the rest of his clothes. She watched him, knowing what would come next and anticipating it. Anticipating the intimacy and the feelings and just being with Thomas. He stood before her naked, dark, chiseled, and beautiful. And then he was back, stretched alongside her and taking her back into his arms.

His kisses became more fierce, but his caresses were gentler. She tensed as she felt him nudge into her. "Sweet, fiery, Patience."

His mouth moved to her breasts and he pulled a nipple inside. She cried out and arched back, and he slid another inch within her, the feeling even more incredible as his hips continued to slowly advance, keeping pace with his mouth's strokes.

She had seen enough statuary and pictures, and been privy to enough gossip to understand what was happening. Well, the motions at least. She had only been able to guess at the feelings before, and they exceeded every expectation.

His slow advance picked up pace, until he drew back, teasing her entrance and making her feel hot and needy. All she knew was that she wanted him back inside. She put her hands on his backside and tried to pull him to her.

He chuckled. "In a moment, lovely. You are so tight, I don't want to hurt you."

He continued the onslaught of slow advances, and it felt like she might die if he didn't stop teasing her and finish what they started. He kissed her, devouring her from the outside while he stroked her on the inside. One hand reached between their partially joined bodies and rubbed. She squealed into his mouth, and he thrust all the way in.

There was some discomfort for a second, as if the remnants of something had broken, but then his fingers rubbed the spot again, and she arched upward. She caught his eye, and there was confusion and questioning beneath the heat and possessiveness she saw there. She arched, wanting to feel the sensation again, and his eyes closed and mouth parted.

Pulling his mouth toward hers, she kissed him with all the passion and love that she felt. He responded immediately, and, instead of the short teasing strokes, he pulled back and thrust all the way in again, seating himself as deeply as possible. She couldn't stop the small sounds that escaped as he moved within her again, and again, and again. And then he was returning her noises, and they were kissing harder and more frantically. The walk up the hill had turned into a sprint and she felt as if she were flying at the top of a mountain peak, caught indefinitely at its apex.

And then he pushed one last time, and she fell, soaring down the side. And he seemed to soar with her as his body pulsed inside of hers. He buried his face in her neck, whispering words that she couldn't identify.

She curled into him as he collapsed next to her, breathing in the moonlight and even the distant smell of the rose gardens, stroking his back as he stroked her hair.

It was minutes later when their breathing had returned to normal that he spoke. "You are new to sex."

She felt a twinge inside at the way he said the word sex. As if they had tried a new type of croissant. "Yes."

"You were a virgin."

She gave him a confused glance at the undercurrent to his words. It was a statement, but she felt compelled to answer anyway. "Yes. Did I do something wrong?"

He stayed silent for a few seconds. Seconds

that felt way too long. Fear replaced her contentment.

"You were a virgin. I don't understand. Everyone says—"

She pushed him away, cutting off his stabbing words and reining in the tears that threatened. She saw confusion and anger in his eyes, eyes that quickly became shuttered against her. How could she have been so naive? She had wanted so desperately to believe . . . and really, that was the crux of the matter.

She threw her dress back on, ignoring the lacings, and draped her wrap to hide the state of her clothes. He stayed silent throughout, obviously needing to say nothing now that he had gotten what he had come to the garden to do. It took every ounce of her courage to meet his eyes.

His face was closed, but there was a hint of something lingering in the air between them. Her emotional pain didn't allow her to analyze it.

"Yes, everyone says . . . they also say you killed your sister. Maybe you did."

Pain washed through her. "And maybe I should stop believing in fairy tales," she whispered. "Good night, Lord Blackfield."

Patience gathered what was left of her dignity and quickly exited the maze without looking back, her hope shattered beneath the moonlight and wicked sky. She had thought she had moved past the rumors and the innuendos and the disrespect. Had moved past her own foolish naïveté to recognize when someone was using her. Someone who was just like the others, wanting to capitalize on the rumors and her ruined name. Someone she had foolishly given straight access to her heart.

Chapter 18

❦

Stupid, stupid, stupid. How long would it take before she learned her lesson? Her father had said one of her best qualities was her ability to forgive. Even to forgive her tormentors. Right then she thought it possibly the worst quality to possess.

She felt no better come morning.

How had she been so naive when it came to Thomas? The man had tormented her during their first week at the castle. Then he had changed overnight to a mostly friendly, seductive devil. And she had completely accepted his transformation! In fact, she had reveled in it after the first few days.

He had been charming, witty, intelligent, eyes always sparkling, challenging her to unlock their secrets. Ah! The man completely validated her hidden fear that there were only two reasons men were interested in her. The first, and most obvious, that she was reputed to be fast. The second, and less used, that she could advance their careers or studies.

She could kick herself for mooning over a man who had coldly seduced her.

Patience flopped into a chair. A tear slid down her cheek.

Great risks reap great rewards. Great risks also wreak great disasters. She had been a great risk her entire life just by being different. It had worked for her in her professional life. Never in her social life. She had wreaked havoc in London, and the consequences still followed her. Thomas had seemed like such a great reward that she had risked again.

She covered her eyes. Heartbreak was just another adventure. She repeated it, but she still felt terrible. She'd have to tell her father that positive thinking was difficult in the midst of an emotional crisis.

Thomas was only one man. Granted, he was the only one who had sparked any sort of real feeling in her. After meeting dozens of disappointments, he had seemed like a diamond. But there had to be others out there.

Just not others necessarily for her, a little voice muttered.

Patience shushed her internal voice and stood resolutely. Quickly pinning up her hair, she got her face into some semblance of shape. She headed for her workroom, to throw herself into her tasks. She had a job to do, after all. And a pillow to cry on.

She avoided Thomas during the morning, and since he skipped the noon meal, he seemed to be avoiding her as well. Patience made no attempt at conversation, choosing listlessly to push her food about instead. Both Caroline and John gave her concerned glances, but she fibbed and said she still had a slight headache from the day before. It was only a minor fib. She had a headache, true, but it was spawned by a tall, dark lord, not chemical fumes. Dark lord fumes instead. The thought was almost comical, but she couldn't dredge up a laugh.

After lunch, Patience stood unseeing in front

of her afternoon's assignments. Try as she might, she couldn't stop thinking of the previous night. She *hadn't* waited to hear him out, true, but he could have either stopped her or sought her out. A part of her wished that she had stayed and argued. At least there would be some closure. Or, dare she still hope, reconciliation?

She was becoming decidedly maudlin and pathetic.

She decided a short lie down was definitely in order, as she felt the press of tears and the grogginess of too little sleep. She flopped onto her bed and pulled the coverlet over top. The usual sounds of the servants, birds, and work noises buzzed around her. She wondered if Thomas was out there working, adding more calluses to his perfect hands.

She buried her head and made good use of her once-dry pillowcase.

"She is not a spy."

Samuel looked baleful. "This again?"

Thomas shook a finger at him. "You say one word about her, and I will do something *you'll* regret."

"But are you sure?"

287

"Quite," he said succinctly. "And all those rumors about her are untrue. Shoddy research, Samuel."

"Oh, ho! You bagged her then."

Thomas punched him, and Samuel went sprawling across the floor. Thomas flexed his fingers. "I suggest you remain in your rooms today to fix that bloody nose. If I hear you've said one thing to her, or to anyone, I will not be responsible for my actions." He turned abruptly and marched from the room.

"But she's just a woman!" Samuel called after him. "What's different about this one?"

Everything. Everything was different about this one.

Thomas approached Patience's workroom, experiencing an awkwardness that he hadn't felt in a decade.

Patience was hard at work. In the late afternoon light her features looked drawn and pinched, as if she hadn't slept much. Lord knew he hadn't slept well.

When she left him he had stared dumbly after her, his mind reeling with the new revelations as she ran from the garden. He could not fathom the revelations nor the idea that she was leaving him.

He had believed the fabrications about her. Fabrications easily seen through if he had looked harder. In hindsight, he could admit that he hadn't wanted to look harder. He had wanted to believe she was experienced. Her natural, open, responsive nature had reinforced the notion, and he had blithely ignored anything that might have suggested otherwise. Because he wouldn't have seduced her if she were an innocent, would he have?

He had avoided virgins. She was his first. *And only*, a voice whispered, *your first and last*. And that was another thing. He had expressly avoided deep friendships or entanglements ever since his sister's death. Somehow Patience had wormed her way inside.

He had spent all day thinking about her, and had come to the conclusion that for her to behave as she had, she had to have a strong depth of feeling for him. He knew she was capable of it, she obviously had strong ties to her father, Jeremy, the man who transported the items, and even her cousin, John. Everything Thomas had learned about her in the past few weeks had pointed toward sincerity, and a somewhat naive sense of others.

So if she had allowed him to make love to

her . . . not allowed, participated eagerly and fully . . . then she had to have some depth of feeling for him. She would see it as an intimate act between two people, unless he was reading her wrong. And he really hoped he wasn't, because all of a sudden he found himself craving that affection from her.

He had really gotten himself into a pickle.

Patience turned to face him, possibly sensing his presence as he stood uncomfortably in the doorway. She lifted a brow in inquiry.

He had no idea what to say. "Do you have a minute?"

She worried her lip. He loved the habit, as it never failed to bring his eyes to her delectable lips. She chewed on them whenever trying to decide something.

"I suppose. Come in."

He entered and after thinking about it for a second, closed the door so they wouldn't be overheard. He felt oddly protective of her. Other than his sister, and to a lesser extent his aunt, he had never felt protective of any female. He pushed the emotions back. They were too confusing at the moment.

Patience's face was a study in uncertainty and nervousness.

How to begin? "I didn't make love to you because I thought you were fast. Wait, no, I can't lie, maybe that was a part of my initial decision to seduce you."

Her eyes narrowed dangerously.

"No, I'm not explaining myself well." He was nearly sputtering. He never sputtered. "I just don't want . . . no, I want . . . what I mean is . . . I didn't mean to hurt you," he finished rather lamely.

Her eyes softened a fraction, and he took that as a good sign.

"I thought maybe I could take you on a tour."

Confusion entered her gaze. "I've been here three weeks and have toured most of the castle."

He had to do this. It was the only thing that would fix his mess, the only thing that would show good faith. "No. I would like to take you on a tour of the perimeter buildings."

She blinked. As peace offerings went, it wasn't a bad one. He would reveal what he had been hiding during the entire duration of her stay and their somewhat strange relationship, if what they even had was a relationship. That line of thought was making her angry again, and she really *did* want to see the perimeter buildings.

"I'd like that."

Relief warred with anxiety on his face, and she marveled at the sudden openness in his expression. She relaxed a bit. Maybe she hadn't been wrong about him after all. Perhaps just a little premature.

Still, it was best not to raise her hopes too quickly. The next hour would be a good way to gauge him. She just needed to trust her judgment again.

Thomas was a complex man. He possessed dark secrets, and Patience had a feeling that this expedition wouldn't uncover them all, but at least it was a start.

"Let's go."

Thomas held out a hand to her and firmly tucked hers into the crook of his arm. He waited until they were outside before speaking.

"I know you've been snooping around the buildings."

She gave a nervous laugh, to which he smiled. "Have you not?"

"With all the strange noises and events, it's hard not to be curious."

He nodded. "I know. That is precisely what we feared when we knew we would have extended guests. It's no problem to shut down operations for a day or two. But difficult to do for a few weeks. That is too much time. The men get restless, and the projects, well, some of the projects don't take kindly to being left lying around."

Patience chuckled nervously. Living things didn't take too kindly to being left . . .

He pulled up short before they could enter the first building, the one in which she had fainted the previous day. "Before we enter, I need your promise that you won't reveal what you see to anyone."

She bit her lip. Her initial reason for sneaking around, other than her curiosity, had been to save the world from his mad schemes. That was before she had fallen in love with the madman though. She looked into his eyes and nodded. "I promise."

He opened the door, and she stepped inside, immediately enveloped by the silence of the hall. Thomas ushered her down the hall to a door at the end. Treading cautiously, she followed as he opened the far door. Sounds of buzzes and pops reached her ears. She was leery of the noise, since it was what had preceded her "nap" the day before, but she gathered her courage and stepped inside.

There were as many as ten men working in

the large, domed room. Workbenches strewn with glass and metal contraptions littered the space, and the men were pouring, peering, or dipping things into the liquids. All at once they seemed to be aware of her presence, and ten pair of eyes darted between Thomas and her. Thomas waved over the rotund man who had helped her move the sarcophagi.

"This is Jim Jones, whom you've already met. Jim is in charge of our chemical and potions projects. The Boyle Building and laboratory are his domain."

She held out a tentative hand, and he shook it after an infinitesimal pause.

"Thank you for helping the other day."

"No problem, Miss Harrington."

Jim turned back to Thomas. "Have you seen Samuel? He was supposed to help with the testing."

Patience felt Thomas stiffen next to her. "Samuel is feeling poorly today. Under the weather. We hope he will be back to full health tomorrow."

Thomas lifted her hand again. "I'm just going to show Miss Harrington around, don't let us bother you."

From his desperate expression, Patience knew

294

Jim wanted to say something, probably to ask why in heaven's name Thomas was showing her, an interloper, their secrets, but he refrained and simply nodded. Tightly.

Thomas introduced her to each of the other men. Most seemed friendly and eager to show off their products. Sleeping potion, headache potion, finish remover, "ground" remover (she shied away from the explanation on that one, the man had looked a bit manic), fertilizer, the list went on.

Their smocks were stained with dark, murky colors, which explained the bloodlike substance that had been smeared on Jim's clothing when she had thought he had been attacked by the monster. One mystery possibly solved.

They exited the workshop and walked down the road that snaked between the buildings. Thomas escorted her into the next building, a long brown structure. Contraptions and vehicles of every shape and description were crammed inside. A team of men were busy. Some were riding and falling from the contraptions and others appeared to be fiddling with them.

Noise and commotion ruled. A bang or crash sounded every few seconds as something or someone fell from its perch. There were two-wheeled, three-wheeled, four-wheeled, and even ten-wheeled monstrosities vying with tiny one-wheeled machines for space on a small track that had been set up in the middle of the chaos. Horses bucked and neighed, and she fancied she even saw a few sheep.

Thomas led her to the tall, thin man who had also assisted with the ill-fated sarcophagus. She was sensing a pattern. Four men, four buildings . . .

"Mr. Tick runs the vehicle, contraption, and mechanical building, also known as the Newton Building. Or more affectionately referred to as Bedlam Physics. As you can see, there is a great deal of chaos in here."

The aptly named Theodore Tick, who Thomas said loved to work with gadgets and clocks, sniffed. "We prefer to deem it 'action.' "

Patience grinned. These men were inventors. Suddenly everything came together in her brain. The strange noises, the lights, men wandering at odd hours across the estate . . .

The noises were almost completely accounted for in the first two buildings alone. Although the stomping and pounding still needed to be explained, Patience had a feeling that discovery was one or two buildings away. And that the discoveries of the lights and smells (besides the solely chemical smells) would soon be apparent.

Warming to the topic, she peppered the men with questions, and after their initial surprise, they perked up and expounded on their designs and what they hoped to accomplish. They were happy to share their excitement with someone else, someone who had been deemed safe by their leader.

Patience realized that they weren't much different from her colleagues, completely absorbed by what they were doing, fascinated by their work to an extent that would bore anyone else, and usually did if engaged in conversation.

The third building, the Galileo Building, was headed by the man who had had the misfortune to kiss the mummy, Peter Yensen. It was filled with glass and light. She learned that astronomers and explorers were charting, mapping, and creating devices. One man was improving a handheld telescope, another was inventing some type of navigational device that resembled a sextant. A third was engaged with setting up a number of pieces of glass to reflect light and form prisms. She would bet that this was the cause of the strange lights.

Thomas whispered, his soft breath tickling

her ear, "Sometimes I don't think *they* know what they are doing either. See that man over there, the one dressed all in purple?"

Patience saw a gangly man madly fidgeting with a compass.

"He has the strangest ideas and always wants to share them. He'll pin you in a corner and babble on and on. He had stationed himself at the back entrance to speak with me the night you came. He does it often enough that I leave the downstairs study window open so I can crawl through to escape him. Kenfield, my butler, won't let me hear the end of it."

She smiled, elated from the discovery of what was really going on at the estate and the trust that Thomas seemed to have placed in her.

The fourth building was the last, although Thomas had offhandedly mentioned something about catacombs and underground facilities. Patience stopped before the door, unaccountably nervous again.

"Why?"

Thomas gave her a questioning glance, but stopped as well. "Why what?"

"Why are you showing me all of this? And why now?"

He paused and tucked an errant strand of

hair behind her ear. "Logically, I know you are innocent of the problems we have been having and that you are not a spy, at least not in the negative sense of the word. The attack on you yesterday is a logical reason for feeling this way. Intuitively, I know you are innocent, because I feel it."

She stiffened at the possible reference to their indiscretion. "Does this have to do with what occurred in the garden and in your study?"

He cocked his head and seemed to carefully select his words. "I'd be lying if I said no. But it's probably not in the way that you think. I'm not doing this solely out of feelings of guilt for believing the rumors about you. I'm doing this because I want you to know what we do here. The types of things that interest me." He cocked his head. "Do you still want to see this building?"

Did she? Yes. She had wanted to see inside this building ever since she had been trapped in the closet eavesdropping on their meeting. But what did he mean, that he knew she was innocent? Something told her that it wasn't in the way that she had been innocent before last night.

"Yes."

"Very well. Be careful not to touch anything."

Too late, she thought, as he took her hand and led her inside.

The hall gave way to the room that had haunted her dreams. In the daylight, the room appeared much less fierce, but the things inside did not. Weaponry of every kind and description covered the interior. Pulleys and chains supported strange-looking barrels and pipes. Gadgets littered the surface in this building as well, accessories to the firearms.

"Come, you can see our monster."

"Wait. Then there really *is* a monster?"

He gave her a strange look and walked toward a cannon with a revolving cylinder. It looked like an improved Puckle Gun. Much improved, if the number of chambers and general machinery were anything to go by.

"This is the monster?"

His eyes had an unreadable look as he, too, examined it. "Yes." His voice was soft.

"How does it work?"

He looked at her briefly, then back at the cannon. "It repeats shot. Up to twenty times. Multiple waves of ammunition. Enough to destroy an entire line of soldiers."

Horrified, all she could do was stare at him as

he stared pensively at the monster. "D-does it work?"

He sighed. "Somewhat."

Richards was in charge of the Hastings Building, but he was too busy putting out a fire, literally, to greet them. He waved and returned to his task.

"Hastings, as in the battle?"

"Yes, the last time England was conquered."

The air in the building became stifling. Whether it was the air or her, she didn't know. Thomas sensed her discomfort and steered her outside.

"The monster. I saw you raising it a few nights after we arrived," she said.

He lifted a brow. "Spying on us from your bedroom, were you?"

"Anyone would be curious," she said somewhat defensively.

He sighed again. "Yes, and that is the problem."

"What do you mean?"

"I started this collective a decade ago. Invited inventors from all over England and the Continent. Some came from farther still. I fund the experiments. For the most part they are useful and even intriguing. Farming, astronomy, mechanics, all scientific study is welcome. However, that includes items of warfare, too." His eyes took a distant cast. "And if I didn't fund and manage it, the interested parties would go elsewhere."

"Other countries, you mean?"

He shrugged. "Even within our own country there are movements afoot. In the wrong hands . . ."

He trailed off, unwilling to say more, but it was obvious what such inventions could do and spawn.

"The mad surgeon you were talking about works on this monster thing, doesn't he?"

Thomas smirked. "You really *were* curious. Perhaps I should call you 'Kitty' from now on?" He leaned closer. "Try and make you purr?"

She blushed.

"But how and why do you keep this all secret? Surely people know."

He nodded. "Of course, they know. And we are wary of spies. Not even counting the warfare division, there are many spies in other industries wanting to steal inventions for their own."

"The retiring room!"

He looked at her oddly.

"The devices installed in the ground-floor retiring room. I had Tilly ask three different servants about it, but none of them would give her a good answer."

He smiled. "The servants and villagers are secretive. Most of them are without price in their devotion to our works. And they are always on the lookout for suspicious people and spies—sometimes they take it a little far. I heard you had quite the excursion to the village."

Patience shook her head. "Loyalty like that is definitely without price."

"We employ most of the village in some way. The village mill employs over half the population. As to the retiring room, I had forgotten that your journey into the bowels of the castle had taken you by it. We are looking to install more within the castle, but they require a lot of piping and engineering. Knocking down walls is a major undertaking."

"And the chandeliers?"

"Noticed the jars, did you? They are powered by gas. Prince George expressed particular interest in them."

She nodded, her mind already on the next question. "What happened the other day? With the explosion?"

Thomas grinned. "An inventor, on his own,

may be a bit inattentive. But get a collective banded together with someone willing to organize it, and you have a lot of dangerous minds. There are traps set around all the buildings. What you saw was one of them being activated."

She was floored. "You have spies. Here, now?"

"Of course."

"You thought I was a spy! That's what you meant."

Suddenly it all made sense. He nodded. "There were a lot of things working against you, namely that you are part French, speak the language, and have current contacts there."

"But Thomas, there are a lot of people who speak French. In fact, most members of the ton do."

Thomas smiled. "But your arrival coincided with a number of incidents, and you were always poking into things. Patience, you are your own worst enemy."

"Are most of your spies French?"

"Some. Monster has created a great deal of government interest. France is especially interested, and we've intercepted a number of their people sneaking about the premises."

She quieted. "What are you going to do with the monster?"

His lips drew tight. "I don't know. We are still thinking that through. Generally our mad surgeon loses interest after he perfects something. Perhaps we will sink it in the ocean and destroy the plans."

He said it lightly, but not lightly enough for her not to believe it an option in his mind.

"Why do you hate antiquarians so much?"

His face pulled tight. "I don't hate antiquarians. I hate obsessions."

She blinked. The inventors seemed just as obsessed as the men from her circle. Before she could say anything, he stepped forward and caressed her cheek.

"Besides, I like things that are alive and full of energy."

She closed her eyes briefly at the sensation, but pulled away before he could continue. She wasn't ready yet. He was starting to show her his layers, and she loved these, too. His passion for the creations he oversaw and his fellowship with the men under his wing drew her deeper. But there were still unanswered questions hidden behind his eyes. She wanted him to trust her with those, too. She had one week left. Time enough not to rush into anything and make another mistake.

* * *

Patience walked back to the castle. The sun was on a downward course. She had spent several hours exploring the buildings, with Thomas answering all her work-related questions.

Perhaps she could make progress tonight.

"—and that is the last."

"I need more time. Darling, please."

Patience looked at the hedge separating the formal garden from the rose garden. The voices were low and heated.

Natural curiosity made her want to hear more, but it sounded like a lover's quarrel, and she didn't want to intrude on a private moment.

"Can't you do anything? Stop them? Make them put it off another week?" The voice turned seductive, and sounded vaguely familiar. "I don't want to lose you."

The woman made some reply, but her voice was too low for Patience to hear.

The man rattled off a series of endearments in French, and Patience paused. The part of her that saw monsters in shadows immediately thought—*spy*! But speaking French wasn't a crime. She spoke French and had never entertained a single traitorous thought against England.

Still, she decided to continue her route through

the rose garden. If she happened upon the couple, well, it was the middle of the day, and actually a poor spot for a secluded rendezvous. What kind of spies chose to meet in the open air, where anyone could see them from the castle windows?

As it turned out, the lovers were gone by the time she reached their spot. Shrugging, she started to continue on when a shiny object caught her gaze.

A bit of metal glinted from a clutch of roses near the edge of the path. She reached down to examine it. It nestled in her palm, oddly shaped and worn. She rubbed it absently and continued her walk through the rose garden, becoming once again lost in thought about Thomas and the end of her stay in the castle. About what would happen to their relationship afterward. About what she wanted. About what *he* wanted. He was about as forthcoming as a clam.

Thomas wanted to meet before dinner. To discuss things, he had said. Patience thought it more likely that he wanted to discuss how his mouth fit perfectly over hers. Not that she minded that "discussion," no, she definitely didn't mind. But she wanted, no, needed answers from him first. And she wasn't likely to

307

get them quite yet. His eyes were still too guarded.

And there was a very good chance that he didn't want the same things she did. A very good chance. She had taken the risk and was willing to accept the consequences, painful though they might be. A part of her pointed to Thomas's reaction after they made love. The rest of her ruthlessly squashed that part. She was going to give him, them, a chance. If he was using her, more fool she, but at least she wouldn't regret knowing for sure.

She walked out of the rose garden, so involved in her internal warfare that she barely had time to register the change in the air as the bittersweet smell caught her nose, and a cloth was clasped over her mouth.

Chapter 19

"What are you doing?" A familiar voice shrieked, and for a second Patience latched onto a name before it dissolved back into the muddied confines of her drugged mind.

"Disposing of an unneeded distraction."

"You can't ki-kill her!"

"Darling, do you want her to expose us?"

"I told you, there is no more us!"

The two voices switched to muffled French as they moved to the other side of the room. Patience strained to hear, her mind becoming more alert with every second, but she only caught a few words. "My love," and "my flower," and "my only." It seemed that the man was trying to placate the woman. They were obviously the same couple she had heard in the gardens. Interestingly enough though the woman's accent was slightly better than the man's, neither was a native speaker of French.

The man's voice grew clearer, and she had the nagging suspicion she knew it. She recalled seeing the colorless concoction on Jim's table. Perhaps it was Jim, the head of the Boyle Building?

"No!" The woman shrieked again.

"I won't discuss this with you anymore. Go back to the castle before I get angry."

There was a definite edge to the threat and the woman must have taken heed, because the door slammed, and one pair of footsteps receded.

Was she in one of the perimeter buildings that Thomas had said they used for occasional testing? How had they moved her without anyone seeing them? If the woman was walking back, they couldn't be that far.

Footsteps came toward her, and Patience stiffened. She really ought not to have shut down her paranoia just because everything about the trip to the castle that had seemed unreal and fantastic had proven to have a rational explanation. She couldn't prevent herself from wincing and shrinking back as the footsteps stopped next to her.

"You're awake. We can't have that. No, not at all. It's still daylight, and since I must wait until nightfall to deal with you, I can't allow you to remain awake. Pity really, as you are quite an interesting woman. Pleasant dreams, Miss Harrington."

The bittersweet aroma once more invaded her senses, just as the nagging memory of his voice and the piece of metal she had been examining coalesced into horrified recognition.

Thomas paced his study and once again checked his pocket fob. Patience was supposed to have met him half an hour ago. It was nearly sundown. If he didn't know better, he would say she was being coy. But *coyness* wasn't even in Patience Harrington's vocabulary.

There was a knock at the door. Finally.

"It's about ti—"

Thomas broke off as Kenfield quirked a brow. "Indeed, my lord. This just arrived for you. The messenger said it was most urgent."

Thomas took the missive, not really caring to read anything not from Patience. He scanned the words, cold washing through him, as fear replaced annoyance. He hadn't felt such fear since he had discovered his sister's body ten years ago.

"Kenfield, who gave this to you?" he asked urgently.

His butler's normally impassive face showed concern. "A boy from the kitchens. Do you want me to detain him?"

"Yes, immediately."

And then he took off running as fast as his legs could carry him.

Patience groggily returned to consciousness. If she never smelled that bittersweet scent again, it would be too soon.

"Don't move."

She froze, terror ripping through her, before struggling against her bonds.

"Stop. Patience, you're safe."

A warm hand caressed her cheek, and she struggled to open her eyes. The room was a blur, and her eyes slowly focused on the dark form sitting next to her bed. Bed? She looked down. What she had thought were bindings were covers tucked tightly around her.

"What happened?" she croaked.

A strong, gentle arm lifted her, and cool water slid blissfully down her throat.

Thomas swam into focus, and she sobbed her relief.

"I was hoping you could tell me." He continued to caress her face and hair.

"Overheard . . . conversation . . . found piece of horseshoe . . . stablehand . . . drugged . . ."

The first time she had been drugged, it hadn't been so difficult to talk. Her terror resurfaced at the condition being permanent.

"Shh. Relax. More than likely you were given multiple doses of the drug, tomorrow you will be fine."

"Yes?" she croaked again.

"Promise." His voice was soothing, but his eyes were dark and dangerous, just like the first night they had met. "You're certain it was the stablehand, Henry, who did this to you?"

She nodded, and his mouth thinned.

"Spy . . . poor French . . . woman . . ."

"I'll take care of him. Just go to sleep. I've posted a guard at the door, and Tilly will stay with you. We'll talk in the morning."

He pressed a light kiss to her forehead. As if his words carried some magic spell, her eyes closed, and she fell asleep, secure in the knowledge she'd be safe.

Soft light flickered in the room as the candle stub fought for life. Patience felt a weight on her midsection, and looked down to see an arm across her waist and a warm body pressed against her side. Thomas's features were warm and relaxed. He was on top of the covers, as if he had dozed off while keeping watch.

A clock softly chimed half past the hour. What hour, she didn't know.

She ran a hand down his face. The touch was light, but his eyes still opened and blinked at her.

"You're awake."

She nodded.

"How are you feeling?"

"Better."

"Your throat, too?"

"Yes," she whispered as she continued to run a hand down his cheek.

"Good." He captured her hand and rubbed each finger with his thumb.

"What happened to Henry?"

His features darkened. "He's been taken into custody by men from London. They are going to question him."

"And then?"

"Depending on what they find, he will either go to jail or be tried for treason. Even if they can't connect him to spying, his actions against you sealed his fate."

"So, he was responsible for all of the accidents in the past few weeks?"

Thomas frowned. "Partially. There is still something that feels wrong."

"The woman?"

"Maybe."

She closed her eyes as his ministrations soothed her. "How did you find me?"

He shook his head. "Someone sent a note. Perhaps his partner was apprehensive."

"The woman was upset. Could have been." Patience shied away from discussing the woman. Upon awakening, she had remembered exactly who the woman was.

"I don't know. Something just feels wrong. Henry was hired just before you arrived. We

315

hired quite a few new people because we are planning to expand our facilities and need more staff. But we had a few problems before that."

Patience entangled her fingers with his. "The woman was being wooed by Henry. I'll bet anything that he was the one leading her. Seducing her for information."

Thomas shifted. "Hmmm. Could be."

"As you did with me."

He looked at her through lowered lashes. "That wasn't the whole reason."

"You thought I was easily seduced, and you were lonely?"

He frowned. "I'm not lonely. And your being easy or hard to seduce didn't factor into it." He shifted again.

"Did too."

"I seduced you because I wanted to." He turned on his back, but the fingers on the hand nearest to her continued to massage hers.

She decided to listen to his actions, rather than his words, and let the conversation drop for the moment.

"Any thoughts as to the identity of the woman?" he asked.

She somehow stopped her body from stiffening. "Perhaps tomorrow I can sort through my impressions."

He sighed. "I was hoping you could shed light on her."

"Perhaps tomorrow."

"Your cousin was quite concerned for you. I had to sneak back in here after he retired."

Patience smiled. "John is a good sort."

"Oh, and I should mention, Mrs. Tecking created a bit of a scene when she saw me enter your room while everyone was still awake. Didn't say anything directly to me, of course, but she wasn't trying to hide her outrage."

"That's nothing new. This whole trip will provide the gossips with endless tidbits. At least some of which will be true this time."

He kissed her head. "Ah, the misery of living among the ton."

"There is plenty of misery if your name is Patience Harrington."

"Why do you let them bother you?"

She sat up and glared at him. "Bother me? I don't think you understand."

"Explain it to me then."

"They take everything I say and twist it. And

317

sometimes because of my errant tongue, they don't even have to twist it! I provide it in a neat little package for them."

"You just need to learn to relax in social situations."

"I've tried. I really have." She was nearly pleading, more with herself than anything else. "I just always end up saying something horribly awful or embarrassing."

He tugged her back against him. "It's because you aren't relaxed. It's because you allow yourself to feel uncomfortable. You see an empty space in the conversation and strive to help by filling it. Better just to leave it there. Let the other person feel uncomfortable."

"I don't want anyone else to feel uncomfortable."

"Well, in society people thrive on it. You earn points for causing discomfort to someone else."

"That's awful."

He shrugged. "So, first you relax. Get in the habit of taking a sip of tea before you speak. Allow a thoughtful pause. Don't rush in."

Patience nodded. She could see where those ploys would be useful.

"And don't say anything about antiquities, politics, work . . . or most anything that you speak of, come to think of it."

She was aghast. "But, I don't want to be some-one I'm not."

Thomas shot her a look. "You aren't being someone you're not, Patience. I don't think you ever could be. It's just a form of restraint. Think of it as testing the players before revealing your hand."

She must have looked unconvinced, because he continued. "Do you enjoy social intrigue?"

"Well, no."

"Are you interested in the type of people that play at social intrigue?"

"They are not at the top of my list usually."

"Then what is the problem with just putting forth a social facade for the times when you have to face them and letting it all go as soon as you are away?"

"It just feels . . . I don't know, dishonest. Like they aren't getting to know the real me."

Thomas threw his hands up. "They are stupid people. They don't deserve the real you."

Patience blushed.

He continued on as if he hadn't just paid her a

very real compliment. "After watching, you will be able to identify those people that you might like to befriend. Then you take things slowly. Comment on the weather. Comment on the crush of a party or the wine or the hall. Inane, stupid things."

She reluctantly smiled. "See! You are calling it inane."

He gave her "that" look again. "Of course I am. It's like a dance. First you watch the other person move, you make small moves together, watching so that you don't step on each other's feet, then, if things are going well, you start whirling around. After a bit of that, maybe you pull the person in closer than you normally would, just to see how she reacts. If that goes well, well, there you are."

He flicked a thread from the bed. She stared at him, speechless. "That's it? That's your advice?"

"Silence first. Get a feel for the other person or people. Small pleasantries. Then maybe a bit of real dancing if they pass muster. Perfect advice. I should hire myself out."

"Wonderful," she grumbled.

"Well, now that I have solved all problems in your social life, is there anything that distinguishes our mystery woman?"

"She spoke French," she said reluctantly. "Not fluently as a native speaker, but well enough. I assume you've narrowed your lists down to those who speak French?"

He nodded. "We can go over them in the morning. I'll show you the note, too."

She burrowed back into his side. Lifting the covers, she said, "Get under."

He gave her an unreadable glance. "You are ill."

"And you are warm. Now get under. You can leave before daybreak."

He smirked. "Don't want your maid to find me in your bed?"

"No, Tilly would probably curse you black-and-blue. In more than one language."

He gave her an odd look. "Your maid speaks other languages?"

"Yes. Tilly was my mother's maid."

He was alert. "So, she speaks French?"

"She is French." She caught his look. "Oh, no, no, you don't. Tilly is *not* a spy."

"But the woman we are searching for isn't necessarily a spy, she's a woman who has been taken in by a man who has seduced more than half the females in this house."

Patience was aghast. "Tilly is ready to retire.

She's forty years his senior. She's not interested in romance."

His eyebrows rose. "Just because she is older? Do you think that makes a difference in someone wanting love?"

"Well, no, and with anyone else I wouldn't have said that. But Tilly? My Tilly? No." She shook her head, dispelling the image. "No."

"Just because she is your maid—"

"She was my nurse!"

He looked amused. "She's a woman, Patience."

She grumbled. "Fine. But it's not Tilly. I'd recognize her voice anywhere. And she's *French*, Thomas. French was definitely not this woman's first language."

His brow furrowed. "Her name is Tilly, and she's French?"

She colored. "Er, no, but I couldn't pronounce her name as a child, and that stuck."

"I won't ask."

"Excellent. Now get under the covers."

He gave her a searching look, scooted under the covers, and pulled her into his arms.

"And make sure you are gone in the morning. I'm not having you shock my maid, French or not."

He pressed his face into her hair. "Promise."

* * *

Light crept through her eyelids as she slowly awakened. She had slept better than she could remember. She was just about to open her eyes and stretch when someone no more than three feet from her screamed bloody murder.

Chapter 20

Patience bolted from bed and fell to the floor. Tilly was standing near her and pointing at the bed.

Guiltily, she turned her head, expecting to see Thomas, but the bed was empty. Trying to discern the cause of her maid's distress, she looked over the counterpane but couldn't see anything.

"Tilly?"

"Hairy, huge!"

Patience looked over once again. She wouldn't

call Thomas hairy, but perhaps Tilly was overly scandalized and he was hiding under the bed?

Then she saw it. A large spider was hanging from the ceiling, suspended as if it, too, was wondering what all the fuss was about.

Patience rolled her eyes and swiped the spider's thread before depositing him on the sill. "Honestly, Tilly, it's a *spider*."

"So sorry, *ma petite*. It dropped right in front of my face, caused me a fright."

On the whole, it was a less-than-pleasant way to start the day. Both pleased and disappointed that Thomas hadn't stayed, Patience wondered when he had left. She was pleased that Tilly's bloodcurdling scream hadn't been due to his presence, yet disappointed not to wake next to him.

A series of knocks sounded on the door—staff wanting to make sure everything was well. Kenfield seemed to take an inordinate amount of time making sure her maid was well. Too much time, really, and Thomas's words about her maid's seeking romance in the castle, and Tilly's own girlish blushes forced bad images into Patience's mind.

She grumpily got dressed and made her way

to the dining room. She would have liked to spend another half hour or so lounging. Stupid spider.

She dumped the obligatory eggs onto her plate and plopped into a chair. John and Caroline joined her a moment later, and Thomas arrived five minutes after that. The regular pink note was delivered, and she reminded herself to ask him about the memos later. He looked amused at this one. She wondered when they had ceased annoying him.

The Teckings were the last to arrive. Although Mr. Tecking looked fully recovered, there was a distinct sense of unease between the couple. Mrs. Tecking's eyes were piercing as they met hers.

Caroline asked after Patience's health, and everyone seemed concerned. Even Mrs. Tecking appeared dutifully affected.

Patience retired as quickly as she could, wanting to work on her last items and also needing to get away from prying eyes. Unfortunately, Mrs. Tecking strode into the room after her. Patience wasn't sure she was ready to deal with her yet.

"Is there something I can help you with, Mrs. Tecking?"

326

The woman eyed her shrewdly. "Have you really recovered?"

"I am quite fine. Thank you for your concern." She paused a moment. "Really, thank you."

Mrs. Tecking hesitated. "I'm glad."

Patience couldn't help it, her jaw dropped. Mrs. Tecking shifted and turned toward the door. Over her shoulder, she said, "I'm not completely evil, Miss Harrington. Good day."

"Wait." Patience's mind was a whirl. "Not that I'm not grateful, but why did you send the note to T—Lord Blackfield?"

Mrs. Tecking's shoulders stiffened. "What note? It is your word against mine."

"But I don't understand."

Mrs. Tecking turned, her gaze condescending. "Don't understand what? Why I saved you, or why I was meeting a man?"

Patience blinked. "Well, both really."

"You don't know what it's like," she said viciously. "You with your charmed life, always getting what you want, making your own way in society. You carouse with the gentlemen, an unmarried woman, and *still* lead your blessed life, your father bowing to your wishes. Doting on you, loving you even as you go against him."

Her eyes closed as if she were in pain and she sucked in a deep breath. "One mistake, and my parents nearly disowned me. I had to fight for my reputation, fight to keep it spotless. My Freddie, my dear misguided Freddie." She opened her eyes, and Patience nearly gasped at the misery in their depths. "I thought we would be happily married. But with his work . . . he forgot about me after a while."

Patience felt a stab of pity for the woman.

"I didn't stray. Not really. I never did anything with Henry. But he brought me flowers, and he wrote the nicest poems, and he didn't seem to want anything in return. He was content to sit for hours listening to me talk about our work and my distress."

"Our work?"

Mrs. Tecking waved a hand, obviously upset at being interrupted. "When the shipments went out, what I recorded and so forth."

Of course. Someone needed to ship information from the castle. What better way than to do it within the museum shipments? At least for a time?

Mrs. Tecking continued, oblivious to Patience's epiphany.

"He made me feel special. Do you know how

long it has been since I felt that way?" She barely held back a sob.

Patience understood all too well and moved to comfort her, but she backed away. Something else occurred to Patience.

"Mr. Tecking saw you two, didn't he? That was the reason for his attack?"

Mrs. Tecking looked guiltily at the ground. "I loved Freddie. I still love Freddie. But I'm bitter, Miss Harrington. A part of me was happy to see Freddie react. React to *something* that had to do with me. You've seen him. You know what he's like." Her eyes were listless.

Patience felt helpless. "I can see your pain. I'm sorry that I never saw it before."

"I don't know what came over Henry when he kidnapped you. We had only been talking—I was breaking things off. There would have been no trouble from Freddie or anyone else."

In that moment Patience truly believed Mrs. Tecking really had no idea what was happening at the estate. She laid a hand gently on her wrist. "Perhaps he was just confused."

Surprisingly, Mrs. Tecking did not move away, but her gaze again turned shrewd. "I see your confusion as well. You be careful with Lord Blackfield, Miss Harrington. He is just as obsessive about his activities, heavens knows what they are, as Freddie is and what Mr. Ashe was reputed to be. Look at Lady Caroline. Don't trust in men. They are flowers and chocolates one moment, then they completely forget you exist after they have you."

Patience knew she was speaking from her own bitter experience, but still found the conviction in Mrs. Tecking's voice disquieting. Hadn't she been saying to herself how obsessive Thomas was?

"What are you and Mr. Tecking going to do now?"

Her chin lifted. "That is none of your business. Freddie and I will work things out. Good day, Miss Harrington."

And with that she swept from the room like a queen leaving her subjects. Patience shook her head. Even with a tentative understanding, she had to wonder if she and Mrs. Tecking would ever get along. She would settle for nodding acquaintances at this point.

A number of things were finally explained to her satisfaction. Mr. Tecking's fit was obvious, he had seen them in the rose garden. Just as she had observed the day before—the windows in his room faced the gardens. She wondered if that hadn't been Mrs. Tecking's plan all the while.

Patience had to decide what to tell Thomas. She chewed her lip. It was obvious Mrs. Tecking had been using Henry in her own way to show her dissatisfaction with her marriage. And Mrs. Tecking had saved her. She must have gone straight from the building to write Thomas the note. No, she would make sure that Mrs. Tecking was not punished. It seemed she had already punished herself enough anyway.

"Patience?"

Speak of the devil. "Good morning, Thomas."

He sauntered into the room, but there was an air of alertness that belied his lazy gait. "You practically ran from the dining hall. Everything all right?"

"Yes. No. Oh, close the door please, will you?"

He raised a brow, but did as she commanded. "Eager to spend more time alone with me?"

She glared. "I know who sent you the note. I know the identity of the woman."

His gaze sharpened. "Who?"

"Mrs. Tecking."

His eyes were blank, much like she expected hers had been when she had realized it.

"Mrs. Tecking?"

"Yes." She sighed and repeated the tale, emphasizing the positive parts Mrs. Tecking had played in her rescue.

Thomas looked thoughtful. "That makes sense although something still seems strange. Henry and Mrs. Tecking couldn't be behind all of the problems."

Patience shrugged helplessly. "Probably not, but we are better off now than we were yesterday, right?"

He smiled and pulled her into his arms, resting his chin on top of her head. "How are you feeling?"

"Better. When did you leave last night?"

"Just before dawn. I heard there was quite a commotion in there this morning."

She grimaced. "I thought Tilly had discovered you and was going to bring the entire castle to my door to discover you as well."

He chuckled, the vibrations heading straight to her toes. "I came to ask if you would like to go riding. Perhaps examine the abbey gatehouse?"

She sighed and pulled back a bit. "I would love to, Thomas, but I'm behind. I need to get the remaining pieces cataloged before the last shipment is sent."

His gaze darkened minutely as he opened the door. "I'll see you later then."

His withdrawal was abrupt. Confusion rushed through her, as he nodded stiffly and walked through the door.

What the devil was the matter with him now?

Thomas was quiet at dinner that night. And he slipped away afterward without speaking to her. She continued to work, trying to make up for the days she had spent with Thomas or the hours recovering from the attacks. Before she knew it the hall clock was chiming midnight and Thomas still had not appeared. Tired from the long night, she prepared for bed, lulled to sleep by the sounds coming from the inventors.

The pattern the next day was much the same, Thomas seemed to be avoiding her. His behavior had become unnerving. Now that the female suspect was uncovered, had her usefulness run out? Irritated and more than a little worried, she decided to beard the lion in his den.

Finishing her work early and figuring she had given him enough time to retire to his study, she set out. She knocked lightly on the door and was rewarded with a deep, warm tone telling her to enter. He looked slightly surprised to see her, but covered it with a smirk.

"Wandering around again, Miss Harrington?"

He was partially dressed, wearing only a shirt, open at the collar, trousers, and boots. His boots were crossed on one of the tables as he lounged in a chair. She pushed aside her response to the sight and pursed her lips. "You've been avoiding me."

His face was unreadable. "Don't you mean that you've been avoiding me?"

"No."

"You didn't come here last night."

"Well, neither did you seek me out," she said pointedly.

"You said you needed to work. That you were too busy."

"You could have stopped by."

He lifted a brow. "And so could have you."

"All right, fine."

His feet dropped from the table. He rose and walked around her, trailing a hand across her shoulders, around her collarbone and up to caress her chin. "So why did you seek me out tonight, dear Patience?" His voice spoke of sin and dark promises. She shivered.

"I thought we could talk."

He whispered against her neck as he pressed hot kisses against her skin. "What did you want to talk about?"

"You looked upset with me before you left yesterday. Were you angry that I didn't accept your picnic offering?"

He continued the melting kisses, and her head tilted back of its own volition.

"No," he answered.

"So, it was something else?"

"Mmmm."

"What?"

He pulled back. "For every question you ask, you lose an article of clothing." He pulled the pins from her hair and then sank to the floor, pushing her lightly into a deep leather chair. He removed her slippers, then reached up to untie her stockings. The silky material caressed her skin as he carefully removed each one.

"But that was five things you removed," she said, breathlessly.

He trailed his finger over her calves. "Ah, but things in pairs count as one item."

"Are you going to answer my questions?"

He slithered, there was no other word, up her body and reached behind her. Deft fingers moved over the buttons. His mouth was near her ear, but he did nothing as his fingers worked. The wait was almost more unbearable than his ministrations.

He pulled the last one free and slowly pulled her gown down her arms. "I may."

"Good to know."

He raised a brow. "Not interested in finding answers?"

She felt bold all of a sudden and unbuttoned his shirt. "Fair is fair, after all."

"Oh, I definitely believe in equality," he said as he latched on to her neck.

She barely pushed his shirt from his shoulders as her head dropped back onto the chair.

A number of questions dancing around the subject of why he had been upset left her with only her corset and shift still attached and her dress half-on. He was down to only his trousers, and they had already been unfastened.

"Did you talk with Mrs. Tecking?"

He suddenly shifted their positions, scooping her up, seating himself in the chair, and depositing her on his lap so she was straddling him. Her eyes opened wide, but he picked up one of her half curls and twirled it around his finger.

"Yes. She helped more than I thought she

would. A maid, Jenny, claims Henry seduced her into helping him as well."

She cocked her head. She would bet a tuppence that it was the same maid named Jenny that always lurked about. "But you don't think that is the end?"

He pulled her forward so her forehead rested against his chest, and began unlacing her corset. "No. But then again, there will never be an end. Merely new players."

His voice was tight. She allowed him to finish with the laces before pulling back to look him in the eye. "You think it is one of your own people, don't you?"

He didn't answer, instead capturing her lips in a heated kiss and discarding her corset to the floor.

"I hope you remembered to lock the door."

She stiffened and started to wiggle from his lap. He chuckled and held her in place. "Oh, no, Patience. This is what happens when you don't plan ahead."

She started to argue, but he leaned down and licked her breast. Gasping, she allowed him to pull her closer as he devoured her like a dessert. She pressed into him, and he scooted a bit in the chair. Her dress pooled around them, hiding their laps, but their upper bodies were bared to anyone who opened the door.

The thought had barely crossed her mind when he leaned back in the chair and his hand reached under the pooled silk and caressed her thigh before traveling north. Already well acquainted with his talented fingers after their two previous indiscretions, she felt them work their magic. Her bare legs rubbed against the supple leather of the chair as his fingers established a rhythm within her body.

His eyes were lazy, but the fondness in them was once more present. Instead of a smirk, his mouth pulled into a languid smile.

"You were upset that our last shipment is almost upon us," she blurted out, having no idea where the thought had originated.

His eyes narrowed, and two fingers slipped inside her, causing her breath to catch and her eyes to nearly close. He said nothing, his eyes never leaving hers.

"Why?"

He leaned forward and blocked further questions with his mouth. The kisses were hungry, far more demanding than before. His hands were suddenly driving her into a frenzy instead of the slow, subtle seduction he had been intent upon. She found that her body quite liked both. His free hand tangled in her hair at the nape and kept her pressed to him.

She pressed right back. The hand under her skirt reappeared, and she was being pulled farther forward onto his lap and directly into contact with his bare skin. He had freed himself without completely removing his trousers. She could feel the material along with the slippery leather as she was pulled forward. His hands gripped the small of her back, and he buried his head into her neck, down her throat, and to her breasts.

The actions were needy, possessive, and wanton. In fact, if someone were to enter the room they would be met with quite a lascivious sight. Her naked breasts, pushed forward as she bent back to allow Thomas better access. Her dress pooled around them, as they moved against each other. His hands pulling her onto him.

And then he was inside her, and her eyes nearly rolled into the back of her head. He had relinquished her breasts and was looking into her eyes. Into her soul. His eyes were fierce. Fierce with possession and unnamed emotions.

They set a rhythm, as she learned the dance. It

was fast and wild, and she could barely hold on to a single thought. If she didn't know better, she would say he were a spirit possessing her soul.

He lifted and pulled her hips down, embedding himself deeper and deeper. With a cry her body pulsed around him and her head fell forward. He followed quickly with a muffled shout, his face buried in her neck.

As their shudders subsided, he caressed her hair. They stayed like that for minutes or hours, she couldn't tell. He finally broke the silence. "What makes your work so interesting?"

"Discovery, story, mystery. What makes yours?"

He continued to stroke her hair, waiting a bit before answering. "Discovery, innovation, creation." He paused. "But what is it about your field that creates such obsessive individuals?"

She leaned back and gave him a pointed look, much as he had given her earlier, before their lovemaking. "I repeat, what makes yours?"

He smiled faintly, but his face was pensive. "My uncle as good as killed my sister, you know."

It was as if he were delivering a report on the weather. She froze, not knowing how to respond.

"Letty was only four. I was away at Eton, but I came home from school every chance I got.

Mother died in labor, and Letty became my world. Father was cold, a taskmaster." He shrugged. "Like most of his station he expected absolute obedience. But Letty . . . Letty was a bright light. Too pure for this realm."

She ran a hand down his arm. "What happened?"

"Uncle sent her nurse to retrieve something for him with the understanding that he would watch Letty. He became preoccupied with something in one of his collections, made Letty sit in the blue room—the one with all of the armor and weapons. She got curious and touched a suit of armor. It toppled and fell on top of her. She was knocked unconscious, never woke up, and two days later she was dead."

"Oh, Thomas, I'm so sorry."

He waved her sympathy aside. "She never should have been in that room. He should have been paying closer attention. Yet he didn't even pay attention to his own wife. Much like your Mr. Tecking, really." He gazed into the fire. "I never forgave him."

She swallowed. "I can understand why you'd be upset with him, but it sounds like a terrible accident. Surely your uncle was distraught?"

He laughed unpleasantly. "He couldn't have

cared less about my sister. He holed himself up even more once he had her out of the way. She used to follow him around when I wasn't there. Drove him mad."

There was an underlying tension to his words. She remembered her parting shot about rumors a week ago and wanted to kick herself. "Surely you don't blame yourself for not being there to prevent her death?"

He gave her a bleak smile. "For years I did. I should have known better than to trust her care to a man whose sole interest was his hobby."

Panic whipped through her languid body at the unspoken words. "But you said Letty had a nurse. And your aunt and father were around as well. It was just a tragic accident, Thomas."

His dark mask was back in place, but now that she knew what had caused his pain, she was helpless as to how to heal it.

"Not all antiquarians are like your uncle, Thomas."

He didn't respond.

"Your line of work produces people who can become just as obsessive as mine. It isn't the work, it is the individual and how he deals with his interests."

He gave her a brief, searing kiss, and tucked

her head under his chin. "Of course, that's true, Patience."

She gritted her teeth in frustration, yet worry filled her breast. Now she knew why he had reacted so badly that first night to finding out she was an antiquarian.

"Thomas, it's not fair for you to tar me with the same brush just because I enjoy and work with antiquities. It's the same thing as believing rumors. I don't believe the things that some of your peers have said about you."

"They are only words, Patience."

"Words hurt, Thomas. No matter how hard you try to convince yourself otherwise, words do hurt. I thought you trusted me. But perhaps it is yourself you don't trust. What do you fear?"

He stiffened but said nothing. Patience wasn't sure if it was a good or bad omen.

Chapter 21

The next morning dawned gray to match her mood. Slipping into the dining room last, she tucked into her food with barely a good morning.

"Good news, Patience."

She looked at John, who was grinning broadly.

"We received word from your father today that there are two new commissions. The Burberry and Crouch estates."

A part of her rejoiced at the new work and opportunities for the museum. "That's wonderful.

The Burberrys are supposed to have an excellent Egyptian collection."

He nodded happily. "And the Crouches were very interested in medieval weaponry. There will be enough work to last the next half year at least."

Patience couldn't help herself, and she stole a glance at Thomas. His face was set in stone, his eyes on his plate.

She sent John a strained smile. "Excellent."

Thomas abruptly excused himself, and Patience was left staring at her plate, fighting back the tears. It was bad enough trying to think of ways to argue against Thomas's irrational view on antiquarians and obsession. It was worse when confronted with a genuine problem. And here she was acting like they had an understanding, had made some sort of commitment. When truly again there had been no promises.

Patience dragged herself through the morning tasks, finishing the final pieces and readying them for transport the next morning. They were then scheduled to stay the weekend at the castle and leave Monday. Truthfully, she didn't know what would be more painful. Staying at the castle with nothing to do but think of Thomas or leaving the castle and Thomas behind.

Having no appetite, she worked straight through, barely noticing the concerned glances one of the maids sent her way.

So it was with some large part of surprise that she found herself looking up to see Caroline hovering above her, arms akimbo in a militant gesture.

"Patience Harrington, you *will* eat."

It took no small amount of will to keep her jaw from dropping, but she did stand up and allow Caroline to steer her to the small table and chairs at the side of the room, where a plate of fruit lay.

No sooner had she taken a bite of a strawberry, then Caroline said, "What is the relationship between you and Thomas?"

Choking on her strawberry, Patience grabbed her water glass and swallowed. "What?"

"You and Thomas. He's been stalking about yelling at the staff and being a veritable bear. And you look like someone kicked your favorite poodle."

Patience looked down. "We had a disagreement."

"Well, obviously. What about?"

Patience gripped her skirt, and decided to

take the plunge. "About your husband and antiquarian obsessions."

Caroline wilted in her chair and heaved a sigh. "What did he tell you?"

Patience summarized their conversation.

Caroline sighed again. "My husband loved that little girl. He always complained and scowled, but he would leave sweets around and conveniently have toys for her to play with."

"What happened then?"

"It was an accident, Patience." She closed her eyes. "A terrible one for all of us. George simply withdrew. He didn't know how to handle it. He blamed himself as much for the accident as Thomas blamed him. He threw himself into his studies and collecting and ignored all else."

Patience saw the pain in her eyes.

"Thomas did the same, but he took a different path. I've seen more of the old Thomas in the last few weeks than I have in the last ten years. And it's because of you, Patience."

Patience looked at her hands, and Caroline took one into her own. "Please don't give up on him. I don't know what is between you, but it is good."

Patience laughed shakily. "I thought so, too,

but you heard John. There is so much work to be done elsewhere, and Thomas has his hands completely full here. I don't know." She looked away before meeting Caroline's gaze again. "And you must understand, Caroline. I don't know what Thomas wants. He has never told me."

"Why don't you ask him?"

She gave her a strained smile. "Perhaps I shall. Thank you for telling me about your husband. I know it was painful. Perhaps it is something you should share with Thomas."

She shook her head. "I've tried before. He changes the subject or leaves when I broach the topic."

"That's what I'm afraid will happen to me, too."

Caroline gave her hand a squeeze and stood with the plate. "Don't wait too long to find out."

As it happened, Thomas sought her out later that day. He spoke as if nothing had occurred, and Patience wasn't sure whether to follow his lead or force them to discuss things. She decided to follow his lead, and they had a long, if somewhat guarded discussion on literature, a neutral topic.

On the one hand it was reassuring that he still wanted to spend time with her. On the other it was very frustrating to act as if having only one segment of their friendship would satisfy.

The rational part of her brain forced her to feel things out before making a move. The idealistic part cried for the lost intimacy and rejoiced when his hand reached for her hair, before he suddenly remembered himself and dropped it back in his lap. Something broke inside her when his hand fell, but her idealism forced her to see it as a positive action only. She even dredged up a smile when they said good night.

The next morning was a bit strained as the last shipment of materials was boxed and moved to the waiting carriages.

It signified the end of the trip. The mood was tense. Mr. and Mrs. Tecking were sending veiled glances to one another, and Patience had noted that there had been a few tentative overtures by Mr. Tecking in the last couple of days. It was almost as if he were trying to make amends for the past. And Mrs. Tecking's chair seemed to magically scoot closer to Mr. Tecking's with each new meal, the lady always leaning in to close the distance further. Patience hoped they continued to work things out, for both of their sakes.

As for the rest of them, Caroline wore a faraway expression. John looked frustrated. Samuel looked preoccupied, and Patience felt somber. Thomas seemed oddly caught between anticipation and anger.

The last box was loaded onto the museum carts, and the castle servants began to disperse. Patience watched a servant stroll toward the castle with a sheaf of papers. She thought nothing of it until she saw Thomas's eyes narrow. He walked briskly after the man, and Patience remembered Mrs. Tecking's words about Henry's interest in the shipment schedules and contents. She started after him, but was almost immediately waylaid by Jeremy.

"Patience! Looking forward to coming home?"

"Yes, of course, Jeremy." She peered around him, watching as Thomas disappeared into the castle. "I'll talk to you on Monday. I just need to—"

"Oh, no, you don't." He smiled. "Your work is done, there is no need to hie off to clean up."

"But—"

"Besides, your father wants to know what you think of the new assignments."

"Tell him I'll discuss them with him on Monday. I'm sorry, Jeremy, but I need to hurry. I'll bake scones to make it up to you."

He looked baffled, but he gave her a wave as

she scooted past him and nearly ran inside, her skirts slowing her a bit.

She came to a stop in the entrance hall and motioned to a footman. "Do you know which way Lord Blackfield went?"

"Aye, Miss, he went up the stairs."

"Thank you." She rushed up the stairs and was lucky to find a maid at the top who pointed her down the left hall. A crash resounded through the hall, like something metal and heavy hitting the floor. She ran toward the sound.

The door to John's room was open. *No, not John, please not John.* She ran forward and as she reached the open door she caught the glint of steel right before she plowed into the man exiting the room.

Chapter 22

‿‿⌒◯◯⌒‿‿

S he stumbled back, catching a glimpse of cold
eyes and set features before an arm steadied
her. Her gaze collided with John's, and fear momentarily gripped her. John had killed Thomas.

"How could you?" she choked out.

He looked momentarily confused, before a loud
thump from across the hall drew their attention.

"Stay here."

He dashed past her to the room across the
hall. Another dull thump sounded, and John
threw open the door.

Patience gasped.

There, lying on the floor, was Samuel, with Thomas standing over him, a trickle of blood dripping down his chin.

John strode forward. "Samuel Simmons, I am taking you to London to be questioned about matters pertaining to both treason and theft."

Thomas wiped his chin and gave Patience a somewhat cocky grin. Perhaps murdering him wasn't such a bad idea. But first . . .

"John, what is going on?"

He looked sheepish as he grabbed Samuel and hauled him to his feet. "My apologies, Patience. I couldn't tell you."

"Tell me what? What is going on? How can you arrest anyone?"

"Well, you see, I've been doing some work on the side, helping to recover stolen artifacts. With the full support of your father, of course," he hastened to add. "A branch of the government asked me to look into the incidents here. Seems there's been some trouble, and they were concerned there'd be more."

Well, that made sense. Somewhat. "And since when do you carry a pistol?"

John had tied Samuel up by this time, and he grinned, holding the pistol up. "What, this old relic? I deal in weaponry, Patience. This pretty thing is only good for a collection." He examined it. "Your father would kill me if I scratched it."

She frowned. "Why didn't you tell me you were investigating?"

"Well, I know you, Patience. You'd have wanted to help." Seeing the outraged look on her face he hurried to explain. "Not that you aren't a good partner. You're great. The best. Really excellent. But you do get rather fantastic ideas sometimes, and . . ."

That she was seriously considering doing him harm must have shown on her face because he pushed Samuel toward the door.

"Wait." Thomas was staring murderously at Samuel. "You didn't answer me, Sam. Why?"

Samuel gave an unhappy laugh. "I didn't want it to go this far, Thomas. But you left me no choice."

"Monster isn't ready. The world isn't ready."

"But I'm ready." His voice was tight. "Ready for the money and the fame. Not all of us have the money and resources to play with toys," he spit.

"I don't treat anything as a toy."

Samuel gave another unpleasant laugh. "Sure you do, Thomas. And you can. But you are holding the rest of us back."

Patience saw the pain cross Thomas's face,

and she felt a surge of anger on his behalf. "How can you say that? He gives all of you the opportunity to fulfill your dreams."

Samuel turned baleful eyes to her. "My dream is to retire a wealthy man, Miss Harrington, and live a life of luxury with a buxom woman or two. Do you know how much monster is worth, Miss Harrington? Do you?"

"No," she said simply.

He looked straight at Thomas. "I trusted you."

Thomas stared back. "No, I trusted you. You betrayed all of us."

"You betrayed me first! We were partners. I should have had an equal say in the future of all the products. Everyone always has to bend to *your* dictates."

Thomas's gaze remained steely. "You always had a say, but your vote is only one. You know there are only five men out of fifty who ever thought exposing the monster machinery was a good idea."

"You are wrong."

"Maybe so, but at least I'll be able to sleep at night. Good-bye, Samuel. I'll send a barrister to help you in London."

Their gazes remained locked. "Good-bye, Thomas."

John exchanged a worried glance with Patience and led Samuel from the room.

The silence stretched. Thomas moved his jaw and winced. Immediately, Patience moved toward him and held up a hand to his face.

"He hit you."

"I'll be fine."

She looked into his eyes. "Will you?"

Thomas didn't hold her gaze. "We should go back downstairs."

She said nothing, just followed him from the room and down the hall. As they approached the steps she remembered the other man. "What about the footman?"

He shook his head. "Just following orders. There is someone on your side relaying the information. He's been taken care of, and if he hasn't, John will do it."

"How long have you and John been working together?"

He smirked, and she was pleased to see the expression. "Since right after he and Caroline talked. He became entangled in one of the traps while surreptitiously trying to fend off an attempt by one of the spies. We had a nice long talk after that. Good thing I came upon him instead of Samuel." His expression darkened.

"Why didn't you tell me you were working together? And how did you know that John wasn't a spy?"

"At first I didn't know. Caroline tried to convince me he wasn't, as did John himself, who, by the way, made me promise I wouldn't tell you, I'm assuming for the reasons he just mentioned. Oh, and it was your father that set me straight about John."

She blinked. "My father?"

"One of his men has been watching the grounds. Kept sending me anonymous notes each morning."

"The pink ones?"

Thomas grinned. "Your father said they would drive you mad. He discovered a spy in his own ranks and warned me about it a few days ago. I was unsure as to who was sending me the notes before. Caroline had worked it out though, and she approached John."

"Dear Lord, is everyone in on everything but me?"

His eyes turned briefly cold before he shook it off. "Obviously not. Samuel was an unpleasant surprise. In hindsight, it shouldn't have been. I didn't want it to be one of my people. Samuel was the one investigating everyone—conveniently for him. And there were so many little clues. He was especially vindictive about your reputation and kept trying to convince me you were the spy."

All of a sudden she was unaccountably nervous. "So, you've spoken with my father?"

He raised a brow. "Only through correspondence. Says he has heard a lot about me. That he sent you here hoping we might find common interests."

Her jaw dropped. They reached the ground floor, and she quickly closed her mouth as the curious gazes of the servants caught hers.

"Are you saying my father was *matchmaking*?" she hissed.

He looked amused. "No, he said we had similar interests in literature."

"Oh." Embarrassment knew no bounds. "Well, we obviously wouldn't be interested in antiquities together."

"Patience, about the antiquities—"

A servant appeared at his elbow. "My lord? You are needed in the kitchens. Kenfield says it's urgent."

Thomas nodded and waited for the servant to leave before turning back to Patience. "Can we talk later? Are you . . . are you willing?"

She had never heard him so tentative. "Of

course I am." She smiled. "You know where to find me."

He tucked the perpetually loose strands of hair haloing her face behind her ears. "At least for the weekend." His voice was solemn. "I'll see you in a bit."

Patience decided to walk around the gardens to clear her head. It had been an exciting day, and it wasn't noon yet and already she felt exhausted. She watched a lazy blue damselfly flit through the rose garden and a lacewing crawl across a leaf. She didn't know what the talk Thomas wanted to have would revolve around, but she hoped it had to do with planning past the weekend.

She returned to the castle after another half hour and headed for the front stairs. As she neared, she could hear the noise of guests even from down the hall. It sounded like a party had just arrived. She slowed her steps. Neither Caroline nor Thomas had said anything about people arriving.

"You must stay the evening, at least." Caroline's voice was pleasant, but neutral.

"That is so kind of you, Lady Caroline. We would love to. We were just commenting in the carriage about how gracious a hostess you are.

And Lord Blackfield, is he in residence? We were so hoping to say hello to both of you." The woman, whoever she was, certainly didn't waste any time.

Patience froze at the drawing room entrance as the women came into view. There were three women, an older woman, a pretty young debutante, and a rather plain companion. Two men stood to their side. The debutante was the one who held Patience frozen to the spot. Their eyes met, and the woman practically glittered with glee.

Celeste Finchford, one of society's darlings. She had taken malicious pleasure in Patience's fate, as it reflected well on Celeste in the hallowed halls of society when she made a cutting comment about those less fortunate socially. Patience waited (and prayed) for the day Celeste would receive her due. Maliciousness had a way of striking those who wielded it.

Lady Caroline smiled and motioned for Patience to join them.

She took a deep breath, squared her shoulders, and walked inside. All she needed to do was relax, just as Thomas had coached.

"May I introduce Miss Harrington," Caroline said, introducing the five travelers in turn. All of them cast her glances ranging from disapproval from the older woman and a sneer from Celeste, to a downright leer from one of the "gentlemen."

Patience nodded and said nothing, remembering Thomas's advice that if she had nothing to add, silence was best. That polite interest was her asset. These people played the social game, one that she wanted no part of. She finally understood why Thomas had been adamant that she wasn't being dishonest if she were quiet and polite.

"It's so lovely to see you, Miss Harrington," Celeste said, eyes fluttering. "Where have you been keeping yourself these past weeks?"

Patience sat in a plum chintz chair, pausing to arrange her skirts before she could spit out her story. "Oh, here and there, Miss Finchford. I was saddened to miss the end of the season. I heard your ball was a marvelous success."

Celeste's eyes narrowed a bit at the lack of provided ammunition. "It was but a small party," she simpered, feigned humility in every motion of her body. She smiled at Caroline. "We would have loved to have had you attend Lady Caroline."

Caroline smiled. "We were sorry to have missed it. There was a prior engagement here that we could not break. Perhaps next season?"

"Of course," Celeste demurred.

Kenfield signaled from the drawing room doors, and Lady Caroline stood. "I will be but a moment. I need to give instructions to the staff concerning your stay. Lord Blackfield has been notified of your arrival as well."

Caroline moved from sight, and Celeste turned to Patience. "Are you planning to return next season, Miss Harrington? It wouldn't be the same without you."

Patience forced a smile and picked up the teacup Caroline had set out for her before leaving. "I appreciate your concern, Miss Finchford."

Celeste's brows knitted noticeably. Patience nearly cheered her small victory, but instead maintained her smile, a smile that had suddenly become real.

"When did you arrive?"

Patience debated how to answer, choosing to sip her tea while deciding. "Three weeks ago."

"You've been here three weeks, without a chaperone?" Celeste's voice was aghast, but couldn't quite cover her excitement.

Patience waved a hand and chuckled. "Oh, most assuredly not, Miss Finchford."

Celeste leaned forward, waiting for her to continue. Patience smiled and sipped her tea.

"And?"

"Yes, Miss Finchford?"

Celeste's eyes narrowed, and the older woman she was traveling with coughed to stop Celeste from responding. The older woman joined the conversation turned interrogation.

"Have you enjoyed your stay at the castle, Miss Harrington?"

"It has been delightful. Lady Caroline has been a most gracious hostess." She almost couldn't hold back a shout of glee as Celeste's mien darkened in frustration. She had just reminded her that she was besmirching Lady Caroline by referring to anything improper in the household.

A cough interrupted the silence. Patience turned to see Kenfield hovering in the doorway. "Pardon me, ladies, gentlemen, but Miss Harrington's presence is being requested. There is a small emergency with one of her traveling companions."

Patience gave Kenfield a smile and excused herself. She could feel Celeste's eyes burning a hole in her back, and she had never felt quite so good about the feeling.

As soon as she rounded the corner with the butler he stopped her. She looked at him expectantly, taking in his apologetic gaze.

"There is no emergency, is there, Kenfield?"

"My apologies, Miss, no there is not. Lady Caroline did specify to excuse you if she hadn't returned in ten minutes."

Patience felt a rush of warmth for Caroline's thoughtfulness, even if she had been managing to hold her own. She thanked Kenfield, who returned to the hall. She was about to head for the stairs when she saw Thomas stride into the drawing room. Now this might prove interesting.

On slippered feet, Patience sneaked back to the drawing room, keeping her back against the wall to listen without being seen. Kenfield raised a brow from his position by the great doors, and Patience gave him a toothy smile. Morbid curiosity caused her to eavesdrop, although if Thomas fell under Celeste's spell, *morbid* wouldn't begin to describe what her thoughts would become.

"Lord Blackfield, it's a pleasure to see you again," Celeste gushed.

"Indeed. I see you've met one of my guests."

"Miss Harrington? I hate to bear bad news, my lord, but—"

"She has to return to London on Monday? I know. We are all sad to see her go."

"But she is a—"

"Wonderful guest, isn't she?"

"No, she isn't a—"

"Person who takes advantage of hospitality? Quite right."

Warmth flowed through her at Thomas's words and Celeste's increasingly desperate attempts to discredit her.

"She is bad." Celeste managed a blurted, but successful sentence. She must have been really desperate in order to show her hand so poorly. Patience allowed a mental smirk.

"Bad? I don't take your meaning."

"You know, bad." Celeste was trying to retreat into coyness, her specialty, having realized her less-than-stellar showing.

"I must ask that you define *bad*."

"Oh, really, my lord. I think you know what I mean." There was a teasing lilt to her voice that was trying to override the desperation.

"I don't."

"Bad, as in not *good*." She stressed the word *good*.

"Well, that is the definition of *bad*, isn't it? But I don't see how that applies to Miss Harrington."

"She is not the kind of person you want to associate with."

"Because she is bad."

"Exactly." This was said with a good amount of relief.

"Bad how?"

"Fast, loose, bad, odd. Strange," she blurted in obvious frustration.

"Ah, that kind of bad . . ." Patience could almost feel the inordinate relief from Celeste at Thomas's thoughtful hesitation. "No, I think not."

"What?"

"I don't agree, Miss Finchlet, was it?"

"Finchford!"

"Finchford. You are wrong. Now, how long are you planning on staying?"

Patience put her fist in her mouth to stifle her laughter. Kenfield looked amused at her antics. Thomas's absolute rude nonchalance had to be stunning—she wished she could see their faces.

She couldn't help but take a peek. Sure enough, the entire party appeared to be in shock. She pulled back, but not before meeting Thomas's eyes. It was as if he had been waiting for her to look. Her heart sped up, both at his gaze and having been caught.

"But, but—" Celeste sputtered. "She is awkward. No one would want to befriend or defend her. And she's nearly on the shelf. Oh!" Celeste seemed to recover. "She's your paramour. I didn't mean to offend you, my lord. Surely you are looking for something more . . . permanent?"

Patience's jaw dropped. She couldn't believe that a diamond of the first water like Celeste Finchford had just bleated her thoughts like, well, like Patience would.

"I'm not sure what you mean by *paramour*." Thomas's tone was deadly. "But, you know, you may have a point, Miss Finchton."

She heard Celeste murmur "Finchford," her voice low and finally cowed.

Thomas's voice turned thoughtful. "Do you think she would marry me? I can't imagine a better wife."

Patience's back hit the wall with a thud.

"Have a pleasant stay tonight, Miss Finchrotten, ladies, gentlemen. I'm sure I won't see you in the morning."

Five steps later he rounded the corner and came into her view. He leaned toward her and held out an arm. "Dinner looks to be quite a trial. I was wondering if you wouldn't mind dining in the study? Perhaps having that talk over a good meal?"

She nodded blankly, and he led her down the hall after giving Kenfield a significant look.

He helped her sit in a study chair and stoked the fire. "I'm sorry for the way I left things last night. I was hurt. And I know I hurt you."

"I'm sorry, too," she said softly.

"The argument was stupid."

They locked gazes and blurted at the same time, "I'm afraid that you won't have time in your life for me once the novelty wears off—"

"I'm afraid that you'll leave me—"

They both blinked, and relief stole across both their faces. Thomas grinned. "Well, that answers that."

Patience returned the smile, but sobered quickly. "But what about our work? I am mainly in London, but I take frequent trips, and you, you need to be here all the time."

He cocked his head. "I spend more time in London than most people know. Plus, there is interest in starting a testing facility there as well. The government is also interested in a facility, but I don't know that I want to deal with them, too." He smiled, a warm, natural smile. "Besides, what good is any of it if I can't share it with you."

"So, you want to continue our relationship?" she asked, a bit tentatively.

"No, silly, I want to marry you. Didn't you hear me propose?"

Her heart started beating so loudly that she could barely form a response. "I wasn't sure that was really for me. What about the antiquarian stigma and your sister."

He picked up her hand. "For the first time in ten years I actually want to let it go. To forgive . . . everyone. Myself included. It seemed easier to cast blame and work myself silly. It didn't matter until it hurt you. I needed a good kick in the backside. And someone feisty enough to deliver one."

She touched his face. "I'm glad."

"Good. Then I'll ask you for real. Will you marry me, Patience? We can divide our time between London, the castle, and the occasional trip. We will have to compromise, of course," he added, airily.

She smiled and squeezed his hand. "That sounds perfect."

Thomas grinned. He would never tire of hearing her voice and feeling her warmth every time she smiled at him.

"You know what sounds perfect?"

She lifted a brow.

"You without any clothes on."

She gave a yelp as he proceeded to divest her of her clothing, kissing each newly exposed area of flesh.

"And I planned ahead so that the door is locked for sure this time. Can't have anyone walking in on my future wife in the middle of the afternoon now, can I?"

He barely removed his own clothing before he was sinking inside her, as if returning home. She smiled up at him again, and he could barely control himself as he worshipped her body with the same intensity and precision that he worshipped her mind. Her soul. This woman that seemed made for him.

He took his time, slowly drawing out sighs and gasps. Her skin turned a delicious shade of pink, and he kissed around her neck, chest, and breasts, as if to taste the color. She was addictive. Like a fine wine or an expensive brandy. Molten, full-bodied, and delectable.

His pace increased. There was a feeling on the periphery of his mind. Something he couldn't quite grasp. Something that had been building. Building at a pace similar to orgasm.

Her movements were becoming more frenzied beneath him. Lord, she was responsive. And she was his. He increased the pace yet again, interlocking their hands together. Her eyes locked with his, small unintelligible sounds falling from her lips. Realization hit him all at once, clear as the midnight sky.

"I love you, Patience."

The realization, the look in her eyes, the clenching of her muscles as his words sent her over the edge, pulled him right along. He gripped her hands tightly as sensations washed over him so violently that he felt as if he had died and gone to Heaven. And what a way to go.

He collapsed next to her, pulling her against his side as their breathing returned to normal. He caressed her hair and whispered the words over and over. She turned to him, and he kissed her gently, needing her with the same burning desire that he had since they had met, but now tempered with protectiveness, friendship, and love. Love. He drew back and stared at her kiss-swollen lips and the warmth shining from her eyes. He smiled. Yes, most definitely love.

She pulled him down for another kiss. "And I love you," she whispered against his mouth.

Thomas felt the last burden lift. They would be fine. She moved against him. Actually, they were going to be much more than fine. And everything would work out. As long as they were together, all their plans, desires, and dreams would be acres past fine.

He planted a soft kiss to her temple, and she lifted her head so that their eyes met. And she smiled.

Coming in May from Avon Romance

Duke of Scandal by Adele Ashworth

An Avon Romantic Treasure

Lady Olivia is a wife in name only, returning to London determined to confront her dastardly husband. But the man who stands before her is her husband's twin, the Duke of Durham, and now Olivia must make a scandalous choice.

Vamps and the City by Kerrelyn Sparks

An Avon Contemporary Romance

Can the undead really find love on Reality TV? Producer Darcy Newhart thinks so. But this sexy lady vampire is distracted by a hot, handsome contestant named Austin . . . who just happens to be mortal, and a slayer! What next?

What to Wear to a Seduction by Sari Robins

An Avon Romance

Lady Edwina is putting on clothes . . . only to take them off again! But she's determined to seduce notorious rogue Prescott Devane, the one man who can help her find a blackmailer . . . and also steal her heart.

Winds of the Storm by Beverly Jenkins

An Avon Romance

Archer owes his life to Zahra Lafayette. Now, in the days after the Civil War, he needs the help of this beautiful former spy again. Posing as an infamous madam, Zahra is willing to help in his cause, but she's unwilling to grant him her love.

Avon Romances
the best in
exceptional authors and unforgettable novels!

Avon Romantic Treasures

Unforgettable, enthralling love stories, sparkling with passion and adventure from Romance's bestselling authors